To Barbara,
Thanks for being so excited over n
finishing the novel. May
you find some truth in
the lines that soothe your
soul.

Being a "Carolina Girl"
you should especially like
the beach scenes.

Love!
Niki

Things Not Said

by
Mitzi G. Tzerman

authorHOUSE®

AuthorHouse™
1663 Liberty Drive, Suite 200
Bloomington, IN 47403
www.authorhouse.com
Phone: 1-800-839-8640

This book is a work of fiction. People, places, events, and situations are the product of the author's imagination. Any resemblance to actual persons, living or dead, or historical events, is purely coincidental.

First published by AuthorHouse 9/15/2008

ISBN: 978-1-4343-5205-7 (e)
ISBN: 978-1-4343-5204-0 (sc)
ISBN: 978-1-4343-5203-3 (hc)

Library of Congress Control Number: 2007909698

Printed in the United States of America
Bloomington, Indiana

This book is printed on acid-free paper.

Acknowledgments

I would like to thank my great, Aunt Lena for giving me a year in my childhood of total love. (Along with Uncle Bob who is deceased.) She continues to be a close friend to me.

A special thank you to Tina Auteri Sweat for helping me to find my voice and for teaching me to speak honestly from the heart without fear. (Truly a benefit for any want-a-be writer.)

A special thanks to everyone who has ever encouraged me to continue to write and to follow my dreams. Thank You to Mrs. Bettie Bland and Mrs. Linda Rainer who were my English teachers in High School. (Thank you for helping to inspire my love of writing.) Thank you to my sister, Dawn for reading and editing the first draft, and I am very grateful to everyone who has read and critiqued drafts of this book. (Hope you like the finished product.) Thanks to all my friends at the county courthouses in South Carolina (employees and abstractors).Thanks for waiting so long for the book to be published and for being excited for me.

The front cover of this book is a picture of the rocking chairs on the front porch of the Shorter Mansion in beautiful Eufaula, Alabama. Thank you to everyone at the Shorter Mansion for allowing me to use it for my first book. As a teenager I used to sit in those rocking chairs and dream of being a writer. So, it represents a dream come true for me.

Thank you to Julie Rhodes for sharing some of her childhood memories with me of Edisto Beach. A special thank you to Bobbie

Ball for allowing me to use Poogan's Porch restaurant in Charleston as one of the favorite places for my characters to frequent. Thank you to Poogan for being such a memorable little dog that a restaurant was named after him.

A special thank you to Pam Collier, Wendy Ziemke, Jan King, Toula Hubbard, Kathi Jo Snipes, Lori Kay Kienzle, Barbie Gogan, Gail Laney, Kay Elmore, and Mary Rutland for believing in me and for your friendship. (Words are just not enough to express my appreciation.) Thank you to Dennis Reeder for being one of my biggest fans.

Thanks to Kimberly Anderson for getting me started on the journey of getting the clutter out of my life. If I had not made those changes, I probably would still be unmarried and I might not have published this book. Thanks to Dr. Leslie Stuck for all her helpful advice for keeping me healthy all these years. Thanks to my dog Sophie who died in 2004. She walked with me hundreds of miles while I thought about the plot for this book. She was a wonderful, loving pet that I will never forget.

I am especially grateful to my husband Jeffrey for all the tenderness and passion he has brought into my life. Thank you for meeting my desires and my needs. Your love changes me a little everyday. I'm certain the books I will write in the future will have a little of you in each one. Thank you for marrying me and for your companionship.

Thank you to my Creator for giving me a shot at this thing called life. What great material for the best book of all. The~Book~of~Life~

This book is dedicated in loving memory of my dad, Mr. M H Rutland~

Things Not Said

The cab driver turned down the last paved road toward the beach house. Melissa knew it would take at least thirty minutes to get there from that point. Her eyes trailed the marshlands on both sides of the country road they traveled. The sun had melted into the western sky. There had been many such skies on her trips to Edisto. Those memories were chiseled in her mind the same way the sea carved its mark on the shore. Etched there in her thoughts, was the peach and orange shadows of the sky at sunset: Reflecting, glistening on the sea in the evening.

She watched the sky waiting for that moment when the sun is no longer visible, when a residue of hue covers the heavens, leaving only streaks in the darkening horizon. Every season the colors are different. Sometimes they're purple and red, other times orange and yellow. This evening they would be more purple and red. It would be winter soon. She longed for that sight, hoping to catch a glimpse before the shades evaporated into the night.

She was grateful to have the quiet and solitude on the ride down. Joe turned the music down when she got into the cab. He had driven her before and taken her to the airport on occasion. He seemed friendly enough. She was glad to have a familiar face to drive her there, someone who wouldn't talk much. She wasn't in the mood to talk.

Melissa took the journal from her purse. She held it close to her chest, believing she held onto the truth about what happened to her friend. Tears filled her eyes. She was finally going to know the truth.

Joe pulled into the driveway and removed her one suitcase from the trunk. She tipped him generously, and informed him she would call a day early to have him pick her up. He nodded, got in the cab, and drove in the opposite direction from the way they had come.

Melissa picked up her suitcase, climbed the steep steps on the ocean side of the cottage, unlocked the door, and went inside. The memories of the past enveloped her thoughts. The smell of salt was caught in the wooden rafters, and reminded her of her childhood. She closed her eyes and breathed deeply. She missed the beach. She missed the smell of the ocean, the sounds of the waves, the gulls, the sand. No place in the world ever made her feel so alive. She couldn't wait until the morning when it was light enough to see. She wanted to taste salt and squeak sand as she jogged along the shore. Nothing soothed her soul more than coming back home to Edisto Beach.

Seashells lined the window sills of the cottage, collections from previous walks. Melissa picked up a virgin sand dollar, a treasure from the past, gently fingered its edges, and tried to remember how simple life seemed then. There were other shells, not all virgins. Some were only pieces of what they used to be. They were decent fragments, embodying some beauty, some uniqueness and were worthy to be saved. They were called keepers. She couldn't help but compare them to herself, no longer whole just a fragment of what she used to be.

The house looked the same way it did when she was a child. She remembered waiting anxiously for her mother to tell her when it was finally time to go to the beach. She would grab her sand bucket and scoop, and take her mom's hand as they walked down the steps to the ocean together. She remembered dancing at the pavilion barefoot, adults and children alike. Something no one ever did anymore. The pavilion had been gone for years. Her thoughts brought a smile to her face. She hoped one day she'd be able to give her own children good memories from these sandy shores.

Melissa unpacked, placed the journal on the table beside the couch, and decided to wait until the morning to begin reading it. When she finally curled up in front of the fire, wrapped in a mountain of blankets, she felt at peace. She breathed a sigh of relief. She was finally home and was finally going to know the truth.

Her eyes closed. Her spirit rested. At that moment she had no fear or concern. She had no idea that someone walked those beaches waiting for her return. Someone was standing there, taking a drag off of his cigarette, looking up at her window, watching the smoke from the fireplace, smiling to himself as he watched the light go out. She had no idea of the danger that awaited her there.

Chapter One

John was nearly an hour late and Melissa was beginning to worry. They had planned to go out and eat at Poogan's Porch, her favorite restaurant and to a movie. John was never late. Early yes, but never late. She was planning to surprise him at dinner with the news she was finally pregnant. They had tried to have a baby for so long, and it was hard on both of them when she couldn't conceive.

Melissa looked at her watch for the third time. It was so unlike him not to call. She picked up the phone and tried the office for the fourth time, still no answer. She waited ten more minutes and tried again. Did he have a wreck on the way home? Where was he?

A sick feeling wrenched Melissa's body. She made some toast and poured a glass of orange juice. She was taking the first bite when John came in the front door. Her heart pounding, she put down the glass, and headed for the door.

"Are you all right? Where have you been?" She looked at his face. He looked so pale and distraught, but he didn't answer. Instead, he started toward the bathroom.

"John, are you going to answer me? What happened to our dinner plans? You could have called, if you were going to work this late."

Despair reflected in John's eyes. "Can't you give me a minute to unwind?" He snapped in a tone she'd never heard before, closed the bathroom door, and ran the water in the lavatory for what seemed like hours.

What could he possibly be doing, she thought? Her insides began to shake, and her hands trembled. It didn't help that she hadn't eaten anything. One thing was certain, tonight would not be the right time to tell him about the baby.

Melissa waited.

The door to the bathroom finally opened. John headed for the couch, avoiding her eyes. He slumped on the sofa and began to speak softly. "I've been riding around thinking about something, Melissa. I've been making some decisions for my life, decisions you probably won't understand."

"Decisions? What kind of decisions?" Her numbness turned to anger.

John stared at the fireplace and began to mumble. "I...I'm leaving you."

"You're leaving me?" Melissa looked at John in disbelief. "Why, for God's sake?" There was silence. "How long have you been thinking about leaving me?" She tried to hide her trembling hands.

"See, I knew you wouldn't understand. There's no need in talking about it anymore. I'm going to bed."

"Going to bed? That's it? Don't you think I deserve an explanation?" She breathed a sigh of disgust. "What on earth could have happened to you between last night's plans to go out and eat, and your sudden decision to leave me?"

John didn't answer.

The room began to spin. Melissa felt suddenly alone and ached inside. She was going to have this man's baby and he was planning on leaving her. Her bottom lip began to tremble. She bit the lower edge to keep from crying and turned toward the fireplace, so she could regain some composure. She wanted so badly to cry, but he was not going to see her cry!

She took a deep breath, wiped the corner of her eye, and turned and walked over to John. She looked at him directly in the eyes. He tried to look the other way. She reached for his chin. "Look at me, John. I want you to tell me what's going on." She leaned down, placed her hands on each side of his face. His afternoon shadow gave him a handsome, rugged look. At that moment she had an irresistible urge to make love with him.

She began to speak softly. "Please open up to me, John. We can work it out no matter what this is really about. I've got so much to tell you, too. We'll go eat a late dinner and talk this out. All right?"

He jerked away from her. "I...I can't, Melissa." He began to unbutton his shirt sleeves.

"You can't or you won't?" She snapped back at him as she stood to her feet. She watched him begin to undress as if he were dismissing any further discussion.

"Whatever, it doesn't matter. I'm not going to change my mind. So there's no sense in talking about it anymore." He got up and headed for the bedroom. Unbuttoning the front of his shirt, he stopped in the doorway, turned and added, "I'm going to sleep. I'll make other arrangements about where to live tomorrow."

John's words were cruel, making her emotions fluctuate between anger and a desire to have him comfort her. Melissa watched him finish unbuttoning his shirt. She felt her cheeks grow hot. Seeing his chest and stomach muscles made her want him even more. Embarrassed, she turned away and walked back to the kitchen. There was no sense in talking. He had obviously made up his mind.

The toast had turned to brick. She tossed it in the garbage, and poured the rest of her juice down the drain. Just the thought of food made her nauseous. Soon anger replaced her feelings of desperation. She began to clean everything: The top of the stove, the refrigerator, the counter tops. She tried to vent her frustration in a productive way. Turning on the stereo as loudly as she could tolerate, she started dusting the furniture in the den.

John came to the doorway. "What are you doing?"

"I'm cleaning. What does it look like I'm doing?"

"Melissa, it's 10 o'clock at night."

John walked over to the stereo and turned the music off. "Can't you clean without all the background music? I need to get some sleep."

"Oh, really? You act like you've just given me a stock report, and now you're going to sleep, business as usual. Well, that's too bad. I'd like to get some sleep, too, but unfortunately you've ruined that for me tonight."

"Can't you just drop it, Melissa?"

"No, I can't, John! In one night, you come home late, you don't call even to have me cancel our dinner plans, and you tell me you're going to leave me. No, I can't just drop it and go to bed. Don't you think I deserve some answers? You think you can just tell me you're leaving and expect me to just say okay, good night?" She waited for some response, but he was silent.

She continued. "Well, that's not going to happen. You've lost your mind, if you think it is." Her voice cracked. She was still fighting the tears. She walked back to the kitchen and slung the dust cloth underneath the sink.

"Melissa, it's late. You look tired. I'll take the couch and you can have the bed."

"John, it doesn't matter where I go to bed. I'm sure I won't be able to sleep, no matter where I am. If you don't want to sleep with me, then sleep wherever you want. Why not just go ahead and leave right now?" Those words made Melissa feel sick at her stomach. She didn't really want John to leave. Suddenly, she felt lonely and frightened.

"You don't mean that Melissa. I'll find something tomorrow. I'm not trying to make this any harder than it has to be."

"Oh, really? Just how hard can it be to say, you've suddenly decided to leave? Last night it never occurred to you. We were making plans to go out and eat. Tonight you've decided not to be married to me anymore. No reason given. That's as easy as it gets for you, but what about me, John. Just say it. You're seeing someone else now. You don't love me anymore. What? Should it matter to me where I sleep?"

John was silent. Melissa walked away, turned the lights off in the kitchen and den, went to the bedroom, got her pillow and afghan from the bed, and tossed them on the couch. This was truly the most exhausting night of her life. Peering out the window, she pondered what to do next. The tears began to slide down her cheeks. She brushed them away, and decided to go ahead and get ready for bed, wherever that might be. After washing her face, brushing her teeth, and slipping on a big T-shirt, she looked in on John. He was lying on his back, looking up at the ceiling.

Melissa stood in the doorway and choked on her words. "Why, John? Why now? I had so many things I wanted to tell you tonight."

4

She grabbed some tissue from the dresser, no longer able to stop the tears.

"Melissa, things happen, things beyond our control. There's no way you can understand."

"Why can't you tell me? Let me try and understand."

Melissa's face was white, pallid looking. Her eyes were the color of stone, not their normal clear blue. The smile and laugh lines around her eyes were lost somewhere in her troubled spirit.

"Melissa, please just get in the bed. You need to get some rest. We both do. This has probably been one of the worse days of our lives and we're exhausted. I shouldn't have suggested we sleep separately. It was a bad idea. I just didn't trust myself sleeping with you. I ...I might not be able to control my feelings."

For one brief moment Melissa felt hope. At least he didn't detest being near her. He must still have some feelings. That fact was enough acceptance to make her think he might change his mind about leaving.

"Okay." She whispered. "Let me get my pillow and afghan."

"I'll get them." John offered and handed her his pillow. "Here, you can use mine."

That's a sweet gesture, Melissa thought. The only problem was John's pillow smelled like John. She held it to her face, breathed in the residue of his cologne before placing the pillow behind her head. She'd have to spend the whole night trying to forget the memories his scent created. The clean smell of John after his shower always encouraged their lovemaking. Now, what always contributed to their closeness would only deepen her feelings of loneliness.

Melissa turned off the light and turned with her back toward John. He decided to take a shower after she finished in the bathroom. She listened as he turned off the water. They normally slept like two spoons for the first hour of sleep. Later, John would hog both sides of the bed, almost pushing her on the floor.

Finally, he got in the bed. She felt his warm body ease under the covers. He was obviously trying not to touch her. She wondered how it would be not touching all night. How would she be able to sleep at all? Every night they told each other I love you, and they kissed good night.

She waited in the silence, no kiss only the silence.

He pulled the covers over his shoulder and faced the wall on his side of the bed.

Minutes ticked by and finally he whispered a soft, "Good night, Melissa." He didn't tell her he loved her.

Melissa's heart ached. She waited a moment before responding.

"Goodnight, John. I love you even if you can't tell me you love me."

He was silent.

She pressed even closer to her side of the bed and cried silently into her pillow. Hours passed and she finally fell asleep.

The night almost gone, they both finally slept. Missing the place of comfort they normally shared at night, their bodies intertwined as if drawn together like magnets.

Melissa was the first to awaken. John's arm was wrapped around her, and he was glued to her backside just like normal. She breathed deeply, wanting him more than she'd ever wanted him before.

She cautiously turned to face him not wanting him to awaken. The warmth of his body comforted her. Having John close to her was healing the rejection she felt earlier. She closed her eyes, letting the moment suffice for the closeness she craved.

Soon she was sleeping nestled in the strength of John's arm; dreaming, resting, wondering why he felt so strongly that he should leave her, wondering if he found someone else, knowing that nothing would ever take the place of his love.

She was sleeping soundly when John realized he was wrapped around her. He wanted her, needed her, loved her. The desire to make love to her was stronger than his ability not, too.

He was looking at her face when she opened her eyes and looked up at him.

The fear he would pull away and leave the bedroom made Melissa start crying. She was afraid of hearing his next words, knowing he might even leave the house.

"I love you, Melissa. I only want what's best for you. I want you to know that."

She sobbed into his neck. "You are what's best for me. I need you, John, now more than ever."

He turned and pressed against the warmth of her body. Kissing the tears from her face, he found her mouth moist, hungry, hurting, swelling under his embrace.

"John, don't leave me. Don't push me away." She whispered as he continued. Her body yielded to his. The pain melted as he made love to her. Neither one of them could control their need for each other. It didn't matter what he had said to her earlier. He was hers for the moment, and she found it hard to believe he could possibly leave.

Exhausted they slept soundly in each other's arms. It was late afternoon and the sun filled the bedroom. John was the first to awaken. Decisions were pounding in his head. It would be harder if she saw him leave.

He slipped out from under the covers, and looked at her one last time as she slept. He searched for some clean jeans and a shirt in the closet, dressed quickly in the kitchen, put on his jogging shoes, grabbed his keys from the table, and closed the door behind him.

Chapter Two

The sun warmed the Hemingway bed where Melissa was sleeping. It was early afternoon, and she slept more soundly than she had for weeks. For days she hadn't been able to keep any food down, thinking she had a virus, or food poisoning. Now, she rested deeply with the knowledge she was pregnant and not battling the flu. Just being close to John gave her comfort and was healing her soul. She didn't want him to leave her no matter what the reason. She was thinking, dreaming, waking in bits and pieces. Reaching out to touch him, she sat up.

"John? John? No." She let go of the sheet and began to moan with the pain of realizing he was gone. She rocked from side to side.

Fear replaced the intimacy of the night before. Somehow she knew he wouldn't be back. She felt a sadness wrap itself around her. Now the joy of motherhood had lost its meaning. Having to raise her much desired child in a home without a daddy, made her stomach churn.

Unable to control the nausea she was feeling, she ran to the bathroom to throw up, not sure if this were morning sickness or a nervous stomach because John left her. She brushed her teeth, rinsed her mouth, and crawled back into bed. She didn't have the strength to face all the trauma going on in her life.

Her head ached with the stress of the responsibility she was being forced to take on. Why? Why now? If he had to leave her why did it have to be after she had finally become pregnant. She sobbed into her pillow. Hours went by before she could catch her breath and make herself get out of bed. She used the covers to try and mask the sunlight that was filling the whole room. Her attempts failed, she finally made herself get up.

Walking into the kitchen, she grabbed a glass and poured some cranberry juice. She knew she should eat something, but just the thought made her nauseous. Tears rolled down her cheeks. She couldn't seem to stop crying. So many thoughts were racing in her mind. She was angry with herself for making love with John the night before. He told her he was leaving. What was she thinking? She had thought he had changed his mind. Wrong.

She sat in the rocker in front of the fireplace and looked forlornly toward the cold logs. In the past she felt so peaceful in her home. Now, she felt as cold as the image in front of her. She kept asking herself why. She'd never known such despair. Sadness filled her eyes and rested there with all the permanence of a portrait, a mirrored reflection of the darkness that enveloped her soul. She continued to sob using one of the throw pillows from the couch to wipe the tears from her eyes.

The next day she tried to set some goals for getting on with her life. It would take sheer willpower to let John go. She would not call his office and she'd have to make herself stay busy. Life would have to go on and she hoped eventually the pain would fade away.

There was some good news. Melissa received a call two weeks earlier from the renters staying at her house in Edisto. She had rented her family's beach home out to some friends of her parents right before she met John. He had never even seen the place. The couple called two weeks before John told her he was leaving to say they would be moving. Maybe it was destiny, but it was perfect timing for her to get away. The beach at Edisto was always so healing for her soul.

She needed a place to get away, a place to get her thoughts and plans together. She was certain the change of scenery would do her good. At least it would give her time to think through her plans for the future. She would take a few days off from her shop, The Cranberry Tree, and drive down to the beach.

She counted off the next days with the mundane obligations of work and household duties. No word, no letter, nothing of the husband she was with for the last seven years. It was like a bad dream. It seemed impossible for someone to just leave that way. The feelings of abandonment, the emptiness of feeling so alone, the anger, the fear, it was so hard to understand how life could be going along one way and the next moment everything can be different.

Melissa chose to stay in town long enough to paint and decorate the nursery. She made arrangements with the ladies at the shop to take over while she was away. She planned on taking her laptop, so she could still work. Even supplies could be ordered via e-mail there.

Finally, everything was ready and she could leave for the beach. Melissa took a deep breath as she drove out of town. She missed John as much as the first day he left her. At least at the beach she wouldn't accidentally run into him. Yes, the beach would definitely be a welcomed relief.

When she arrived, Melissa unlocked the door to the beach house. This was her first visit after picking up the keys from her friends. She immediately started opening all the windows to let in the fresh air. She walked to the back porch, closed her eyes and breathed in the smells of the sea. Listening to the waves crashing beneath her, she couldn't help but have some sense of peace. It was wonderful that she had held onto this place for all these years.

Melissa went back inside and began to unpack her things. She needed to eat even if she didn't feel hungry. She made a salad with Romaine lettuce, garden tomatoes, carrots, cucumbers, and red onion. She dipped fresh strawberries in homemade whipping cream for dessert.

After dinner she walked through the den and looked at the fireplace. An ache surfaced inside of her. She wished John could be sharing this moment with her. She was glad it was summer not winter. At least she wouldn't have to look at a fire in the fireplace. Seeing those flames flicker always brought out the romantic side in her. She threw an extra pillow on the couch and went back outside.

The sky was radiant. Blues, purples, and reds streaked above the water, reflecting there in a rush of foam and waves. She patted her abdomen and spoke softly to her unborn baby.

"You're going to love this place. You'll play in the water, build sand castles, and run up and down the beach. Don't you worry about anything, honey. You and mommy are going to be just fine." She was talking to herself as much as to the baby, hoping all her anxiety and fear would not affect the health of her fetus in anyway.

Melissa went for a short walk down the beach. Slipping off her shoes, she let the water run through her toes and back out to sea. The sand squeaked with each step she took. She wanted to run as fast as she could, but decided this might not be good for herself or the baby.

She missed John. She remembered for the hundredth time their last night together. She relived it over in her mind, cursing him silently for coming into her life in the first place. Why had he left her so suddenly without any explanation? Why hadn't she picked up on any discontentment he may have had with their marriage? And why didn't he call? It just did not make sense. Well whatever, she had determined never to let anyone for any reason get close to her again.

It was getting late and the sun had already gone down. She walked slowly back to the house trying to quiet her troubled spirit. She climbed the creaky stairs to the back door of the cottage. She turned, looked at the ocean one last time, and went inside.

Melissa tried to read the book she brought with her to the beach, but found it hard to concentrate. She was thinking about hiring someone to work at the shop before the baby was born. Later she might need someone to manage the store full time. She would just have to see what would be best. The thought occurred to her to purchase another store in Atlanta and perhaps move there.

That's what she would do. Get someone to help manage the store and then take it over in a year. Melissa finally put down the book and wrapped the sheet tighter around herself. She attempted to push her thoughts aside and go to sleep. Her slender long legs were curled up near her chest with her knees drawn close in a fetal position.

Sleep came quickly, but her dreams more than once interrupted her night. Had it not been for the waves to lull her back to sleep, she might not have slept at all. Something about the sound of waves crashing in the background was the very thing she needed to bring peace to her waking moments.

The sun challenged her laziness early the next morning. She woke with very little sign of morning sickness. Even as a child, any morning at the beach was an exciting one. She put on some shorts, a wind breaker, and jogging shoes. Melissa then headed for the shore feeling almost like a little girl again. Except for the hurt in her heart, the beach stirred up all kinds of good feelings. She let the waves crash upon her body, hoping they could somehow pull her pain and confusion back out to sea.

It was the beach, the ocean, and the wind that gave her comfort. It did not matter that she had been abandoned and left behind. She would always have the land, the one thing that would always remain faithful to her. It was the good earth that gave her strength. Seems like she remembered reading Pearl S. Buck's book by that title years ago.

That's what it's all about, a place we call home. People may come and go in our lives. We may be left behind, but it's where we stay, where we live, the place we call home that gives us real security. Everything that was good about her childhood always came back to her beach memories. South Carolina was her home. Charleston and Edisto were her roots. Could she move to Atlanta? Not unless she could return to Edisto.

She watched the gentle cycle of the waves as they returned to the sea. In only moments a white cap beat against the shore. She sat right in the middle of the waves in hopes they were restoring some balance into her life. Melissa liked that image. She sat with her eyes closed and imagined her hurt being pulled out of her. She began to feel better. Every moment she spent by the shore the better she felt.

It would be hard to leave and head back to Charleston. She would have to face the circumstances of her life with determination or she wouldn't make it. She won track meets in college by setting her mind on the goal ahead of her. Staying focused for the baby's sake was something she had to do. Life had to go on no matter how she felt.

She wouldn't allow herself just to curl up and die over some man's leaving her. The baby needed her to be strong and she would let that motivate everything she had to do in the months ahead. It was a part of her southern heritage to survive, no matter what was going on inside.

Feelings of loss could never be what held her back from living her life to the fullest. She would just have to fake it until she made it because there was someone else to live for now.

Melissa stopped walking and sat on the driest part of the sand closest to where the waves were breaking. If it were possible, it was time to purge herself from all this sadness. She looked out as far as she could see, and sobbed over the loneliness she felt. She cried releasing her tears in the crook of her arm until she couldn't cry anymore. She had to get it all out and then leave it behind her. Finally, the tears stopped. She stood up, carried her shoes in her hands, and headed back to the beach house. The ocean had done its job, and it was time to head back to Charleston.

Chapter Three

JOHN ISAACSON

John could not help but think about everything that happened on the day he decided to leave Melissa. Everything was as clear to him as when it first happened...

"Dr. Smith will be right with you, Mr. Isaacson. You need to undress and put on this hospital wrap."

John hated going to the doctor for tests and sitting on wax paper that rattled every time he moved. It was humiliating having two people look at his private parts and as usual he was freezing.

The door swung open and startled John. "Dr. Smith is going to need a urine specimen. You can use the facility to the right of this room."

He returned with what little urine he could get and waited.

The nurse interrupted his thoughts again. "I'll take that sample now, Mr. Isaacson. I should have instructed you to leave it in the other room. The doctor will be right with you." She smiled routinely.

Several more minutes passed and Dr. Smith came in with John's records.

"How are you, John?" The doctor asked without looking up from his files.

"Fine, fine." He replied without thinking.

"Let's see what we've got here." The doctor skimmed through John's charts.

John waited. The muscles in his stomach began to contract with each minute he waited.

He felt like throwing up. He waited.

"John, I've gotten some results back from the test we did the last time you were here. There appears to be a problem with your prostate."

"What do you mean, Doc? What kind of problem?"

"Well, the last time I examined you, I did a classic digital rectal exam. Your score on that exam was around 375. To be honest with you, John that's not a good score. What I want to do now is a TRUSP. That stands for Transrectal Ultrasonic Examination of the Prostate."

John felt the blood leave his face. "What does that mean? I...I thought I was finished with all my tests."

"This will be the next step. Using sound waves, the urologist can pass a fiber optic probe through the rectum. It's about the size of a thin straw. It may sound badly, but it's actually less uncomfortable than the digital exam you already had. The second test helps us to be more specific about your condition."

John felt his stomach begin to churn as he continued to listen.

"The first test classified your condition between stage C and D. If this is correct, we need to start some kind of therapy right away. The ultrasound image gives a remarkably clear picture of the tissue density of the prostate and we can detect any changes immediately."

"It sounds awful to me." John's face turned almost white.

"In reality the office biopsy is a relatively painless procedure."

"I don't understand, Doc. I'm only 36 years old. How could I possibly have such a serious case of prostate cancer?"

"I don't know, John. There aren't very many known cases of anyone your age having prostate cancer. That's why it's so important that you have this second test."

"And what if the first test were right? Then what?"

"We'll have to start treatment right away."

"What kind of treatment?"

"First we try hormone therapy, then radiation, then ..."

"Then, what?" John looked like a frightened boy.

"Then medically indicated castration as a final resort."

They were both silent as those words tore inside John's thoughts. He stood to his feet and barely made it to the trash can near the sink where he began to throw up. The doctor started to reach out to him, but stuffed his hand in his pocket instead.

"That's a last resort, John. The first two treatments normally work. You're young and you have a very good chance the hormone therapy will take care of the problem."

"If I have to do the radiation treatment? How will that affect me?"

"Well, with radiation you can take oral forms of the treatment. Some men have lived to be seventy, even eighty years of age after radiation treatment."

"What about sex and the ability to have children? What about that?"

"During and sometimes after the radiation some men can't have intercourse and are sterile. There is always the possibility of a transplant if necessary."

The disappointment was overwhelming. John wished the doctor hadn't said those last words. They played over and over again in his mind.

"When will you do the test?" He finally asked.

"We can do that right now. The urologist is available. If you can stay a little longer?"

"Then what?"

"We get the results back and schedule treatment."

"Doc, what am I supposed to say to my wife? She wants to have kids so badly and I do, too. We've been trying for several years. I just can't face her with this, right now."

"Maybe you don't need to, John. Let's just wait on the results and go from there. The office will call as soon as we hear anything. I'll have them set up an exam right now with the urologist."

"All right." John's voice trailed off. He felt like a zombie just going through the motions.

Doctor Smith reached up and touched John's shoulder. "I know this is a lot to think about, but at least we found out as soon as we did."

John nodded his head, too emotional to talk anymore. He followed the doctor down the hall to the urologist's examination room.

When the exam was over, John left the doctor's office, walked to the elevator, and watched the doors close behind him. Tears began to drip from the corners of his eyes. He brushed them aside with the back of his hand. His relationship with Melissa may as well be over. She deserved to have children and a healthy sex life with her husband. He would never tell her. No one was going to stay with him out of pity. He would just have to get out of her life.

He reached the car and began to retch in the parking lot. Finally, he opened the door, got in and buckled the seatbelt. He leaned forward against the steering wheel and sobbed. The pain and hopelessness tore at his insides. He cried, not like a man, but like a little boy, like an abandoned child. He started the car and drove around for the next couple of hours, trying to figure out what he should do next. He decided to leave Melissa.

Chapter Four

JENNIFER CRAWSON

Jennifer walked in The Cranberry Tree to apply for a managerial position. She waited while Melissa completed a job order from one of the wholesale distributors that supplied lace and ribbon for the shop.

She watched Melissa, curious about her life. No ring, obviously pregnant and she seemed sad. There was this forlorn look in her eyes, yet she appeared to be self-confident with her business skills. Melissa was a very striking attractive lady, long dark hair, deep blue eyes, skinny though pregnant. Wonder if she's married and just doesn't wear her rings? Jennifer thought.

"Sorry to keep you waiting. I'm Melissa Johnson. You must be Jennifer Crawson." Melissa was using her maiden name now. She extended her hand and received a firm shake from Jennifer.

Jennifer nodded. "Yes, I am. So, nice to finally meet you in person."

"Would you like some coffee? I was just about to have some myself."

"Yes, I would, thank you."

"I'm trying not to drink as much since the pregnancy, but I haven't been able to give it up completely. You like yours light? Sugar?" Melissa asked pointing to the coffee server.

"No, I like mine black. I've been drinking it that way since college."

She poured Jennifer's first and then her own. "I hope you like Almond Amaretto. That's the kind I made today."

"That just happens to be one of my favorite flavors." Jennifer smiled and thought to herself, I can tell we're going to get along great.

Melissa continued. "So tell me, Jennifer, what makes you think you want to manage a shop like this one?"

"Well, I have an extensive knowledge of your basic product line, and I have a good business mind. I suppose I have a little of my mother and my dad in me. Fortunately, I was adopted by two wonderful parents who were very proficient in art and business. My creative background and my seven years of experience in retail and management would certainly contribute to my proficiency at, The Cranberry Tree."

Melissa made a mental note of how articulate Jennifer seemed during the interview with lots of eye contact. She interjected, "You said your parents were proficient in business. Are they still living?"

"My mother is, but she is retired now. She still paints some, but just in her spare time."

"How about siblings? You said you were adopted, any brothers or sisters?"

"I have one brother. We were separated initially. Unfortunately his first family treated him terribly. My parents adopted him later, but the damage was already done. He ran away and I believe may have gotten in trouble with the law. I'm not sure where he is now, but I would love to help him get his life straightened out."

"Maybe one day you'll be able to do that. With all those programs on the internet you may be able to locate him, as well as your real parents, if you wanted to find out who they are."

"I've never had a desire to do that. My adopted parents were so good to me. Sometimes adopted parents are better for you than your biological parents would be. Sometimes being abandoned can lead you to a better destiny than you otherwise would have had." She noticed the color change in Melissa's face.

Melissa drank a swallow of her coffee, and hoped Jennifer's last statement would be true for her baby as well as herself. She and

Jennifer seemed to have a lot in common. They were both abandoned and neither of them knew why. Maybe it didn't matter why, only what you choose to do with your life after that happens.

Jennifer interrupted her thoughts, "Melissa would you mind if I used your restroom? I just drove in from Atlanta this morning and I didn't have time to stop on the way in."

"Sure, its straight down the hall to the left." She watched Jennifer excuse herself. Her appearance was impressive as well. Melissa couldn't help, but feel a little insecure looking at Jennifer's tiny waist. She was feeling very fat this last trimester of her pregnancy.

Jennifer's hair was thick and brown and hung in waves down her back. She favored Andy McDowell in her face. Her eyes were brown with long lashes. Sensitive eyes that kind of drew you in, very compassionate looking. The turquoise blouse under her suit was a very good color for her. Yes, this lady was very sharp and Melissa instantly liked her. As far as she was concerned she already had the job.

Jennifer returned and took a sip of her coffee.

"Is there anything you want to ask me?" Melissa inquired.

"Are you married?"

Melissa turned two shades redder. "Well, you don't beat around the bush, do you?"

Jennifer wished she hadn't asked such a personal question. She tried to think of something else to say, but was drawing a blank.

For the first time Melissa was having to admit her failed marriage. "Uh, I was married, but I'm not anymore. We're divorced and yes, I'm very much pregnant with his child." She looked away and pretended to be straightening one of the handcrafted clocks from Switzerland, one of her favorite places to shop.

Jennifer read the pain in Melissa's face. She decided to change the subject by asking for the job.

"Melissa, I really believe I'd be perfect for the job, and I think we could work well together. I believe you'll be very glad you hired me for the position." She smiled warmly and waited.

Melissa liked her confidence. There was something about Jennifer that made her want to tell her everything about her life. That thought scared her in a way, but it was also a comfort to her. Instant trust was not something she had ever experienced before.

"Well, let's go eat lunch, talk about your salary, and decide when you can start work." She gave her an encouraging smile.

"Sounds like a great idea to me!" Jennifer replied.

Melissa put a sign in the window that said 'Gone to Lunch. Be back at 2:00.' She locked the door and headed toward Queen Street.

"I thought we could go to my favorite restaurant, Poogan's Porch. Have you ever heard the story of Poogan's Porch?"

"No, I haven't. My knowledge of Charleston is very limited, I'm afraid."

"Oh, it's a wonderful story about a little dog that was abandoned. Poogan's family had to move up north. He stayed behind and faithfully waited for their return. He would go from house to house perhaps looking for his owners. The neighbors began to feed him and when this house became a restaurant it was named Poogan's Porch in honor of Poogan. The patrons of the restaurant would feed him scraps from the table and scratch him behind his ears.

Poogan never left the house on Queen Street and would forever call Charleston his home. I'm not sure I have all the details right about his life, but I think it's such a nice story about abandonment and our destiny. He died in 1979 and the restaurant is a memorial unto him. That little dog statue in the yard marks his grave.

You'll have to look at all the pictures on the wall. Several celebrities have visited here. Barbara Streisand, James Brown, Jim Cary to name a few. It was a favorite place to eat for Paul Newman and Joanne Woodward."

"I just love true stories about the history of a place. Isn't that something we were just talking about abandonment and our destiny? See what I mean, sometimes our lives are better for it when we're abandoned. Poogan could have moved up north, felt disoriented and walked the streets until he died an early death. In Charleston, he has his own restaurant that continues to carry his name even after his death."

"Here we are. The place has so much personality. There are rumors Poogan's Porch has a ghost. Some stories are fabricated others supposedly true. Regardless, I love the food here. My favorite is fish and chips, but the other specials are delicious as well. I think you'll end up coming here as well when you come to work for me. I hope you can start right away."

Jennifer extended her hand. "That would be great. Thank you very much, Melissa. Maybe I'll be like Poogan and live here for the rest of my life as well."

The staff was excited to see Melissa at Poogan's Porch. She had not been there in two months. She of course got the fish and chips. Jennifer had the Charleston Chicken.

"Are you familiar with Charleston at all?"

"Not really. Other than reading, *Gone With the Wind*, I've never visited here before."

"Well, let's walk down to the Battery after we eat. You need to see Rainbow Row. If you have time, we could do a little tour of Charleston."

"Sure, I'd love that and you're right, this is a wonderful restaurant. It has such atmosphere and personality. I almost feel like Poogan is here with us."

Melissa smiled. She could tell Jennifer was going to love it in Charleston. They'd have to do a horse and buggy ride after lunch. She could learn the history of the buildings. The structural dynamics of preparing for a hurricane or an earthquake.

"Charleston is so full of history. You'll love learning about it. Including the horse and buggy tours. We can take a ride later if you want to."

"That would be great!"

Chapter Five

John had been on radiation for almost six months. His treatment did not cause his hair to fall out, but he did feel nauseous. He didn't have the energy to work out at the health club anymore, and he no longer stayed at the office late. There were very few people who knew he was sick. His boss knew, and his friend Alex had driven him to a couple of his doctor's appointments when he had been too sick to drive himself.

He rented tons of movies and read three or four books a week. He always had been an avid reader, but now he read as a form of therapy. After five months his sexual drive had decreased tremendously. He attributed it partly to his separation from Melissa, and partly to the medication he was taking. He was grieving and he didn't know if he would ever get over his having to leave her. Memories flooded his dreams and his waking moments. There wasn't a day that went by that he didn't think of her.

The doctor scheduled exploratory surgery in two weeks to see how well the radiation was working on eliminating the cancer. Perhaps after all his treatments, he would make plans to leave Charleston. Although he wanted to see Melissa, he knew it wouldn't be right to drift in and out of her life. It wasn't his desire to cause her any more pain, so his plan was to stay as far away as possible.

It was Thursday afternoon and John would have to hurry to make it to his doctor's appointment on time. Traffic seemed unusually heavy. He should have left earlier.

He parked on the third level adjoining the hospital and walked the crosswalk to Dr. Smith's office. The exhaust from the cars as they entered and left the garage was stifling. He began to jog to escape the fumes. He noticed his shoe was untied and bent down to tie it.

"John Isaacson! John?"

Turning around, John saw a young woman motioning for him to wait. She was too far away for him to see her face, but she continued to call to him.

"John, wait. It's Jennifer Crawson. Wait a minute!"

He squinted toward her. "Jennifer? Jennifer, what are you doing in Charleston? I haven't seen you since we graduated from college."

She finally reached him and threw her arms around his neck. "My God, it's been so long and you look so skinny. What on earth are you doing here?"

"I might ask you the same thing. I've been living in Charleston for almost 12 years. I moved here not too long after I finished school." John informed her.

"Has it been that long? It seems like only a couple of years ago. I guess I've been so busy with graduate school, working during and after school that the years slipped by." She studied his face with all the intensity of a sculptor and noticed he failed to tell her why he was going to see the doctor. He seemed sad even though he was obviously glad to see her.

"Jennifer, what about you? What are you doing here? I must say, you look terrific. Whatever happened with you and Andy? Did you two finally get married?"

She blushed. "Andy? No, after eight years, we finally called it quits. His idea actually. It seems he was seeing someone else for the last couple of years we were together. Other than the fiasco in my relationship with Andy, I've been doing great. Eating right and exercising daily helps to keep me as healthy as I can be under the circumstances, and I recently started a job here in Charleston. What about you? Are you all right? Married?"

"I was married."

Jennifer saw that pained look in his face again and he still didn't tell her why he was going in the medical building in such a hurry.

John glanced at his watch. He was five minutes late for his appointment and needed to catch the elevator to the fifth floor.

She picked up on his anxiety. "Don't let me hold you up." She said apologetically.

"Well, I'm a little late for my appointment, but I do want to catch up with you later. Let me get your phone number and I'll give you a call tonight, if that's all right with you?"

"Sounds great. She fumbled in her purse for a pen and paper as they both got on the elevator. Here's my number."

"Okay. I'll call you this evening, if you're going to be home."

"I'll be there after work and a jog. Give me a call anytime after 8:00."

The doors opened on the 5th floor and John started running out. "I'll call around 8:30 tonight. Look forward to catching up on everything then." He yelled as he headed down the hall.

The doors closed behind him. Jennifer was still wondering what kind of doctor John was seeing. She was so glad she ran into him. It was like having an old family member in Charleston with her. She pressed the button to the 6th floor, and hoped Melissa hadn't been waiting very long.

Melissa was having her last weekly checkup before the baby was due. The discomfort of her large abdomen made her pray daily that she would have the baby early. Jennifer had dropped her off at the doctor's office over two hours earlier and she would be returning any minute. They hadn't even called Melissa's name yet. She looked at her watch. She was glad Jennifer was running late. Having read all her favorite magazines, Melissa began to get tired and irritable. She wished they would hurry so she could get back to the shop. She wanted to do some bookkeeping and there were orders that needed to be placed. If it were at all possible, she wanted to leave early and go right to bed.

The door opened and closed as Jennifer's smiling face met Melissa's frustrated one. "Hi, I see you're having a great time here in the waiting room. I hope you haven't been waiting for me long."

"No, I haven't even seen the doctor yet."

"You're kidding. I thought I was the one who had caused that irritated look." Jennifer picked up a magazine and sat down next to

Melissa. "Well, you look totally disgusted and your shaking your foot that nervous way you do when you wish you were doing something else. I'm just glad I wasn't the source of your irritation."

"Unfortunately no. I wish you were. I'm glad you were running late. I'd hate for both of us to be wasting so much time this afternoon. I hate to be doing nothing when I've got so much that needs to be done at the office."

"Maybe I can do something for you. I could come back and pick you up later." Jennifer suggested.

"I guess you could. I'm just so tired of sitting here. Looking at my swollen ankles is not helping my mood any."

"That's normal Melissa. I don't know of a single pregnant woman who is easy to be around during the last two weeks of her pregnancy. So don't worry, the baby will be here before you know it, and then you won't have any time for yourself."

"Thanks for the encouragement. Now, I really have something to look forward to." She smiled sarcastically.

"Should I go back to the office or just wait for you?"

The nurse called out Melissa's name before she had time to respond to Jennifer's question.

"Melissa Johnson, the doctor can see you now."

"I suppose you should just stay. I'll leave my purse with you, if you don't mind."

"We'll be right here." Jennifer smiled at Melissa and flipped through the magazine she held in her hand. Her mind began to rehash her conversation with John. She couldn't believe she ran into him today. It concerned her that he looked so badly, but she was so glad to see someone from home. She couldn't wait to talk with him tonight.

Maybe the two of them could go out and eat this weekend. She could find out what had been going on in his life, tell him about Andy, her decision to move to Charleston, and of course her new job and her boss. She couldn't wait to tell Melissa about him. Maybe they could all go out sometime. Once again she was seeing how life always has a way of coming full circle. Everything is always connected in some way.

Chapter Six

John's doctor arranged for his admittance to the hospital to be in a week. This part of his treatment would indicate if any cancer had spread to the bone or to his organs. The next test would indicate if castration would be necessary.

It all sounded like a terrible nightmare to John. The cancer was not the only thing that made him sick. The torment of what might happen next was frightening. His appointment lasted 30 minutes and he was heading back to the office before going home for the weekend.

On the way home, he stopped by his favorite Chinese restaurant and ordered chicken cashew with chicken fried rice, no MSG. He got it to go so he could call Jennifer after he ate. He was thinking about running into her on the way into the hospital. It gave him some comfort having at least one friend to talk with. Maybe they could go see a movie this weekend. He was tired of renting movies and watching them by himself. Sometimes he just wished he had someone to go out with just as a friend.

He ate right out of the carton with chop sticks and poured club soda. He ate too quickly, and was feeling a little indigestion. He was anxious about talking with Jennifer as soon as he could. At 8:20 he dialed the number and the phone rang several times.

"Hello?"

He was about to hang up when he heard her answer. "Jennifer, is that you? This is John Isaacson. I thought for a moment you weren't there."

"Hi, John. I was just walking in the door when I heard the phone. Do you mind holding on a moment while I lock the door and put my groceries away? Or if you want, I can call you right back."

"I can hold unless you think you need more time."

"It shouldn't take me long. Hold just a minute."

"All right."

Jennifer put down the phone, locked the door, and pulled her shoes off. She threw the milk and salad ingredients in the refrigerator. She washed her hands, grabbed some cheese and a diet Coke, and then ran and got the mobile phone.

"I'm back." Somewhat out of breath, she continued. "So what's going on with you?" She wanted to find out if he were sick or something. He looked so thin and depressed. The divorce must have been so hard on him.

"Oh, not much. Just working too much. How about you? It's been so long, Jennifer. Seeing you brings back so many memories."

"John, is everything all right? What were you doing in such a hurry at the medical building today? Are you sick?"

John was quiet for a moment. Thinking of where to begin. "Well, about nine months ago I found out I have prostate cancer. I am currently going through radiation treatments and I'm scheduled for surgery in a week. Nothing has been the same in my life since I found out. I've been going through a divorce in the process. I don't guess I look so good, huh?"

"Well, to be honest you look thinner than I remember. I'm so sorry, John. Is there anything I can do for you?"

"I guess it helps just having someone to talk to about it."

"There's no need in your going through this alone. I could take you to the doctor, look after your place, or water your plants. I'm already doing that for my boss. Her baby is due at anytime."

"Is that why you were at the medical building today?"

"Yes, I was picking her up from her last doctor's appointment before the baby is due when I saw you. So it's not a problem if you need me to take you somewhere or run an errand for you."

"I appreciate that, Jennifer. I don't know what the doctor is going to find or what I'll need to do next. Sometimes I wish my parents were still alive so they could be with me right now."

She remembered that John's dad died of a heart attack and his mom died of cancer when John was in his first year of college.

John continued. "I miss my parents so much. It was hard when I lost them just a year apart, but for some reason I miss them even more now."

"I'm sure you do, John. Don't worry, you don't have to go through this alone. We'll walk through this, one day at a time. I'll go with you to the hospital and if you want me to, I'll even stay there until you find out the results of the tests. The only other commitment I have right now is to drive my boss to the hospital. As long as she doesn't go into labor at the same time, we'll be okay."

John smiled for the first time in months. "You'll never know how much that means to me, Jennifer. Thank God you moved to Charleston."

"Good, that's settled. Now tell me what they've told you so far about your condition. I know of older men who have prostate cancer and it has not been life threatening for them."

"There aren't very many cases on record of anyone my age having prostate cancer. I don't understand it, Jen. I'm in the prime of my life. I wanted to start a family and now it may be impossible. I may never be able to have kids or a normal sex life again because of the treatment."

"Don't think that way, John. You're going to be fine. There's no telling what they'll be able to do. The medical field is coming up with new treatments all the time. Just keep thinking as positively as you can. That's probably the only reason I've made it as long as I have. None of us could make it if we didn't believe the best. There is always the possibility of a new beginning. By this time next year, you may be married. You never know."

"Yeah, right."

"I'm serious."

"Who's going to want someone who may not be able to have children or sex?"

"You don't know that for certain, John. Just concentrate on getting better."

"I'll try. Anyway, I've kept you on the phone long enough with my problems. Maybe we can get together this weekend for dinner."

"Sure. I'd like that."

"Do you want to talk sometime on Friday to make sure we're both free for the weekend?"

"That sounds like a good idea. My boss may go into labor at any time, so that would be better for me."

"Yeah, me too. The doctor may decide to send me early for surgery if they can see me any sooner. Should I pick you up at your apartment or would you rather meet somewhere?"

"We'll talk on Friday and if everything is still good for both of us, you can just come by my apartment and pick me up. Sometimes I have to work late. If you'll give me your phone number, I'll try to call and let you know when I'm leaving the shop."

"Okay, I might as well give you my address as well."

"All right. Let me get a piece of paper. I left my address book at the shop." She put the phone down and grabbed her purse. "Go, ahead."

When he had finished, she gave him instructions to her apartment. "John, I'm so glad we ran into each other. It seems like old times minus a couple of people." She was referring to Andy and several of John's old girlfriends.

"Boy, that seems like a hundred years ago for me. I never was real serious with anyone. Those were some fun times, all those ball games and parties, we seemed so carefree then."

"You and Andy were carefree. I was struggling with so many things: Andy, my health, and then my career for another. I'll have to say things definitely got better when I got Andy out of my life."

"Knowing Andy I can believe that. I guess we can talk about the past when we get together on Friday. I feel better already, Jennifer. I'm so glad you saw me today. What were the odds of that happening?"

"It's destiny, I guess. Maybe an old friend from the past is just what you need in your life, and I just happened to be in the neighborhood. It's my last good deed for the year."

32

"I'm just glad I got to cash in on it before you ran out. Well, I can't wait to see you this weekend. That is if your boss doesn't go into labor." John added.

"Sounds great to me. It'll be good seeing you again, John. You have a goodnight. Bye now."

"Goodnight, Jennifer." John hung up the phone.

Chapter Seven

Jennifer stuffed John's phone number and address in the side pocket of her purse, and hoped she'd remember to put it in her address book the next day. She was still hungry so she made a salad and decided to check on Melissa. The phone rang and rang. There was no answer. She dialed again and still no answer.

"H'm, that's odd. I wonder where she is?" Jennifer mumbled out loud. She let the phone ring four more times. There was a nagging feeling of unrest beginning to settle over her.

Melissa had complained of false contraction pains earlier that day. She certainly hoped she hadn't gone into labor on the way home.

"Ah, that's crazy. I'm just paranoid." She continued to talk to herself. She finished eating her salad, crunching on raw carrots and broccoli. It had been an exhausting week. She longed for a hot shower. This was one night when all she wanted to do was read a good book, write in her journal, and go to sleep early. As she undressed, nagging concern for Melissa overshadowed her thoughts.

Wrapping her robe around her nude body, she delayed getting into the shower long enough to make another call. Steam began to fill the bathroom as she let the phone ring. Still there was no answer. It was already after nine o'clock.

"That's strange. She should have been home hours ago. She left early, said she was going home and getting in the bed as soon as she ate something." Jennifer continued to mumble out loud. She hung up the phone.

The shower was hotter than usual, but comforting. Jennifer's mind was retracing her own steps when she left the office. She had taken the mail to the post office in five o'clock traffic. Then she went to the grocery store and talked on the phone with John for almost an hour. Why wasn't the answering machine working? If Melissa were there and nothing was wrong, she wouldn't just let the phone ring.

The water beat hard against Jennifer's face. She pressed herself into the stream allowing the heat to draw the tension from her shoulders. She turned exposing her back and legs to the same healing effects of the spray.

She recalled John's words and felt badly for him. He had never looked so sad and empty in college and she had never seen him look so frail. She hoped after his treatments, he would go on with his life, and get out and meet new people.

Turning the faucets off and the shower nozzle upward, she wrapped a white towel around her thin body, and twisted another one around her hair. After slipping on her bedroom shoes, she tried calling again, ten rings, and then another five.

"Where is she?" She shouted into the silence of her apartment. It was 9:30. She finally called the hospital to see if Melissa had admitted herself. Maybe she had gone into labor early. There was no record of her arrival, no admittance into labor and delivery. Jennifer's heart sank.

"Well, could you connect me with the emergency room? She may have needed emergency care while driving home this evening."

They complied, still nothing. "Thank you very much." She hung up the phone. Oh well, maybe she's just asleep and forgot to turn the answering machine back on after checking her messages. None of those thoughts eased Jennifer's mind.

"This is driving me crazy. Where is she?" Her heart began to pound. Something was wrong and she knew it. Call it women's intuition, but in her gut she knew something was terribly wrong.

She threw on some jeans and pulled a sweater over her damp hair. She ran her fingers through her hair instead of using a comb and put her running shoes on without socks. Grabbing her purse and keys, she rushed to her car. Her mind was fighting with her heart. What if all this were just her imagination? It didn't matter, something inside kept pushing her to check on Melissa. The tires squealed as she pulled away from the apartment.

"God, help me. What should I do? Where do I go first?" She whispered out loud. "I'll check her house first and then back track to the office."

"Hold on, Melissa. Whatever's wrong, I'm coming. Hang on just a little longer."

Jennifer slowed down, looked both ways, and then ran two red lights when no one was coming. She decided she'd have to plead for mercy if the police came after her. She was thankful Melissa had already given her a set of keys to her house, so she could take care of her plants for her while she was in the hospital.

She continued to battle with her emotions. "What am I doing? Melissa said she wanted to go home early and get some rest. Maybe she was so tired, she turned the ringer off and didn't realize the answering machine wasn't on. I should just go home and go to sleep myself. She's going to think I'm crazy if I wake her up."

The headlights hit the corner of Melissa's house. Jennifer pulled into the driveway and turned off the motor. She hesitated a moment, then decided she might as well go in and see if Melissa had made it home. She searched frantically for Melissa's keys. Snatching them from her purse, slamming the door, she ran up the driveway to the door.

Chapter Eight

It was ten minutes after 6:00 when Melissa turned the corner into her driveway. Glad to be home she had felt more tired than usual. The baby was pushing on her cervix and there had been a series of hard contractions all day, about two hours apart. Perhaps having to wait in the doctor's office for so many hours had stressed her out.

She waited for the garage door to open and pondered what to eat for dinner. She really wasn't hungry. She looked at her nails, picked at a chip on the nail on her ring finger, and wished she had the strength to paint them tonight, but was just too tired. She slowly pulled into the garage. There were a few more things she needed to pack to take with her to the hospital, but everything would just have to wait until tomorrow. There was no way she was going to do anything tonight, but go to bed early. Grabbing her purse and attache case, she locked the car door. The garage door clicked shut as she headed for the steps to the back door.

As she reached up to put the key in the lock, a sharp pain wrenched her body.

"Oh, my God!" She screamed. Dropping the attache case, she grabbed her abdomen with one hand, and reached out for the door knob with the other to try and catch her balance. Her foot missed the step and she tumbled into a dark corner of the garage. Blood began to puddle around her thighs. Her nose and mouth were also bleeding.

Minutes ticked by taking more of her life with each moment that passed. Her pulse beat with the same consistency of a clock that loses time, slowing down as the minutes went by. She regained consciousness for just a few moments only to drift back into the darkness that shadowed her mind and body. She was lost in the emptiness of her surroundings, struggling to stay alive, struggling with the word help. It was as though she were in a dream where she could neither speak nor run. She was helpless and it did not matter that she couldn't cry out. There was no one who would hear her anyway.

In those moments when she was cognizant she tried to form the words with her lips even if she couldn't make a sound. She wasn't sure where she was or what had happened. She only knew pain throbbed through her whole body. Finally, she screamed out into the darkness. The horror that no one knew where she was or would even miss her until the morning was overwhelming. She collapsed as her body continued to empty itself of life. The contractions began to come even closer together, blood continued to spread on the garage floor, and her pulse grew even fainter.

The phone was ringing inside her home. Her semi-conscious mind wanted to respond, to answer, to scream out for help. The phone continued to ring with an urgency to be answered. The caller and the unconscious were communicating in that unspoken language of the soul. There was the knowledge that time was running out, that one life, maybe two would be lost.

John switched the channels with the remote for the tenth time. He felt so much better after talking with Jennifer. It somehow gave him the strength to believe everything was going to be all right.

He was feeling up, but restless. He wanted to eat, but didn't know what he wanted. He started watching one show and then turned to something else. He missed Melissa. He wanted to call her, but didn't want to hurt her any more than he had already.

Maybe he could just call to hear her voice. He knew he shouldn't, but for some reason he could not get her off his mind. Finally, he couldn't resist this urgency to call her. Remembering her number, he dialed slowly, deliberately. His heart was beating loudly in his chest.

The phone rang and rang. Where could she be at this hour? The thought occurred to him she might be on a date. He continued to let the phone ring, wondering why she didn't have on her answering machine.

Finally, John hung up the phone. So much for hearing her voice. He breathed deeply. He deserved this ache in his heart. He never should have left her. Of course she would be out on a date. Why wouldn't she be dating? He couldn't expect her to be alone for the rest of her life just because he might be.

He made popcorn and found the movie, Casablanca on television. Bogart also had to say goodbye to the person he loved. How could Bergman just walk away? Obviously, for the good of both of them.

John tried to sleep, but spent the next hour turning back and forth on his back and stomach in the bed. "What's the use?" John whispered. He went to the bookshelf and pulled out one of his favorite books of poetry from college. As he opened it to read a poem, a piece of paper fell out. It was a poem he had written when he was in school. He read it out loud:

I am hungry for love like the ocean is hungry
For the shore. Always coming back for more
And more with each wave that laps across the sand.
When I find you, I'll be content and in gentleness
I will hold you close. For if I find true love, I'll
Never let you go. Forget You? I could not. For I
Have carved you in my heart. Letting nothing, not
Even death, pull us apart. For true love burns like
A roaring fire that can not be quenched, though
Man or life or ocean demit. And if I be the one to
Blow out the candle of love, may I be cursed
With hours of aloneness, with no other lover, with
No true friend to hold.

Those words were written so long ago. He may have been influenced by Heathcliff in *Wuthering Heights*, and it might sound a little corny, but tonight it seemed like a self-fulfilling prophesy. Why had he left Melissa? Why did he walk away from the one person he truly loved?

He tried to call again still no answer. He was sure she must be out on a date. He shouldn't be calling anyway. She needed to go on with her life.

He wept. What he had said so many years ago, in a feeble attempt to write a poem had somehow come to pass. He certainly had become a cursed and lonely man. He was truly alone.

Chapter Nine

Jennifer rang the doorbell several times before she took the initiative to go inside. The house was totally dark. She called Melissa's name as she slowly opened the front door and continued to do so as she walked into the house. There was no response. The thought of being shot as she entered her friend's house, crossed her mind. She continued to call into the dark, so Melissa wouldn't think someone was breaking into her home.

"Melissa, it's Jennifer. Melissa, are you sleeping? Oh!" She stumbled over a chair, caught her balance, and continued to skim the wall for a light switch.

"Melissa, are you home?" She finally found the light and turned it on in the living room. She reached the hallway, turned the light on in there, and headed for Melissa's bedroom. Jennifer's pulse was pounding in her ears as she discovered Melissa was not in the bed and it had never been unmade.

"God, where is she?" She mumbled to herself as she headed for the den to see if she had fallen asleep on the couch. She wasn't there either. It looked as though she had never made it home.

Jennifer's mind was reeling. What should she do? Maybe she should call the police and report Melissa as a missing person.

"Melissa may have gone into labor and decided to drive herself to the hospital. Maybe the first time Jennifer called Melissa, she hadn't gotten there yet." Jennifer mumbled out loud to herself.

"Now is no time to panic." Jennifer told herself. "I've got to keep my head on straight. Where could she be?" She picked up the phone and dialed the operator.

"Yes, operator, this is an emergency. Could you dial the Medical University Hospital for me? I'm at the home of Melissa Johnson and she never made it home. She's pregnant and could go into labor at anytime. Before I dial 911, I want to make sure I'm not overreacting. She may have gone into labor and admitted herself into the hospital."

"Hold please."

Jennifer waited.

"Labor and delivery"

"Yes, could you tell me if there is a Melissa Johnson there?" She waited.

"No, she's not. I checked on the computer and there is no listing for a Melissa Johnson."

"She was going straight home from work and that was three hours ago. I'm at her home now, and she never made it here. At least there is no evidence she ever made it home. Could you transfer me to 911?"

"Emergency Assistance."

Jennifer repeated the situation and waited for their response.

"What's the address and full name again? I'll also need the make and model of the car."

"Melissa Johnson." She gave her the number for the office on King Street and continued with Melissa's home address. "She drives a new white BMW." She waited a moment and gave them the phone number.

"I'll give this number to the police. They can patrol the area and see if the car has broken down somewhere, or do an APB to see if there are any accidents reported for the make and model of her car. Which way does she normally travel to and from work?"

"I'm not certain. I don't know if she gets on I-26 West bound for part of the way home or if she just goes straight through downtown traffic on Meeting."

"Okay, I'll report your concern. Are you planning on waiting there on a patrolman to fill out the report?"

"I was going to drive by the office and see if I can locate her car somewhere on the side of the road."

"Okay, call back if anything new turns up."

"I will. I'm leaving right now." Jennifer hung up the phone. She felt panic grip her like the swell of a tidal wave. She was choking with anxiety and could envision Melissa dead on the side of the road somewhere. She shuddered and tried to force all the negative thoughts from her mind. Her head was pounding and she had the urge to throw up.

"Where are you, Melissa?" She cried. Grabbing the keys, she locked the front door behind her. Leaving all the lights on in the house, she ran for the car, unlocked it, and threw Melissa's keys in her purse. She started the engine, turned the headlights on, and backed out of the driveway.

Tears were streaming down her cheeks. As she backed out, the headlights flashed against the garage windows. The reflection of Melissa's car antenna penetrated the darkness of the garage only slightly. Jennifer didn't recognize it or it didn't register what she had seen. She drove on.

Halfway down the block, it dawned on her the reflection in the garage may have been Melissa's car. She slammed on the brakes, screeched back around, and fumbled in her purse for Melissa's keys to the house. Once in the driveway, Jennifer jerked the gear shift into park, raced to the door, unlocked it, and slung it open. Jennifer ran to the kitchen door and peered into the garage. There was Melissa's car, but it appeared to be empty.

She began to tremble. From the window's view, no one was in the car. Not satisfied, Jennifer opened the door and peered into the darkness toward the front seat. The light from the kitchen wasn't enough to see entirely into the car.

Walking out onto the steps to get a better look, she suddenly noticed a dark puddle at the bottom of the stairs. As she walked down two steps, she saw a body crumpled on the garage floor, and the dark puddle appeared to be blood.

Jennifer heard the scream, but was unaware that it was her own throat that had released the sound. Her heart was pounding as she ran down the remainder of the steps. Melissa had collapsed on the right side of the stairwell and her legs were covered in blood. Jennifer squatted to check Melissa's pulse.

"Melissa, Melissa? Can you hear me? It's going to be okay. I'm going to call for an ambulance." There was a clot of blood in Melissa's mouth and nose. Jennifer refrained from gagging as she scooped the blood out of her mouth with her finger, and continued to call her name. Melissa's heart was still beating, but her pulse was slower than normal.

"Melissa, hang on! I'm going to call for help." She squeezed her hand. Thank God, she's still alive. She ran up the stairs, two at a time, and dialed 911.

"Yes, I need an ambulance. There's been an accident. A pregnant woman has fallen down the steps of her garage and is hemorrhaging from the mouth and nose. She is laying in a pool of blood. I believe she's in labor." After giving them Melissa's address, she dropped the phone, left it dangling from the kitchen wall, grabbed a clean dish towel from the drawer, wet it with cold water, and hurried back to Melissa.

When she got to her friend, she wiped her face and checked her nostrils to see if the passages were clear. There was very little air coming from her nose, but she was breathing through her mouth. Jennifer suspected she was having contractions and only hoped she didn't go into full fledge labor before the emergency team got there.

The minutes ticked by like hours. She ran to the top of the stairs again, turned the switch at the top of the stairs to open the garage door, and watched for the ambulance to get there. Again, she checked Melissa's pulse only to discover it was slowing down even more.

"Oh, God, I wish they'd hurry. Hold on Melissa! Don't you dare die!" She yelled at her unconscious friend. "Do you hear me? Fight, Melissa! For the baby's sake, for your sake, for my sake." Her voice cracked. At that moment she heard the sound of the ambulance coming in the distance.

Normally a siren was a dreaded sound, but now it was the one bit of hope she had that Melissa might make it. The ambulance suddenly screeched around the corner into the driveway.

"Thank God, they're here."

The doors slammed closed. One attendant ran toward the house, the other attendant got the stretcher out of the back of the ambulance, and placed the medical bag on top of it.

"We're in here!" Jennifer yelled out.

"How long has she been like this?" The ambulance attendant asked as he observed the amount of blood Melissa had already lost. She also appeared to be suffering from a concussion.

"I don't know for certain. Possibly three hours. I'm not sure if she came straight home from work or if she was stuck in traffic. We left the office around 5:30 this evening." Jennifer was very pale and felt like she needed a shot of insulin. The trauma of seeing her friend so close to death, suddenly hit her nervous system. She began to tremble.

The other attendant came up with the stretcher. They turned Melissa over on her back and preceded to prepare the stretcher to lift her onto it. They grabbed her one on each side, and then simultaneously lifted her up.

"Tom, we're going to have to get her blood type. She needs a blood transfusion. Her blood pressure is dropping and her breathing is almost non-existent."

They addressed the next question to Jennifer. "Do you know where she's planning on having this baby? Which hospital? We need to find out her blood type."

"The Medical University Hospital."

"Tom, go ahead and check her records for blood type with the hospital. I need to see what's going on with this baby. She's having close contractions. Let's get rid of this bloody skirt and I'll see if the baby's head is visible. Give me that sheet to wrap her in and for the record, I've never delivered a baby before." Mike looked over at Tom and hoped Jennifer would not be alarmed by that bit of information. He hoped she hadn't heard his last comment.

Tom looked over at Jennifer's face. She was obviously shaken by Mike's inexperience. He tried to alleviate some of her fear. "I've had to deliver twice on an emergency run and both were successful. Believe me, it's no picnic, but every time I have to do it, it gets a little easier."

"Good." Mike said, glancing at Jennifer. Her face was ashen white from fear.

"Everything's going to be all right. Don't worry. It looks like we made it here just in time. It's a good thing you found her when you did or she probably would have died before anyone could get to her."

"Yeah, thank God." She whispered.

Mike swabbed Melissa with some diaper sized gauze pads and examined her to see if the baby's head were visible.

"No crown yet!" He yelled at Tom. He left the pad against her to absorb the blood and wrapped the sheets around Melissa's naked body.

Tom radioed the hospital to get Melissa's blood type so they could start the transfusion. They told him he would have to wait a few moments. The computers were down."

He sighed. "Okay, but please hurry. This patient is in critical condition." He continued to check her pulse.

"Do you mind if I ride with you?" Jennifer interrupted Tom's thoughts.

"Yeah. That'll be all right."

"I'm going to run in and get the things Melissa already packed for the hospital."

"She ran inside before he had a chance to answer. Going straight to the nursery, she picked up a neatly packed diaper bag for the baby. Then she headed for Melissa's room and found the suitcase that was already packed. She turned off the lights as she went back through the house, leaving only the hall light on to give the appearance that someone was home. She carried the baggage with her, got her purse out of the car, and hurried back to the ambulance. She met Tom on the way back.

"We need to hurry. Her blood type is 'A' Positive. We don't have that blood type with us and there is no way we can save her without it. There is such a shortage of Type 'A+'."

"I'm type A+". Jennifer responded. "She can have some of mine."

"That's great! We'll have to strap you down in the ambulance. Is that a problem?"

"No, of course not."

"We'll take yours first and then administer to her. You don't have any infectious diseases, do you or viruses?"

"No, nothing that would prevent me from giving blood. I'm diabetic, but that doesn't prevent me from giving blood. I had a physical three months ago and everything is fine. No diseases." She blushed only slightly.

"That's good. We really don't have a lot of options if we're going to save her life." Tom and Mike lifted Melissa into the ambulance and Jennifer got in behind them. Tom stayed in the back to begin the blood transfusion. Mike closed the back door, ran around to the front, and jumped behind the wheel to drive to the hospital.

Tom began to prepare Jennifer to draw blood. She looked like a frightened little girl as she watched Melissa lying on the opposite side of the ambulance.

Jennifer looked at her friend's limp body. One arm was dangling down from the side of the stretcher. For some reason that lifeless sight reminded her of a corpse. She began to tremble all over. She suddenly realized that Melissa might not make it.

She continued to pray that her fears would not come to pass. Tears trickled from the corner of her eyes. The ache in her heart, the tiredness and the sadness of the moment, all made her begin to whimper as the tears continued to fall. She never had a close friend die and she wasn't sure she had the strength to go through it. And the baby, dear God, what if the baby made it and Melissa didn't? All of these thoughts were racing through Jennifer's mind. Suddenly she began to sob out loud. She just crumbled under the fear and anxiety of what might happen next.

Tom was alarmed by her emotions. "Hey, there's no need for all that crying. She's going to be all right. You really saved the day twice by having the right blood type, but if you don't stop shaking we won't be able to transfuse to your friend. The worst is over now. When she gets enough blood into her system, she'll begin to climb out of the critical stage." Trying to keep his eyes on Melissa, Tom patted Jennifer's shoulder.

He prepped Jennifer's arm, stuck the needle in, and began drawing the blood. He glanced down at Jennifer's face. It was pale, the color of ash. In reality she was the one who looked like she needed a blood transfusion. He was aware of how pretty she was even without makeup. Even in the darkness filled with fear and worry, her beauty came through.

Jennifer felt a little dizzy. She closed her eyes and tried thinking about being at the beach, riding horses, or jogging on a country road. She thought Tom was cute, although he was probably lying to her when he said everything would be all right. It didn't matter if he were telling the truth. His voice was so comforting, he could have told her anything, any lie and she would have believed him. His touch made her realize how much she missed having a man in her life. She sighed with the impossibility of that ever happening again.

Her thoughts turned toward the day's activities. She couldn't believe she ran into John and what a change she saw in his life. Sickness didn't seem to bypass anyone, no matter who they were or how successful. Just look at Melissa, she really has so much going for her, but death could touch anyone at any time. Who would have thought she'd be fighting for her life? Jennifer breathed deeply.

"All finished." Tom interrupted her thoughts. He pulled the needle, removed it from the vile of blood, and taped cotton to the puncture wound in Jennifer's arm. He prepared another needle and attached it to the side of the flask he had gotten from Jennifer.

Then he inserted it into a tube to administer the IV and stuck the end of the needle into Melissa's limber delicate arm. She did not flinch. He waited, checking her pulse. The muscles in his cheeks tightened. He tried not to show his concern, but was afraid the baby would peak before they had Melissa ready to deliver. The contractions were just minutes apart. It was uncanny how the human body worked regardless of the consciousness of the human mind.

In only moments the ambulance pulled into the hospital. Mike jerked the back doors open and he and Tom began to pull Melissa's stretcher out while encouraging Jennifer to stay there if she felt dizzy.

"I'm fine. I want to go with her if that's all right?"

He nodded yes.

She followed them inside as they took Melissa through to the emergency room. She stopped at the main desk to give them all the information she could for Melissa's paper work. Afterwards, she got some black coffee from the machine in the lobby and winced as she forced it down.

Jennifer felt sick. She gulped the bitter blackness hoping it would be strong enough to give her a lift. Ignoring her own fatigue, she looked for a nurse who could tell her when she could see Melissa or at least what her status was.

"They'll let you know. It's possible they may have to do a C-Section, but they're not certain she's strong enough to go through any kind of surgery right now. To be honest with you she might not make it. We'll do the best we can, but she lost a lot of blood before anyone got to her. As soon as they tell us something, we'll come and get you."

Those words penetrated Jennifer's hope like a pin deflating a helium balloon. Fear and rage, despair and sorrow; the gamut of her emotions was pulled from one extreme to another. She walked over to a chair in the waiting room, sat down and began to sob into the sleeve of her sweater. Her head was pounding. She waited.

It was 1:00 A.M. and she still hadn't heard anything other than Melissa's doctor being paged over the intercom. She heard several code 9's which alarmed her. She knew that meant possible death for some of the patients. She prayed and wondered if there were anyone in Melissa's family she needed to call. She wasn't sure where Melissa kept her address book.

Her mother died when she was in college, and her father died when she was a little girl. So, the only close relative she knew to call was her sister in Oregon. Jennifer decided not to call. She wasn't prepared to upset anyone from Melissa's family, and besides her condition could go either way.

Jennifer hated going through all of this alone. She wanted to call John and tell him everything that had happened to her boss. Also, she needed to cancel their date. She would have to walk down the hall to make the call, so she decided to wait. She was afraid they might come to tell her about Melissa's condition and she wouldn't be anywhere nearby. It would kill her if she left and something happened to Melissa or the baby.

Chapter Ten

The doctor ran an ultrasound on the baby and could still detect life. There was clearly a heart beat. They had feared the baby would be stillborn, so this was a good sign. Melissa's irregular heartbeat was of some concern, but her breathing was improving. However, she had lost so much blood, she would need another pint.

The attendants decided to approach Jennifer to see if she would be willing to donate more blood. It would be a great help in saving Melissa's life. Finding another donor was almost impossible at this time of the night, and there was none of her type at any of the hospitals in the surrounding counties.

One of the interns went out to see if he could find Jennifer in the waiting area. She was crumpled over in a chair, sleeping, obviously exhausted. He hated to awaken her, but had to.

"Excuse me, Ms. Crawson, Ms. Crawson." He gently shook her.

Jennifer jumped up. "What's wrong? Is she all right?"

"I'm sorry to frighten you. Yes, she's improving, but we need to know if you would donate more blood? That is if you are up to it?"

"Sure. Anything."

"Follow me to the back and we'll get you set up. You look very pale. Have you eaten anything yet? We don't want you to get sick. You need to be putting something nutritious in your system."

"No, I haven't eaten a bite. I've just been drinking black coffee out of that machine and I'm feeling very nauseous."

"Any preference to having breakfast, lunch, or dinner?"

"No, right now I don't care what I get, just so I get something."

"Soon as I finish this we'll go by the nurses station, and I'll have them send up some breakfast. How about a cheese omelet, grits, whole wheat toast, coffee, and orange juice?"

"Sounds great." She followed him up the hall and asked if she could stop by and see Melissa.

"Let me do the blood transfusion first and then I'll let you visit for a moment. She's been a little restless which may be a good sign, and keeps mumbling something, but she hasn't totally regained consciousness yet."

"What about the baby?"

"She's still in labor."

"Is the baby still alive? Is there still a heart beat?"

"Oh, yes. He has a very strong heart beat."

"Thank God." She followed him in the room where he would administer the IV.

He prepped her left arm this time and made her recline on the examining table. She closed her eyes and thought about how much she disliked giving blood, especially being stuck with a needle, but she was willing to do whatever it took to save Melissa and the baby.

"Ouch!"

"Sorry about that. It might pinch a little. I seem to be having a hard time finding a vein."

"Ugh. Don't tell me. I'm feeling sicker by the minute."

"Sorry. It won't be much longer." He tried to comfort her as he continued to struggle to find a vein.

Jennifer winced, closed her eyes again, and tried to meditate on something pleasant. She thought of college times when she and Andy double dated with John and one of his girl friends. She thought of Melissa and wondered what in the world had gone on in her life. Where was the baby's father? What kind of man would leave her right after Melissa found out she was pregnant?

"That's it, Ms. Crawson. I'll get your breakfast for you. Rest for a few moments and after you've eaten something, I'll come back and take you to see Ms. Johnson."

Jennifer was a little dizzy. She mumbled a soft, "Okay" and kept her eyes closed. She was having to fight not to lose consciousness.

"Here you go, Ms. Crawson." The nurse handed her the tray with her breakfast on it.

"Let me know if you need anything else."

Jennifer tried to lift her head. She whispered a faint, "thank you".

"Just ring the nurses station when you're finished and Mr. Anderson will come and get you." The nurse closed the door behind her.

Jennifer wasn't hungry anymore. Her blood sugar level seemed to be way off. She knew she needed to eat something to get her strength back. A few hours earlier she would have gulped down the eggs, but now she moved them around on her plate like a child dreading spinach. Even the smell made her stomach churn. She drank some juice, ate a couple of bites of toast, and pushed the plate away. She attempted to move the tray to the other side of the room. Her head was spinning. She almost dropped the tray before placing it on the bedside table. She came back to the bed and started to ring for the nurse when the door opened.

"Oh, it's you. I was just about to call."

"Hi, I'm Barry Anderson. I should have introduced myself to you earlier. If you're finished eating, I'll walk with you down the hall to the Intensive Care Unit to see Ms. Johnson."

"Barry, I wish you'd call me, Jennifer." She stood up, but felt a little woozy. She waited a moment.

"Are you sure you're ready to do this? I could come back after you rest a little."

"Oh, no, I don't want to wait any longer. I want to see Melissa and be there when the baby is born." Jennifer's head was still spinning as she reached the door. She held the door knob to steady herself.

Barry extended his arm for her to hold onto him. They went down two corridors until she saw the sign that had I C U. She stiffened as she walked passed all the patients. The smell of sickness permeated the hallway. The whole floor reminded her of death; the rasping forced breathing of the patients, their twisted forms wrapped in sheets, the sad desperate eyes peering out of their rooms, and some were screaming out in pain. It was obvious that most of them were dying. She struggled to keep her mind free of doubt. Jennifer suppressed her fear that Melissa might not make it and tightened her grip on Barry's arm.

"This is it, I C U room 4C." He opened the door for Jennifer and left. Two nurses were there hooking up the IV for the second half of the blood transfusion. There was a monitor hooked to Melissa's abdomen to record the severity of each contraction. Jennifer stopped and stared at her friend's lifeless body. It would be an absolute miracle if she lived.

The baby's heartbeat was strong. She watched both monitors and breathed a sigh of relief. Melissa and the baby were still alive. That thought was the only hope she could cling to. As long as they were both breathing, she would fight in her mind for both of them.

She suddenly felt her own tiredness. Every limb ached for rest. She found it hard to keep her eyes open. Her mind soon gave up the fight to stay awake as the dull repetition of the machinery rocked her to sleep. She dreamed for the moment that everything was going to be okay. She slept soundly and did not hear the nurse when she came back into the room.

"Excuse me, Ms. Crawson. We need to unhook this IV now." She spoke softly trying not to startle her. She didn't want Jennifer to accidentally snatch the needle from her arm.

"Sure." Jennifer was still half asleep.

"Dr. Peters is on his way. He may need to induce labor. Also, Dr. Rayburn will be checking in on Ms. Johnson concerning her head injury. He wants to make sure there is no possibility of brain damage or a blood clot."

Jennifer sat straight up on the table. "What do you mean? You don't think she'll have brain damage, do you?"

"We don't think so, but until the doctor does a thorough exam, there's no way to tell."

Jennifer smiled faintly. It was hard for her not to worry even more. What if Melissa survived, but had brain damage and couldn't take care of the baby? What if she couldn't function normally at the shop either?

"Right now we're concerned about preventing any blood clots from going to the brain. Dr. Rayburn will do a CAT scan before and after the baby is born. In the meantime, you're welcome to stay with her until the doctors get here."

Jennifer nodded as they shut the door behind them. She tried getting up, but felt a little dizzy. She waited a moment, walked over to Melissa's bed, and gently squeezed her hand noticing how fragile and delicate it looked. She whispered, "I'm right here, Melissa. Don't give up. You need to keep living for the baby's sake." Jennifer brushed her hair away from her forehead.

She watched Melissa sleep wondering what had put such sadness in her eyes. Melissa never talked about any of her pain with Jennifer. She almost opened up when they went to dinner one night, but she became emotional and couldn't talk. Jennifer suspected it was the baby's father. Only a man could make her look that sad.

Suddenly the monitor showed Melissa having another contraction. The contractions began to come closer and closer together. Jennifer rang for the nurses.

They answered her on the intercom, "Yes?"

"Her contractions are coming more frequently. I think you need to come and check on her."

"We'll be right there."

Jennifer waited.

When they arrived, they immediately checked to see how much Melissa had dilated.

"You're right! She's between eight and nine centimeters!"

Jennifer panicked. "Can't you give her an epidermal? I don't want there to be any chance she's feeling any pain."

The nurses looked at each other.

"I suppose it couldn't hurt." One of the nurses responded.

Jennifer sighed in relief and squeezed Melissa's hand.

...Melissa could hear voices in the distance. She wanted to speak, but could not. She fought the darkness, yet was swallowed up by it over and over again. The brief moments of light brought voices, memories, and pain.

She wrestled and rested. Torn between two worlds: Life and death, light and darkness, peace and pain. She thought she heard a baby cry right before the darkness kept her from hearing any more sounds. Silence wrapped itself around her.

It was day and night again and a new wave of pain pounded in her head. She screamed, but the sound never left her mouth. She felt someone squeeze her hand. She tried to squeeze back to communicate her semiconsciousness, but there was no strength left in her body. The effort was lost amongst the activity that was going on around her. The pain eased, sleep was enveloping her, and she didn't have the power to hold out any longer. She slept.

Chapter Eleven

Jennifer waited in the lounge and drank more bitter, black coffee. What she wouldn't give for some fish and chips from Poogan's Porch or one of their delicious breakfasts with cheese grits. It was 5:00 in the morning and she began to doze off. Things had happened so fast with Melissa, sleep was not a luxury Jennifer had been able to indulge in. Her own health needs had to be put on the back burner. Although she always took her vitamins and her medicine first thing every morning, this morning was the first time she had remembered to do either. Black coffee had sustained her for the past couple of days. Now she just didn't have the strength to stay awake.

Even in her sleep, questions kept going through her mind. What if Melissa didn't make it? Would she need to try to adopt her child? What about her own life and needs? Well, she just couldn't worry about that right then. Melissa was going to make it, she just had to make it.

After only an hour, Jennifer woke up and felt an urgency to check on Melissa. The nurses were coaching Melissa as if she were conscious. It was Jennifer's first time to ever see a baby being born. It was remarkable to see how the body responds to child birth even when the mother is unconscious.

In only fifteen minutes the doctor was holding a beautiful baby boy. Tears began to trickle down Jennifer's face. She wished Melissa could be the first one to see her son.

She walked over to Melissa and whispered. "Melissa, he is absolutely beautiful. You need to wake up so you can see him for yourself." She put the baby's hand in Melissa's hand and swallowed hard to keep from crying out loud.

"Please wake up, Melissa. I don't know how much longer I can hang in here without your help." The tears began to roll down her cheeks. It was hard to suppress her emotions any longer. She began to sob. Turning around she saw Dr. Rayburn walk in the room. Somewhat embarrassed, she wiped her cheeks with one free hand.

"Dr. Rayburn, I didn't know you were here."

He saw the hurt in Jennifer's eyes and the trace of tears falling down her cheeks. He wanted to go to her and let her cry in his arms. He refrained to maintain a semblance of professionalism.

"Hello, young lady. I've heard you've been through quite an ordeal with your friend. Don't worry. We should have her back to normal in no time. From the x-rays it looks like we've got everything under control. The injury to her skull doesn't look as bad as we suspected and there is no sign of hemorrhaging or blood clots in that area. The sooner we find out exactly how deep the injury is to her skull, the sooner we'll be able to correct the problem. We're also going to monitor her to make sure no blood clots go to the brain. One less worry is that her son seems to be a totally healthy baby. His breathing is normal with no need of a respirator. He seems fully developed with a full head of dark hair."

Jennifer looked at Melissa's son and agreed. "What about Melissa, Dr. Rayburn? Will there be any complications because of the length of time she's been unconscious?"

"If we hadn't done those blood transfusions as soon as we did, there would have been an even greater risk of that happening. As long as we don't have any blood clots obstructing the blood flow, she should be fine. You should feel very good about your contribution to her survival. She wouldn't have made it without you."

He smiled warmly at Jennifer and continued, "The nurses will be in to take the baby for his first bath. I'll have them call you when we're finished with our exploratory surgery. Then you can come back and stay with Ms. Johnson if you'd like to."

She smiled faintly back at him and shook her head yes. She prayed silently that he wasn't oversimplifying Melissa's condition. Jennifer had a sad foreboding feeling come over her. It may have been her own need for food, or the fact that her blood sugar was so out of balance, but she was feeling depressed. She hated going through this alone.

She wondered if she should call John and see if he would come sit with her until Melissa regained consciousness. For some reason Jennifer wished John could be with her and put his arms around her and tell her everything was going to be all right. Again she wondered where the baby's father was. He's the one that needed to be with Melissa.

Jennifer's stomach began to cramp. She was headed for an ulcer if she didn't stop worrying about everything. She couldn't make everything all right, but she could put something other than coffee in her system. Poogan's was open at 8:00 A.M. and served a delicious breakfast. She loved their cheese grits and homemade biscuits. Right then anything sounded good. Even a Big Mac or a Biggie Fry and Coke would be great.

Chapter Twelve

John tried to contact Jennifer to confirm their dinner date, but couldn't seem to catch her at home. He hoped she hadn't changed her mind about their meeting, or forgotten about their plans to go out and eat.

Regardless, he thought she would have called him by now. He wished he had gotten the name of the place where she worked or the phone number. Maybe her boss had gone into labor and they were both at the hospital.

Well whatever, she said if he didn't hear from her by Wednesday she wouldn't be able to go that weekend. He couldn't help but feel disappointed. He wanted so much to be able to talk about everything that had happened in the last few months.

He hung up the phone, grabbed his keys, and headed for the door. He couldn't stand the thought of staying home alone another weekend. Even if he just went and got another video or got something to eat, at least he had gotten out of the house for a little while.

In a couple of days he was going to be in the hospital and he wouldn't be able to go anywhere. He made a call to the video store closest to his house and asked them to get him three very funny movies.

"Who do you like?" The sales person asked rather absentmindedly.

"Bette Midler always makes me laugh, as well as Steve Martin and Goldie Hawn." He got the attendant to get one of each of their movies. After he picked them up, he reached in the bag and pulled out, *Beaches, Private Benjamin, and The Out of Towners.* He wasn't sure but he thought all three of those were chick flicks. At any rate he hadn't seen any of them. He paid the guy, stopped by the deli, and headed home to eat his sandwich.

Jennifer finally got change for the pay phone and tried calling John. He didn't have his answering machine on and she let the phone ring for a couple of minutes. Finally she gave up trying. The disappointment was overwhelming. She needed so much to tell him everything that had happened to Melissa.

The nurses had told her this would be the best time to leave if she needed to go home because surgery would last at least a couple of hours. She gave them her mobile number where she could be reached in case of an emergency and waited outside for a cab.

The ride to Melissa's was quiet. The cab driver didn't have much to say and she was grateful. All she wanted was a hot bath. When she got to Melissa's house, she didn't go inside. She got her keys from her purse, opened the car door, and slid behind the wheel. The reality of what had happened began to sink in. Resting her head against the steering wheel, she began to sob. She couldn't wait until this was over. Her emotions erupted into 20 minutes of weeping.

"God," she prayed out loud. "Please let this be over soon. I'm so weary."

She finally regained her composure, drove home, and began to concentrate on taking care of business. She packed more clothes to take back to the hospital, started making all the calls Melissa had wanted to make when she went into labor, including the rest of the staff at The Cranberry Tree. Then she called the next door neighbor to let her know that Melissa had already gone to the hospital and given birth to a baby boy. She asked her if she would mind taking care of things around the house for a few days until Melissa came home from the hospital. She decided not to tell her about the other complications. This lady was in her 70's and there was no need to make her worry.

The shower felt great. It seemed like months since she had been home. The hot spray did wonders on the tension she was feeling. Putting on clean clothes helped also, but it took all the control she could muster not to crawl into the bed and sleep for a couple of hours. She was feeling numb all over. It was probably her blood sugar again. She needed to go somewhere and get something to eat. Before leaving she grabbed her journal so she could jot down some of the things that had been happening and to express some of the emotions she was feeling. She also grabbed one of her favorite books, *To Kill a Mocking Bird.*

Finally she made it back to the hospital. The ride back seemed to take forever. It was hard to concentrate on anything but Melissa. She needed to call Melissa's sister. She had mentioned that her sister lived in Oregon, but until she found the address book Jennifer had no idea where she lived.

When she got out of the cab back at the hospital, she almost started crying again. She wasn't sure why she was so emotional but everything seemed so depressing. The sun was setting. She felt a lonely, empty feeling settle over her. Surely God would give Melissa back her life. She wished it were herself and not Melissa who were dying. Melissa had so much more to live for than she did. She on the other hand had no one who was dependent on her to be their mother.

Chapter Thirteen

"Dr. Rayburn, Dr. Rayburn. Paging Dr. Rayburn. Code 9. Code 9 on the fifth floor."

Dr. Rayburn heard his name being paged as he entered the cafeteria. He left his tray on the counter and headed for the fifth floor. Melissa Johnson's blood pressure was dropping for some unknown reason. The nurses were already working on her when he entered the room.

"We'll need to take her back into surgery. There must be a blood clot somewhere." He shouted and began to rattle off a list of procedures that needed to be followed.

"She needs to be prepped immediately and given some morphine for pain. Get the anesthesiologist in here! We don't have a minute to waste."

He told the assisting aid, "Check her pulse again and be prepared to do CPR." He left the room to wash up for surgery.

Jennifer walked through the lobby of the fifth floor in search of a nurse who could tell her the status of Melissa, but she couldn't find any nurses.

She walked down the hall and saw Dr. Rayburn leaving Melissa's room in a big hurry. The closer he got to her the more distraught he appeared.

"Is Melissa all right? Has something happened?"

"Ms. Crawson, I'm afraid I don't have time to talk. I've got to take Ms. Johnson back into surgery. I'll let you know her status as soon as I know something."

Jennifer felt her legs become weak. She began to tremble inside. She felt sick at her stomach as she waited. She prayed silently and paced back and forth in the waiting room.

"God, please don't let her die. Please give this baby a mama." She cried even more. She couldn't stand going through this alone any longer. She looked at her watch. It was 9:30. She ran to the phone to call John. The phone rang twice and John answered.

"Hello."

"John, this is Jennifer. I'm sorry I haven't gotten in touch with you sooner. I tried to call a couple of times, but there wasn't anyone home and your answering machine never picked up. So I wasn't able to leave a message."

"Jennifer? What's happened? I left you so many messages and I never heard back from you. I was beginning to worry."

"My boss went into labor that night we talked. She fell down the stairs in her garage and the fall induced labor. It was awful, John. The baby seems fine, but I'm not sure my boss is going to make it. There are complications and they just took her back into surgery. I'm so worried about her John." Jennifer burst into tears.

"Do you want me to come be with you? I was just packing a few things to take with me to the hospital tomorrow, but I can finish up in the morning and come up there and sit with you tonight."

"No, it's too late and you need to get some rest. You've got a big day ahead of you. I'll come by your room tomorrow if I can. I just needed to talk with someone. I've just never gone through anything like this before." She began to sob again.

"Look, I'm leaving right now. I can't stand hearing you cry like this."

Jennifer's voice cracked. "No, John. I'm okay. I just needed to talk to someone. I was upset that the doctors had to take her back into surgery. Don't come here tonight. I'll call if anything happens. Just get some rest and I'll come by your room tomorrow."

"If you're sure, but promise me if anything happens you'll call me back."

"Okay, I promise, and thanks John. Good night."

"Goodnight, Jennifer." They both hung up the phone.

Jennifer went back to the same hard chair she had been sitting in for days. She was so weary and exhausted, but too worried about Melissa to sleep.

The elevator door opened and closed. Another stranger took a seat near her. Everyone there seemed to be waiting for life and death answers. Jennifer didn't even smile at the newcomers.   She just waited for the doctor to return.

Chapter Fourteen

The nurse woke Jennifer to see if she wanted a cot moved into Melissa's room. Somewhat groggy, Jennifer nodded her head yes. She got up, reached for her purse and journal, and followed the nurse back down the hall toward Melissa's room.

Melissa was sleeping peacefully when Jennifer walked into her room. The nurse told her the surgery was a success. There had been a blood clot, but they got it in time, and she should regain consciousness as soon as the medication wore off.

The nurse finished putting sheets on the cot and Jennifer hugged and thanked her for the good news. Tears were swelling in her eyes. Melissa might just make it after all. God, she hoped so.

Jennifer slipped between the sheets of the cot, relieved and exhausted. For the first time she had hope. Sleep came quickly. The next sound she heard was Melissa moaning. She went to her side and reached for her hand.

"I'm right here. Are you awake?" There was no response. She went back to the cot. This happened several times during the night.

It was almost morning when Jennifer heard Melissa calling for John. She smiled. That was so sweet to hear her already calling out for her son. She must subconsciously be afraid John Michael didn't make it or have some concern about his safety.

"Melissa, it's Jennifer. I'm right here and you're going to be all right." She squeezed her hand again.

Melissa squeezed her hand back, only slightly, but there was definitely a response. Jennifer smiled and cried at the same time.

"Melissa, I'm here. I'm right here!"

Melissa had a dull headache. She could hear Jennifer's voice, but she was too weak to squeeze her hand any harder. She tried again to no avail.

She tried to speak. "Jen, Jennifer." It was barely a whisper.

Jennifer heard the cracked sound of Melissa's voice, barely audible. She saw her lips move. She pushed the hair away from Melissa's face so she could see her eyes.

"Can you hear me, Melissa? Squeeze my hand if you can hear me."

The nurse came into the room and checked the heart monitor.

"Her heart rate has increased. Has she shown any signs of regaining consciousness? She should be waking anytime now."

"She squeezed my hand twice." Jennifer smiled through her tears.

"Well, it shouldn't be long before she can carry on a conversation with you. Those first ten hours were crucial. We've been watching her progress all night."

"This is the morning after the operation. You probably slept 16 hours."

"You're kidding me. I slept that long? No wonder I'm so hungry." Looking at the clock she suddenly remembered John. She needed to check on him as soon as possible.

The nurse interrupted her thoughts. "If you need to take a shower, there is one on the 2nd floor. I'll send some food up if you'd like."

"That would be great!" She had a pounding hunger headache.

The shower and fresh clothes were wonderful. This was the best she had felt since the accident. Now she was actually excited about going back to Melissa's room.

Jennifer's breakfast came ten minutes after she had ordered it. The coffee was better than the coffee from the machine in the lobby. She sighed deeply and drank slowly savoring the peace she finally felt. She decided to see if she could go get John Michael from the nursery, just in case Melissa woke up. Jennifer wanted the baby to be the first person Melissa saw when she opened her eyes.

The nurses consented. Jennifer was so excited. She took John Michael to the side of his mother's bed and placed him under her arm with him facing Melissa.

"Melissa, you need to wake up and see your precious little baby. He's beautiful."

Melissa's eyes flickered and she began to mumble something.

"Can you hear me?"

Melissa reached her hand toward Jennifer.

"Oh, my God, you're awake. Here Melissa, look at John Michael." She positioned him closer to Melissa's left side and he nestled close to her face.

Focusing was not easy for Melissa and she still had a slight headache. It was hard for her to determine if she were just dreaming. She was finally holding the baby she had waited so long to have, and it suddenly did not matter all the heartache concerning John. Seeing her son for the first time seemed to dull the rejection Melissa had felt before.

She couldn't remember one thing about the labor and delivery. She didn't even remember coming to the hospital. She had a headache, a baby in her arms, and Jennifer was standing beside her crying her heart out. Melissa was holding the one person she could love forever. Tears dripped down her cheeks and onto the pillow.

Jennifer leaned down and gave Melissa and John Michael a big hug.

"Boy, am I glad to see you with your eyes open. I was so afraid you might not regain consciousness. Finding you after the accident, not sure if John Michael was going to make it, it has been the longest couple of days of my life."

"What accident? What happened?" Melissa asked.

"You fell down the stairs in your garage, went into labor, and started hemorrhaging. I found you there. You lost a lot of blood and needed a transfusion. I have your same blood type so I gave you some of mine."

"Sounds to me like John Michael and I are alive because of you. We both owe you so much." She leaned forward to give Jennifer a hug, trying not to squish John Michael in the process.

Jennifer pulled the blanket a little tighter around John Michael and Melissa and tucked it in on one side.

"Thank you sounds so shallow. You've turned out to be a dear friend. I'm sure John Michael will feel the same way about his aunt Jennifer." They both laughed.

The nurse came into the room while they were laughing. "Well, I see you're doing much better. From the sound of it, you're both doing much better."

They agreed.

"I hate to break up this little reunion, but its time to take Mr. John Michael back to the nursery."

Melissa helped to hand him over to the nurse, wincing a little from the tenderness in her lower abdomen. "When will you be able to bring him back to me?"

"Well, we need to give him his bath and you need to eat something. So, it will probably be some time this afternoon."

Melissa smiled. "I'll be anxiously waiting to hold him again." She looked at Jennifer.

"Can you believe I finally have a precious little baby boy? What a miracle! It's just a miracle we're both here at all."

"You can say that again." Jennifer smiled warmly back at Melissa.

"I suppose you should try and get some rest. You may need all your strength to feed John Michael."

Melissa nodded. "Jennifer, I don't know how to thank you. Words seem so inadequate for everything you've done. I will forever be grateful to you for everything." Melissa's voice trailed off. Her eyes were already closed. The light in the room seemed to make her head hurt.

Jennifer leaned down and hugged Melissa. "You're very welcome. I'm going to run down the hall to check on another friend of mine while you take a nap, but I'll be back before you have a chance to wake up."

Melissa was already sleeping before she heard Jennifer's last words.

Jennifer slipped out the door to find John.

Chapter Fifteen

John's doctor did an ultrasound on him, which showed that he had a smaller mass of tissue in the prostate than he was originally diagnosed with, and that was good news. It meant there was a possibility he could have some of the more advanced treatments administered to him. There was new hope as to what the results could be as well.

"Your score on the digital rectal exam was 375 only a few months ago. Now your score is 320. That's still not where I want it to be, but it is so much better than it was and it happened in such a short period of time. Your condition is still serious, but we know now that it's possible for you to get even better with the right treatment.

John, I have a colleague at John's Hopkins in Baltimore. His name is Dr. Patrick Williams and he has devised a procedure for the removal of cancerous prostates with a nerve sparing technique, leaving most patients potent and continent. There is a possibility your condition is still in an early enough stage for the procedure to work. Otherwise, it could take as much as ten years of therapy to correct your problem.

I think it would be in your best interest to be transferred there. What have you got to lose? Your insurance would cover it. I know that you've been upset that you might not be able to have children. With this procedure, the side effects are not the same, so it would not do anything to prevent you from having a family. I highly recommend you try it, John." Dr. Philips waited for his words to sink in and continued.

"Well, what do you think?" Again the doctor waited.

"I, I don't know what to say. I can't believe it. That would be great!"

John was elated and continued, "I'll be able to have a normal family life? Children and everything?"

"That's right, if everything goes as planned, you can enjoy your family once again. Just so you realize this procedure is still in the experimental stage. Everything is questionable, but you have a very good chance for it to work. Your age is a big factor. After the laser treatments, you have a 90% chance of recovery."

"In that case, I'm ready. Let's go right now!" John was ecstatic. His adrenalin was up, and he felt like he could run a marathon.

The doctor continued. "I could make a call to see if they could schedule you sometime next week. You'll need to stay here another day so we can monitor your progress, and I'll see how soon they can take you."

"I'm ready, whenever you are. Thanks, so much, Dr. Philips." John extended his hand.

The doctor grabbed his hand. "I'm not sure I'm the one you need to thank. You might want to thank your God for this one. You still need to get as much rest as you can. We need to keep progressing in a positive way or this new treatment might not work as well as it could. Do you know what I'm saying? I want you to keep a positive attitude, John. That's more important than any treatment you can get."

"I will, Doc. I'm very grateful for what you've done so far".

"Well, I've got to finish my run of the hospital. Let's start on that rest right away. I suggest you try to get a good night sleep and I'll check on you in the morning."

"I will and thanks again. If it were not for you and God, I probably wouldn't have made it. Good night, Dr. Philips."

John could not wait to tell Jennifer the good news. She had come by the day before when he was still groggy from the surgery. She called earlier to say she would be there in an hour. He had not gotten the good news then, but now she could rejoice with him.

There was a gentle tap on the door. "John, it's Jennifer." She began opening the door before he could respond.

"Come in."

He looked so thin and weak, but he had a huge grin on his face.

"Well, you certainly look better than the last time I saw you." She leaned over and gave him a hug.

"I've got some great news to tell you. The test came back on the first few treatments I've had and the report was very good. Now, I can go to Johns Hopkins Hospital in Baltimore for a new treatment they have there. This treatment will allow me to have a normal married life, as soon as the effects of the chemotherapy wear off."

"That's great. How soon will you go there?"

"Maybe as soon as next week. The doctor is checking on that right now."

"Oh, John that's wonderful. I'm so excited for you. Let me know if you need me to help you in anyway. I could drive you to the airport if you need me to."

"That would be great. I'll let you know as soon as they let me know something."

"I won't be able to stay but a few moments today. I've got some things to do at the shop. I can check on you again in the morning, if that is okay?"

"Sure, that would be perfect. The doctor is coming by in the morning to let me know when I'll be going to Baltimore."

"Should I call first?"

"No, just come on up whenever you get here."

"Well, it's a date. I'll see you then."

"Let me walk with you down the hall. I'm so excited I've just got to get out of this bed and walk around a little bit."

"All right. If you think you're strong enough, let's go for it." She smiled warmly as they headed for the door.

They walked together passed the nurse's station and John gave her a hug at the elevator. He thanked her for being such a good friend and for coming to see him. She hugged him back and got in the elevator.

Chapter Sixteen

Melissa was going through her daily walk up and down the hospital hall trying to do whatever she could to regain her strength. Feeling exceptionally strong she decided to take the stairs and walk up and down all the floors to the hospital.

The door to the second floor rattled shut behind Melissa as she headed toward the hallway. She hesitated for a moment because she wasn't sure she wanted to walk down the cancer hall.

Before she had gone two feet, she stopped and stared intently at the couple who were walking toward the elevator. She could not believe her eyes. There was Jennifer and John walking down the hall both of them smiling. Jennifer hugged John and got in the elevator.

Melissa took a deep breath and felt sick at her stomach. She lifted her hand to her mouth to suppress the cry that almost came from her lips. There was no mistake. She turned and went back through the door hoping they had not seen her. She walked as quickly as she could back to her room. The pounding in her head increased as she got closer to her bed. Her stomach wretched. She was totally nauseous.

Pressing her aching body against the pillows. Melissa sobbed out loud. How could this be possible? How could John and Jennifer even know each other? She felt her heart grow cold. She had to get better and get out of the hospital. She and John Michael could go to the beach house for a while or move to Atlanta, but she had to get out of John and Jennifer's lives.

There was no way she could stay here and watch the two of them. It was like having her heart ripped open again. What was the possibility that Jennifer and John would know each other? Jennifer never said anything about knowing John.

Melissa wished she had died rather than survived and have to relive all this pain again. Not just seeing John, but seeing him hugging Jennifer made her sick at her stomach. Her head began to spin. She grabbed the trash can and vomited.

She would not tell Jennifer she had seen the two of them together. She would just go on with her life, leaving the past and her two best friends behind her. It would not be easy to push the feelings of betrayal behind, but she had to regardless of how empty that would make her feel. How could Jennifer keep this from her? What a twist of fate that Jennifer and John would end up together. She was obviously very close to him.

Melissa wrapped her body around the pillows like a baby in a fetal position. The anger, the coldness, and the sorrow of losing both a friend and a husband were more than she could handle. Thank God she had her baby, the only source of joy left in her life. She prayed she would never have to fight the two of them for custody of her son. Just the thought of that made her even sicker. She wept in total abandonment, letting the coldness and sadness envelop her soul again. She began to feel the void inside. Death and darkness seemed to creep into her heart and silence filled the room.

One of the aids came in to check on her, removed her trash can and asked if she were doing all right.

"Do you need anything, Ms. Johnson? Looks like you've had an upset stomach. Do you want me to bring you a coke or something to settle your stomach?"

"No, thank you. I'm fine. I just need to sleep some more."

"All right, if you're certain you don't need anything. If you should change your mind, just buzz the staff and someone will bring you whatever you need." She closed the door behind her.

Food was the last thing in the world she wanted right then. She tried to sleep but could not. She opened her eyes searching the white wall beside her bed for answers. There were none, just the sick smell of the hospital. She was forced to feel the pain and rejection without the ability to escape into sleep.

It was obvious she needed to back away from Jennifer. She didn't want to ever hear her talk about her relationship with John. She would move away as soon as possible. That way the two of them could be free to have a relationship together.

Melissa dreaded seeing Jennifer. She dreaded even hearing her cheerful voice. She wished she had the strength to get up and walk out of the hospital right then. All of her thoughts seemed to be filled with only negative feelings. It was hard enough seeing John again, but to see him with Jennifer was too much. She knew it was bound to happen sometime. She was bound to run into John somewhere in her everyday routine, but never in her wildest imagination, did she think she would see him at the hospital with Jennifer.

Suddenly there was a tap at the door. She pulled the covers up over her head trying to hide, trying to feign sleep.

"Melissa, are you already asleep? It's Jennifer." She opened the door slowly in case Melissa was asleep. She waited.

"I'm awake." Melissa answered in almost a whisper. She kept her head down so Jennifer couldn't see she'd been crying. The only light in the room was from the monitors and the crack in the door. Melissa had the curtains drawn closed so there was no way to tell if it were day or night outside.

"Were you already trying to go to sleep? It seems awfully dark in here." Jennifer thought it was strange that Melissa was keeping the room so dark, so early.

"I'm tired that's all." She said rather sharply.

"Is something wrong, Melissa? Has something happened to upset you?" Jennifer thought she seemed mad about something or irritated.

"I'm just tired, Jennifer. That's all." She knew she was lying, but she felt justified in doing so.

"Well, I have some good news I wanted to share with you, but I guess it can wait. Is there anything I can get you before I leave to go to the office?" She waited.

"If not, I can check back later." Boy, Melissa was in such a bad mood. Maybe this is the post labor depression some women go through. She'd been through so much trauma lately, maybe she just didn't feel well.

"That's really not necessary. I don't need anything and I'll probably be asleep later, so there is no need to check in on me." Melissa bit back the urge to cry. She wished Jennifer hadn't come back to her room so soon after seeing her with John.

"Look, Melissa, are you sure nothing's wrong? You seem so upset over something and I wish you'd tell me what it is." Jennifer was hoping to make eye contact with her so she could tell for certain if she were just imagining this whole mood thing.

"I'm all right, Jennifer. I've just been through so much and I need to rest. You shouldn't be worried about me. You should just go on with your own life." Melissa knew she sounded cold, but she didn't know how else to get rid of Jennifer. She wished she didn't have to talk to her at all.

"Okay, if that's how you feel then I better go."

Melissa's words hurt a little. If Jennifer didn't know better, she would think Melissa was trying to get rid of her. She wasn't sure why, but it seemed Melissa's feelings had changed so drastically toward her. Well, she'd just try and ignore it for now. Maybe it was Melissa's medicine making her act that way.

"I'll see you tomorrow then." She replied as she opened the door to leave. She was trying not to feel so rejected.

"It really won't be necessary for you to come by tomorrow since John Michael and I are doing so well. I'm sure there is plenty to keep you busy at the shop." Melissa never did turn around and look at Jennifer.

"Look, Melissa, I know it's not necessary, but I really would like to see you and John Michael tomorrow. If you're upset with me about something, I just wish you'd go ahead and tell me. To be honest, it hurts me to have you talk to me like this. I'm not real good at rejection. Maybe it's something about my past, but I can't deal with it very well and Melissa, I've never seen you this way. What's going on with you?"

Melissa could tell it wasn't going to be easy to get Jennifer out of her life, so she tried to soften up her tone a little.

"I'm sorry, Jennifer. I realized today you have a life other than taking care of me. I just don't want you to be consumed by mine."

"Believe me, Melissa, I realize I have a life of my own, but sometimes things happen that put us together with other people and it can be for everyone's good. If you're so ready to be by yourself that's fine, but I don't feel the need to suddenly separate myself from you. If that's what you want then I guess I'll just have to accept it, but the change in your attitude hurts me. You won't even look at me. I don't know what's wrong, but something is and I know it."

Jennifer didn't wait for Melissa to answer. She just walked out and closed the door behind her. As she walked down the hall, it took all she had not to start crying. Those sad feelings from her childhood began to surface. It was a feeling of abandonment that was the hardest in life for her to deal with. She reached the car and began to cry. Why did this emptiness continue to be with her as an adult? She had to get a grip. Maybe she should go write in her journal for a while, make some effort to locate her brother, or go to the shop and work. Whatever, she had to do something constructive to get rid of the pain she was feeling from Melissa's words.

Melissa cried as soon as Jennifer left the room. She felt she had lost John and Jennifer in one brief moment. She knew it wasn't fair to be so mean to Jennifer, but it wasn't fair that she had lost her husband to one of her best friends.

Chapter Seventeen

Jennifer made all the flight arrangements for John and drove him to the airport. The rest of the week was very grueling. Melissa had been unusually cold and distant. Being around her was not just uncomfortable, it was painful. Jennifer pulled her car into her usual parking spot at the shop and just sat there behind the wheel. She was dreading going inside to be rejected by Melissa. She could just hear the cold sarcasm in Melissa's voice. If she didn't hurry up and go inside soon, Melissa would also be upset with her for being late as well.

She put a fake smile on her face, walked into the shop, and said cheerfully, "Well I got all the errands run and it looks like we're all set for the weekend."

"Did you remember to take the changes on my invoices to the printer?"

"Yes, Melissa, I did." Jennifer tried to keep the warmth in her voice, but was beginning to feel irritated. Melissa seemed to be looking for something to be mad about. She never acted this way before the accident.

"What about the bank? Did you remember to bring the deposit slip back?" Again she snapped at Jennifer.

"Here it is! Yes, I remembered everything, Melissa. Look, I think we need to talk. What's wrong with you? You have never treated me like this since I came to work here. What could I have possibly done to you to make you treat me this way?"

"You tell me, Jennifer. There's nothing I could be upset over, is there? I'm leaving to go to the beach house for the weekend, and I just want everything to be done right before I leave."

"Have you ever had a problem with my not doing my job?"

"No, but-"

"But what Melissa? And another thing, don't you think it would be unwise for you to go to the beach alone so soon after your surgery?"

"Excuse me. I don't think that's any of your business. If I want to go to the beach, I don't have to ask you or the doctor. I'm doing just fine now."

Jennifer's face burned with anger. She had to refrain from telling her boss she was sick of her attitude and she was quitting. Instead she replied, "I know it's none of my business, Melissa. I'm just concerned about what's happening with you. Maybe you shouldn't be by yourself. You're still having those dizzy spells and the doctor said-" She didn't get to finish her sentence.

"I know what the doctor said, Jennifer. I need to get more rest and I can't get any rest hanging around here. I need some time to be alone. I know what he said about another blood clot, but if I die, I die."

Jennifer slammed her purse down and the deposit slip went flying.

"You ungrateful-"

"Go ahead say it. Just say it. I'm waiting." She glared at Jennifer like she just dared her to say something that would give her the right to let her go.

Jennifer took a deep breath and tried to control her feelings. "Something is eating at you, and I hope to God whatever it is, you'll consider John Michael needs a mother. You can treat me as coldly as you want, but I haven't done anything to warrant this kind of behavior."

Melissa softened a little. "I'm sorry I have to be cold to you, but I need to be alone and you can't seem to accept that."

"Well, I can accept that you've got some issues to work out, but I'm not going to let you go to the beach by yourself. I don't care what you say or do. I'll follow you in my car if I have too, but I'm going. For goodness sake Melissa, don't shut me out of your life like this. We've been through so much together." Jennifer's voice began to crack. She was on the verge of crying.

"Jennifer, I'm grateful for what you've done for me, but that doesn't keep me from having to go on with my life. I need to make plans for mine and John Michael's future, and I don't need you around when I do that."

"I don't buy it. There's something deeper going on here and you're not being honest about it. I can't make you open up to me, but I can keep you from leaving town by yourself."

Melissa was furious, but knew there was no way to keep Jennifer from driving down to the beach.

"Okay, I can't keep you from going down to the beach, but I'm going to warn you, Jennifer, you haven't begun to feel coldness. If you come with me, it will not be a fun weekend. If you are determined to go, then I'll just come by and pick you up after I pack my things."

"I'm serious Melissa, if you try to trick me and leave Charleston without me, I'll drive down to Edisto by myself. I know the address. I've seen it every time I paid the electric bill there. So don't try to pull any tricks."

"I'll be there, Jennifer." She was irritated, but knew it was useless to fight any more about Jennifer's going. Melissa wished she had never said anything to her about her plans for the weekend.

"Do you mind if I go by the grocery store on the way home and buy some groceries to take with us?" Jennifer asked trying to sound light hearted.

"Do whatever you want. Why should it matter what I think?"

"I just didn't want you to get there early and not see me, and think I had changed my mind about going. Anyway, I'll go to the store on the way home, so give me a little extra time to get ready."

Being at Melissa's mercy was humiliating, and a part of Jennifer wanted to run away from the whole situation. In the back of her mind she kept thinking Melissa might be sicker than they all realized.

She'd rather take the heat now than regret that she hadn't gone with her gut feelings. If something happened to Melissa at the beach and she hadn't gone with her, she'd never forgive herself.

Chapter Eighteen

A knot had begun to form in Jennifer's throat and her stomach felt a little jittery. Everything was packed and she was waiting for Melissa to come by and pick her up. She was beginning to have some doubts about insisting on going on this trip. There was nothing worse than being stuck somewhere with someone who didn't want you there.

If she didn't believe it was dangerous for Melissa to drive alone, Jennifer certainly wouldn't go. Maybe Melissa's sickness was the only reason she was acting this way. She hoped this was true, but had her doubts.

Melissa pulled in the drive, began blowing the horn, interrupting Jennifer's thoughts.

Oh, God, I better hurry or she might just leave me. Jennifer thought.

"I'm coming. Just a minute!" She yelled toward the door. Jennifer picked up her luggage and grabbed the grocery bag of food sitting on the counter. With both hands full, she struggled to open the door and hurried toward Melissa's car.

"Just put your things in the back. The trunk is already packed with my things." Melissa shouted through the closed car window.

"All right." Jennifer hoped against hope Melissa would be in a better mood.

"Jennifer, I just want to say one thing. I resent your forcing me to let you come this weekend, and I have no intention of talking to you about anything that's going on with me. If you still want to go knowing that I want to be by myself, then that's up to you. Don't get upset or feel rejected if I don't talk to you or discuss anything going on in my life. Is that understood?"

Jennifer shook her head yes. She resisted the urge to tell Melissa to stop the car and let her get out. She wanted to run back inside and lock the door. It didn't help matters that she didn't have time to eat. As a matter of fact, she hadn't eaten anything all day. She wished she had grabbed something before Melissa got there. Her insides had a nervous tremor, but there was no way she was going to suggest they stop and get something.

Jennifer slipped her sun glasses on and closed her eyes. Her head was pounding so the silence was a welcomed relief. The strife between the two of them had created a sick gut feeling in her stomach. She may be keeping her mouth shut, but in her mind she continued to fight with Melissa. She wanted to cry, to scream, to do something to make the sick feeling she had inside go away. Jennifer wanted to tell Melissa she was just being selfish and cruel. Even if she had been in an accident there was no reason for Melissa to be treating her this way.

Oh well, regardless of the inward battle, Jennifer knew it would be better for them both if she kept her mouth shut. Thank God John Michael didn't come on this trip. Maddie, his nanny, was keeping him for Melissa until Sunday.

Melissa's own mind was whirling. Why did Jennifer insist on coming? She was the last person Melissa wanted to be with on a trip to the beach. It made her sick every time she looked at Jennifer. Now there would always be the memory of John and Jennifer together in her mind.

Poor Jennifer. She was like some metaphor for goodness. She had to make sure everyone was all right even if she has to be crushed in the process. It seemed the worse she treated Jennifer the more committed she was to helping her.

It had been almost an hour since they left and the traffic had finally thinned out. Melissa was certain Jennifer must be hungry. She was still upset with her, but it would be cruel not to stop and get something to eat. She didn't want to make the trip pleasant for her, but it wasn't her desire to be cruel either.

"Would you like to stop and get something to eat?" Melissa asked.

Jennifer couldn't believe her ears. Was Melissa actually going to act human? It was the first considerate thing she had done in weeks.

"Yes, if you don't mind. I didn't have time to get lunch today." Jennifer rubbed her left temple, trying to massage her headache away.

Melissa felt a twinge of guilt. She should have asked her if she were hungry before they left town. She was so upset about Jennifer wanting to go with her to the beach, she didn't realize Jennifer hadn't eaten all day.

"I'm sorry, Jennifer. I should have asked you sooner."

"That's all right. I should have grabbed something to eat at home. There just wasn't time after I went to the grocery store."

"I suppose I didn't really give you the opportunity to say anything after the little speech I made?"

Jennifer smiled only slightly. "Well, not really."

They stopped and got two turkey sandwiches on wheat. Neither of them said two words the rest of the way to the beach, but at least there was a little less coolness in the ride. Jennifer wasn't sure what would happen once they got there, but at least Melissa had finally shown some compassion toward her. It might be all the compassion she received all weekend, but it was a start. Maybe just maybe, Melissa would eventually open up to her. If not, Jennifer brought her journal and she could catch up on her writing. There were so many feelings she needed to express and if Melissa continued with her silent treatment, Jennifer would have some way to spend her time other than walking the beaches alone.

Chapter Nineteen

It was 10:30 p.m. when they finally arrived. The ocean was refreshing as always. A cool breeze brushed against them as they unpacked the car. The air was salty. As they climbed the stairs to the beach house, they stopped a moment to look at the sea. There was a rush of white waves surrounded only by the darkness of the night.

Melissa turned on the hot water heater as they entered the house and started a fire in the fireplace. She let Jennifer choose what bedroom she wanted. She chose one of the four upstairs and they both began making their beds for the night.

There was still silence between them, but the anger seemed to have subsided. For this, Jennifer was grateful, even though the long term silence made her uncomfortable.

It wasn't long before they were both in the kitchen putting away all the groceries they had brought.

"I was going to make some hot chocolate, would you like some?" Jennifer asked as she started making her own.

"Yes, thank you."

The room was still cold, but the fire had already begun to take the chill away. Melissa walked out onto the balcony of the deck and took a deep breath. God, she needed this. Nothing soothed her soul like a trip to the beach. The deck had been weathered by the salty spray and storms, but it was still very sturdy and solid.

The iciness of the wind swept over her, she pressed her hands deeper into the pockets of her jacket in hopes the numbness in her fingers would go away.

Jennifer walked up and brushed the mug of cocoa against the arm of Melissa's jacket.

"Here be careful, it's hot."

"Thanks, I was beginning to freeze out here. This wind cuts right through." She wrapped her hands around the cup to absorb the heat.

Jennifer looked longingly at the waves. "Would you like to go for a short walk?"

Melissa contemplated her answer. She didn't want to be too chummy with Jennifer, but she did want to go walking. She decided to give in.

"Yes, let me put on my running shoes, and I'll meet you at the bottom of the stairs."

"Okay." She waited for Melissa to return. Jennifer had already dressed for a short walk even if she had to go alone. She breathed a sigh of relief. Maybe they could talk, maybe Melissa wasn't going to be so difficult. She could only hope that would be the case.

They walked for almost an hour without saying a word. Melissa's thoughts were of John. She wondered how he and Jennifer ended up together. The more she thought about them the more bitter she became.

Jennifer knew Melissa told her not to ask any questions about what was bothering her, but she seemed to be in a better mood. So she decided to give it a try.

"Melissa, could we stop a minute?" Jennifer reached out and touched Melissa's arm.

Melissa stopped. She wanted to run back to the beach house without answering any questions.

"Melissa, I can't stand this silence between us. I want you to tell me what I've done to upset you so much. I just can't go on like this."

The fierce gray and white waves twisted with the wind as Jennifer waited tensely for Melissa's response. She looked into her eyes and waited for an answer. The pain seemed to deepen in Melissa's face as she obviously searched for a way to reply. She suddenly seemed even sadder than when Jennifer first met her. Was it the baby's father? It could be, but Melissa's anger seemed to be more toward Jennifer than towards someone else.

Melissa still did not answer. Her silence made the air seem even colder. Jennifer took another deep breath and waited for her to respond.

Melissa stared out at the ocean. Searching for some answer or for some way to escape.

The sadness of it all permeated Jennifer's whole being. She shuttered, wrapped her jacket even tighter around her waist, and began thinking of someway to start walking again. She could feel the rebuke she was about to receive and the silence was making her sicker by the moment.

Melissa cleared her throat and Jennifer's heart began to beat wildly. It seemed to be beating so loudly, Melissa could probably hear it above the pounding of the waves. She wasn't sure she had the courage to hear what Melissa was going to say.

The minutes ticked by like hours. Jennifer shifted her gaze from Melissa to the white caps that were breaking closer and closer to their feet. Melissa cleared her throat again and spoke with the softness of a frightened child. Her voice quivered under the hurt she was trying to suppress.

"There are times Jennifer when we have to let things die and then go on living. There are times when we have to separate ourselves from the pain, and there are times we have to hold onto our relationships because they are more important than what has to be forgiven. I'm not sure right now what to do. I'm groping for the answers to those questions, and I just need time to figure it all out. I need some time to be alone and think. I'm sorry if you've gotten hurt in the process. I never intended to hurt you."

"I guess I just don't understand what this has to do with me. Your feelings toward me, or should I say your attitude has become so cold and distant. What have I got to do with your decision?"

Melissa was silent and Jennifer became fidgety. She waited, still nothing. Jennifer wasn't sure how much of this she could take. Nothing made any sense. Why couldn't Melissa just talk about it and get everything out in the open? Finally she couldn't take it anymore.

She nodded toward the beach house. "Melissa, it's getting cold. I'm going to head back."

"Wait." It was nothing more than a whisper and her voice sounded so lonely and empty. God only knew what was hurting her so badly.

Melissa's voice quivered, partly from the cold, and partly from the need to suppress her tears. "I wish I were able to talk about everything Jennifer, but right now I just can't. I may not ever be able to talk about it and I'm sure this will inevitably affect our friendship. I regret that, but I can't do anything about it."

Jennifer wanted to scream out at Melissa but resisted. "Yes, you can do something about it. Just talk to me, Melissa. This is ridiculous. There's nothing you can't tell me." She paused a moment and finally gave up. "Forget it, Melissa. Let's just go back to the house."

They both started walking back. It had gotten colder and the wind pressed against them as they reached the top of the porch steps. Melissa groped in the darkness for the light in the den. There were two remaining embers in the fireplace. Just a flicker of warmth lingered in the house.

Jennifer wanted to leave, but couldn't. She wished she'd never ridden down to the beach with Melissa. She looked nervously around the room in hopes of finding something to occupy her time. She remembered her journal. She'd get ready for bed, then write in her journal before she went to sleep, and avoid Melissa as much as possible for the rest of the time she was at the beach.

"Well, I don't guess there is anything else we're going to talk about tonight, so I'm going to bed."

Melissa wanted to reach out to Jennifer to explain everything but couldn't.

"Goodnight, Jennifer. I hope you sleep peacefully." She reached out and touched Jennifer's shoulder, backed away and went into her bedroom.

"Yeah, me too." Jennifer mumbled to herself. She wrote in her journal for thirty minutes and finally turned off the light. She wrestled throughout the night with the speech Melissa gave her on the beach. She was tired. It had been a very long day, a very long week, a very long month.

Chapter Twenty

It was raining when Melissa finally opened her eyes. She was disappointed that walking would not be an option this morning, but it was comforting to hear the rain. She slumbered for another hour until she smelled coffee brewing in the kitchen. Jennifer must have already gotten up.

Melissa slipped on her robe and headed for the bathroom. Passing through the den to check on the fire she saw Jennifer curled up in front of it wrapped in a blanket. Jennifer obviously had already added more wood and appeared to be sleeping peacefully.

Jennifer looked so innocent as she slept. A twinge of guilt filled Melissa's thoughts because of the way she had been treating her. She was a great friend and employee. Melissa and John Michael would not be there, had it not been for her. Maybe when she finished taking her shower, and Jennifer got up, she would try and convince her everything was going to be all right. She could suggest they call for a cab to take Jennifer back to Charleston.

The hot shower was soothing to Melissa. She relaxed. She still didn't have the strength to talk about John, but she'd try not to be so guarded and defensive toward Jennifer.

When Jennifer heard the shower running, she got up and started making breakfast. She had decided earlier that morning not to talk to Melissa about anything personal. It was fruitless anyway. They had one more day and then they'd be leaving. She would just have to make the best of the situation. If Melissa didn't open up the night before then she probably wasn't going to. Breakfast was ready by the time she heard Melissa cut off the water in the shower. Nice aromas filtered through the house.

Melissa walked in the kitchen dressed in sweats and a T-Shirt with a towel still wrapped around her head. She stood beside Jennifer and breathed deeply.

"Um, good morning. Whatever you're cooking sure smells great." She noticed the two place settings and steam coming from an omelet cooking on the stove. She smiled.

Jennifer noticed the smile. "Thanks, I've made a mushroom and cheese omelet. I've got some croissants heating in the oven, fresh strawberries in the fridge, and there's some Georgia pecan coffee over there, if you want a cup."

"Gosh, that sounds wonderful. I'm starved. Let me go comb my hair and I'll be right there."

After they had finished eating. Jennifer took her shower, dressed, and pulled her journal out to finish writing in it. It was pouring down rain, so it would be a perfect day for staying inside in front of the fire. She only wished she had someone special in her life to share the romantic setting. The rain combined with the sound of the waves and the crackling of the fire had a soothing effect on her. She wanted to sleep and write all day. She hoped nothing would develop between her and Melissa to spoil the peace she was feeling.

Melissa seemed so much better this morning. She had already called twice to check on John Michael. Jennifer watched the joy come over Melissa's face as she attempted to talk to him on the phone. Maddie who had been with Melissa at the shop for years was a perfect nanny for John Michael. She could tell Melissa was struggling with guilt for leaving him for the first time. She was reluctant to hang up, but finally told him good-bye.

"How's he doing?" Jennifer asked.

"He's fine. Maddie was about to put him down for a nap. I didn't realize how much I would miss him."

"Maybe you just needed a little time away and now everything will be better. You've seemed so stressed lately. I've been really worried about you, Melissa."

"I know, Jennifer. I've been thinking about moving to the Atlanta area to open a new business and I'm nervous about making that big of a change in my life. I'm still trying to figure out the best time to move."

"You're kidding right? I didn't realize you were planning on moving. When did you decide that? You don't mean really move away for good do you?"

"I've been thinking about moving for a long time, even before I hired you for the manager's position at The Cranberry Tree."

"Melissa, when were you going to tell me? Does this mean I'll need to find a new job?" Jennifer could feel herself getting upset again.

"I wasn't sure when to bring it up, but I thought you could continue to manage the shop, and I could hire one extra person to help you. The regular staff would be staying except for Maddie. She'll be coming with me as a full time nanny."

"You didn't think I should know about this sooner, so I could decide what I wanted to do?"

"Well, that's up to you. No, you don't have to stay, but it's not going to change my plans one way or the other. I feel a need to leave Charleston."

Jennifer was silent. All of these changes were more than she could handle at one time. She had the urge to get her things, call a cab, and leave Charleston, too. If it were not for her desire to try and locate her brother, she probably wouldn't have come to South Carolina in the first place.

Melissa's nonchalant attitude was making her crazy. Jennifer had to burn off some steam. She decided to go for a run even if it were raining and cold. She jumped up, tossed her journal on the couch, got her jacket, and put on her running shoes. She was mad, frustrated, and sad all at the same time. There was no way she could stay in the same room with Melissa without losing her temper.

The door slammed behind her as she headed for the beach. She said nothing to Melissa about where she was going and Melissa watched her go without trying to stop her. The rain was cold as it beat against Jennifer's face. She started running and the coldness of the air filled her lungs making them ache. It became very hard to breath.

That's it, she thought. I've had it with this situation. Angry tears began to burn down her cheeks. She ran even harder choking on the thoughts that were racing in her mind. She finally stopped when she could take the pain no longer. She was soaked and freezing.

Jennifer sat down unaware she was sitting in the middle of a puddle that had formed in the sand. She was crying so hard it didn't matter where she was sitting or that her pants were completely soaked. She began to shake all over. No longer able to suppress her emotions the shaking and the tears seemed to erupt at the same time like a dam overflowing its boundaries.

She was powerless to control either. The rain came down in sheets, and torrents of cold wind blew against her back making her shake even more. She needed to go back as much as she hated to do so, knowing if she didn't get out of the cold soon she would probably end up sick.

The walk back seemed to take forever. The farther she walked the colder she became. Now all her anger had been replaced with pain. Not only were her feelings hurt, now she was hurting physically. The cold had settled in her lungs and she felt feverish. Her head began to pound with the same crashing effect of the waves.

As she walked the last ten minutes to the house, she felt disoriented. The freezing rain became so thick she couldn't see any lights in either direction. It was getting darker instead of lighter as the morning went on. The darkness of her soul mirrored the blinding effect the storm was having on the beach. Now she worried that she'd not be able to find the beach house. She wished so much she could go home to her own apartment. She hated the fact that she had forced Melissa to let her come with her to Edisto.

Chapter Twenty-One

Melissa watched Jennifer rush out the door. She was obviously upset. She wanted to run after her and tell her everything, but couldn't. Jennifer's face had shown such despair and anger. She knew it was wrong to allow her to be so confused, but she couldn't tell her about John. She just couldn't.

No matter what happened Melissa was still going to leave town and purchase a new store. If Jennifer wanted to stay and manage the store, fine and if not that was okay also. In the future if Jennifer wanted to buy her out, she would sell her The Cranberry Tree without question. Melissa felt like she owed Jennifer that much for saving her life, not to mention John Michael's as well.

She certainly didn't want to come back to Charleston for any reason. In the end it would be for the best. She would be free from having to see Jennifer and John together, and she'd be away from the one place where the memories of John were so painful. She could still go to Edisto to visit and maybe move there one day for good.

Melissa tried to pass the time by straightening things around the house. She did the dishes in the kitchen and poured another cup of coffee before grabbing a book to read in front of the fire.

She was thinking Jennifer was out in the cold and rain longer than she should be. The fire began to die a little so she brought in more wood from the porch. Her eyes scanned the beach trying to get a glimpse of Jennifer walking along the shore. It may have been raining too hard to see very well, but there was no sign of Jennifer in either direction.

Melissa was sorry Jennifer was so upset over her decision to leave Charleston. She hoped she didn't get sick out in the cold and rain. If Jennifer did get sick then she would feel guilty. Melissa knew she should have told her the truth. She rationalized some of the guilt away by thinking Jennifer shouldn't have come on the trip in the first place. She tried justifying her actions, but knew she was ultimately responsible for all the pain Jennifer was going through.

More time passed and Melissa was really beginning to worry. She turned on the porch light and looked out towards the sea. There was still no sign of Jennifer anywhere. Melissa tried to busy herself in the kitchen. She got two steaks out of the refrigerator and started marinating them in olive oil and garlic. She wrapped the container in Saran Wrap and put them back in the fridge. They could eat steaks on the grill that night or the next if the rain let up. There was a grill at the end of the driveway under the beach house. It was possible to cook on the grill even when it was raining, but it would be easier to cook outside if it wasn't so cold and wet.

Melissa began making a big salad for lunch, chopping cucumbers, tomatoes, and carrots. She covered the salad ingredients and put them in the fridge. The fire was toasty and still there was no Jennifer. She poured some seltzer and added a slice of lime, then went out on the porch again to scan the beach for her. Again nothing. Where could she be? Melissa went back inside, sat on the couch, and sipped on her seltzer. She touched the edge of the glass with her forefinger letting it squeak as she sat worrying about Jennifer. She carried her seltzer with her to the fire and turned so her back would be warmed by the flames. The fire crackled and sparks flew upward.

The door suddenly opened and Jennifer walked in looking pale and drenched. She was shivering, gave Melissa a mean look, headed for the bedroom to get some dry clothes and turned on the shower, all without saying a word.

"My God, Jennifer, you could catch your death of cold out there in this weather. Why did you stay outside so long?"

Jennifer shot another angry look at Melissa and replied, "Don't even start in on me, Melissa. Just do whatever you came here to do and leave me out of it. There's nothing else to talk about. You made that clear when we left Charleston and I should have believed you." Jennifer was freezing and could not stop her lips from quivering.

Melissa decided to wait until Jennifer got some dry clothes on before she asked her about dinner or lunch. She didn't blame her for being angry. Everyone's angry or hurt right now. She only hoped Jennifer didn't get sick. Melissa went into the kitchen and began to boil water for hot chocolate.

Jennifer took her dry clothes and towel into the bathroom and decided to take a bath instead of a shower. She stripped and got in the tub before it was completely full. The hot water did not take the chill away. I must have a fever, she concluded. Just my luck I'd end up with a fever all because of my stupidity. I should have just called a cab and gone home. Melissa hadn't wanted me here in the first place. She could have dropped this bomb on me at the shop on Monday. I could have already been looking for a new job. All of this is just too emotionally draining and I certainly don't need all of these problems on top of trying to keep myself healthy.

The bath helped to warm her externally, but she was chilled to the bone. She wrapped her hair with a towel and slipped a fresh warm-up suit on. She sat on the edge of the tub contemplating on whether she wanted to open the door and face Melissa. After about 15 minutes, Melissa knocked on the door.

"Jennifer, I've got hot water ready. Would you like some hot chocolate or some tea?"

Jennifer hesitated. She didn't want to answer.

"Jennifer, are you all right?" It was obvious that Melissa was really concerned about her.

"Yes." She said nothing else.

"Would you like something hot to drink?"

"Hot tea would be good." Jennifer's arms were still shaking as she hung the towels over the shower curtain rod. She opened the door and headed for the laundry room to put her wet clothes in the washing machine. Her lips were trembling.

"I'll get that, Jennifer. Why don't you go wrap up in the blanket beside the fire and I'll bring you your tea?"

Jennifer started to argue with her, but didn't have the strength. Her hair was still wet, but she was too fatigued to blow it dry. She grabbed a pillow from the bed, lay down in front of the fire, and doubled the blanket around her aching body. The heat from the fire only slightly helped to warm her trembling body. She was exhausted and longed to sleep.

"Jennifer, here's your tea. Do you want anything to eat?" She handed the cup of tea to Jennifer with a napkin.

"No thank you. Just the tea." Jennifer answered without looking at Melissa. She took a couple of swallows and put the cup on a coaster on the coffee table, and snuggled deeper into the blanket.

Melissa picked up her own empty cup and placed it in the sink in the kitchen. She definitely decided to wait until the next night to prepare the steaks. She ate salad and cleaned the kitchen. Afterwards, she grabbed her book and a pillow. Melissa found another blanket in the hall closet and curled up on the couch.

Jennifer's face looked flush. Melissa wondered if Jennifer were sleeping too close to the fire. She went over and touched her forehead. She felt like she was burning with fever. Melissa started searching for some aspirin. She thought she had a small bottle in the bottom of her purse.

"Jennifer, here are a couple of aspirin and some water." She gently shook her shoulder, handed her the pills and then the water.

Jennifer turned around and took the medicine without even a little argument. After swallowing the pills, she turned over and immediately went back to sleep. Her lethargic behavior frightened Melissa. She wrapped another blanket around her and felt her forehead again. It felt even hotter.

She went and got another glass of water and brought it back for Jennifer to drink. Again it was very hard to awaken her. Finally, Jennifer sat up, drank the water, and sank back under the covers.

Melissa got a damp cloth and put it on Jennifer's forehead. She had to do something. She knew Jennifer had a doctor she saw on a regular basis. She decided to try and find his number and call him. Jennifer might need to go to the emergency room.

"Jennifer, can you hear me? I need the name and phone number of your doctor? Did you bring your address book with you?" She gently shook Jennifer and asked her the question again.

"What? Who?" Jennifer had no idea where she was or who was talking to her. Delirium had already set in.

"Your doctor? I need the name of your doctor?"

"Doctor Epstein. His number is in my purse in my address book." Jennifer mumbled and dropped her head back on her pillow.

Melissa found his name and left a message with his answering service. They would page him and he'd call her right back. She hung up the phone. She was beginning to feel sick at her stomach. It seemed wrong now not to have told Jennifer the truth. She promised herself if Jennifer got better, she'd tell her everything. If she wanted to have a relationship with Melissa's ex-husband then there was not anything she could do about it.

The phone rang and startled both of them. Melissa knew it had to be the doctor.

"Hello, Dr. Epstein. This is Melissa Johnson. I'm a friend of Jennifer Crawson. She seems to have gotten sick from exposure to the rain and cold at the beach. She is burning with fever. I gave her some aspirin and water, but she's so lethargic that I'm worried. Do you think I need to take her to the nearest emergency room? We're at Edisto Beach, so it may be too far to go all the way back to Charleston."

"I don't think that will be necessary, unless you can determine just how high her fever is. She needs some juice. Do you have any orange juice? It's important that she get some sugar in her system. She needs orange juice rather than just water. Call me back if her condition gets any worse and I'll call for an ambulance in that case. You should notice a big improvement once she gets the juice in her. If she's not totally better within 24 hours, we may need to find the nearest emergency care facility at the beach."

"Thank you, doctor. I'll get back with you if there's not an immediate improvement. I believe she brought orange juice and cranberry juice with her. Bye." She hung up the phone, went to the kitchen, and poured Jennifer a large glass of orange juice.

"Jennifer, Jennifer. Sit up! I need you to drink this juice." She helped Jennifer sit up while she drank the juice.

"Do you want to go get in your bed or just continue to stay out here beside the fire?"

"No, don't make me go to bed. It's warmer here. I don't want to move." Jennifer took another gulp of juice and flopped back down under the blankets.

"Okay." She wrapped the blankets tighter around Jennifer. Melissa needed more wood for the fire. When she came back inside with the firewood, Jennifer was mumbling something.

"Don't worry. I'll be leaving as soon as I get back to Charleston. I'll leave the shop and you can find someone else to work there. That way you don't have to move at all."

"You're just talking out of your head. I don't want you to quit working at the shop. Just drink some more of this juice and rest. That's all I want you to do right now. Just get better and we'll talk about everything later."

"Yeah, right." Jennifer turned over on her side and faced the fire.

"You're mistaken, Jennifer. I don't want you to leave. Do you hear me? I just want you to get well. I'll talk about anything you want to talk about, I promise. Just get well."

Jennifer didn't reply.

Melissa was getting thirsty. She went to the kitchen and got a glass of cranberry juice and got ready for bed. She decided to sleep on the other couch across from Jennifer, so she could keep an eye on her. She brought in more wood to keep next to the fireplace. Melissa took a few minutes and called her house to check on John Michael. Maddie said he had eaten a good supper, but he did seem to be missing his mother.

His mother was missing him, too. Melissa was feeling guilty about leaving him for the first time. She couldn't wait to get home and hold him. Hanging up the phone, she grabbed another piece of wood and put it on the fire. She reached down and touched Jennifer's forehead again. Her face was still very red, but it did feel a little cooler.

Melissa walked over to the back porch window and looked out. It was still raining and the wind was blowing hard against the house. She paced back and forth, walking to other windows and peering out. She was praying silently that Jennifer was going to be all right. Melissa was feeling so badly about the way she had been treating Jennifer. She went in the kitchen and poured Jennifer another glass of fresh orange juice. She checked her face and neck to see if Jennifer still had a fever. The fever did appear to have broken some and beads of sweat were forming on Jennifer's brow.

Melissa stretched out on the couch. She was exhausted just from worry. If Jennifer pulled through this, she was determined not to hurt her again and she would tell her the truth. She promised God if He would let her be all right, she'd tell Jennifer everything. No matter how hard it was to hear Jennifer say she was in love with John, she would just have to let her say it. What is it they say? "The truth will set you free."

Before Melissa knew what was happening, she had fallen asleep. She and Jennifer were both restless in their dreams, both struggling with their demons, yet sleeping until the sun came up the next morning.

Chapter Twenty-Two

Jennifer got up first. Her fever broke during the night. She went to the bathroom, took some of her medicine, drank some juice, and got back under the covers. The fire was almost out, but she didn't have the strength to put any more wood on it. She wrapped herself tighter in the blankets. She was sweating although the room was beginning to feel cooler. Jennifer was glad because that meant she no longer had a fever. She hoped to get more sleep before Melissa got up. She certainly didn't want to talk to her about anything.

Unfortunately, Melissa began to stir a little. For a moment she forgot about Jennifer being sick. Looking around, she suddenly realized where she was and what had happened the night before.

She got up and checked on Jennifer and the fire. She placed her hand on Jennifer's forehead again. She was clammy and sweaty and Melissa sighed with relief. Thank God, she thought, Jennifer's fever had broken. The room on the other hand was very cold. She put another couple of logs on the fire and relit the embers.

Melissa went to the kitchen and poured two glasses of cranberry juice and started brewing the coffee. She took one of the glasses of juice to Jennifer.

"Jennifer, Jen? Here's some juice. Wake up, Jennifer." Melissa's voice was a lot more compassionate.

Jennifer sat up, but was obviously irritated with Melissa. She did feel better, but she hated being stuck at the beach with Melissa. As soon as she was well enough to travel, she was calling a cab.

Melissa could see the anger in Jennifer's eyes. In a way that was an encouraging sight. Her change from sadness and fear to one of anger was a welcomed improvement.

"It looks as though your fever has broken. You really had me worried last night. I'm glad you're better. How do you feel?"

Jennifer thought to herself, I'll tell you how I feel. I feel like getting out of here as soon as I can. Instead she replied with the easiest nonfeeling reply she could muster.

"Fine, Melissa. I feel fine." She answered with a sarcastic tone in her voice.

Melissa detected her hostility. She started to comment on it, but decided to get a cup of coffee instead. She turned and asked, "Would you like a cup of coffee? I have some Almond Amaretto or will juice be sufficient?"

"I'll just have juice." She wished she could have some coffee. Almond Amaretto was her very favorite coffee.

Jennifer seemed to feel well enough to fight, so Melissa decided now might be a good time to try and talk with her.

"Jennifer, you have every right to be mad at me. I was wrong and if you'll give me a chance, I'll tell you everything."

"Don't bother, Melissa. I don't want anything to do with your mysteries. I don't care if you talk to me. I don't care if you move to Atlanta and frankly I quit my job at The Cranberry Tree." She pushed the covers off and started to get up.

"Wait, Jennifer. Please give me just a minute. I just want to say one thing to you. I can't make you hear me out, and no I don't deserve it after treating you so badly. When you were gone for so long and came back obviously sick, I realized how much I made you suffer. I ask you to forgive me for everything. You had no idea why I was hurting so much and now I want to tell you if you'll let me. I promised God if you'd get well, I'd tell you everything."

Jennifer's head was pounding. She was still mad, but she wanted to know the truth. At least she could know everything before she left. If she didn't hear her out, she might not ever know the answer to all of these questions. She lay back down, looked at Melissa in disbelief, and replied quietly. "I forgive you."

"Thank you." Melissa wished John could have forgiven her for whatever it was he couldn't tolerate about her. She took her coffee with her and sat on the couch in front of Jennifer. She cradled the cup as she searched for the right words to begin telling Jennifer about John. Her stomach tightened as she tried to talk without crying.

"Jennifer, I don't really know where to start. I, I...." The tears began to flow.

Jennifer watched as the tears slowly dropped down Melissa's face. She just couldn't imagine what was behind all of that pain and why in the world it was somehow connected to her. None of it made any sense. They'd only known each other for about a year and it was the strangest relationship she'd ever been in. Melissa always looked sad even though she had everything going for her.

Melissa stood up, walked to the bathroom, got some tissue and wiped her tears. She continued to talk as she walked back into the den.

"Jennifer, there is so much you don't know about me, and there is something I need to ask you." She blew her nose and stood in front of the fire.

Jennifer wondered what Melissa needed to ask her.

"I've never talked to you about John Michael's father. I really never intended to bring his name up to you, but something happened right after the accident, something that's forcing me to talk about him now. I don't even know where to begin."

"Are you sure you want to do this? You really don't have to, Melissa. If it's going to hurt you then I don't have to know anything about him." Now she felt badly for making Melissa talk about something so personal and painful.

"No, you need to hear me out. I know now that it's the only way we can go on with our lives. I'll just start from the beginning." She took a swallow of coffee and continued.

"The night I found out I was pregnant, my husband told me he was leaving me. He never told me why. He just left. It was one of the most painful things I've ever gone through in my life. I decided then, as soon as the baby was born, that I would move. I hired you with that plan in mind. I never wanted him to know I was pregnant or to see me with his child." She waited a moment before telling Jennifer she knew she was dating John.

"Melissa, that's terrible. That must have crushed you. So, he's never tried to contact you and he doesn't know about John Michael?"

"No, he hasn't. He doesn't have a clue we were having a child. He thought we couldn't have children. I don't know how you're going to take this and I'm sorry I couldn't talk about it before now. Anyway, I want you to know who John Michael's father is."

"You don't have to, Melissa. I don't really care who he is. He must be an awful person and I don't care if I ever know his name. Let's just forget about it. It's not important to talk about him."

"No, you're wrong, Jennifer. I think it's very important. It's important because you know him." She waited a moment to let those words sink in.

"I what?" Jennifer's mouth dropped open in disbelief.

"You know him, Jennifer. I think you probably know him very well. You may be very good friends. As far as I know, you may be dating him."

"No. Now I know you're wrong. I'm not dating anyone."

"Okay, but I know you're good friends. I saw you with him. His name is John Isaacson." She waited and watched the color drain from Jennifer's face.

The words were spinning around in Jennifer's mind. She kept hearing them over and over again. His name is John Isaacson. My God, she thought.

"It can't be. It just can't be John."

"Yes, it is Jennifer and yes, you do know him. I don't know how well you know him, but I believe you must know him very well."

Jennifer suddenly felt weak and dizzy again. "It's not what you think, Melissa. How did you know I knew John?"

"I saw you walking together to the elevator at the hospital."

"Oh, Melissa, why didn't you tell me? I could have explained everything. No wonder you were so bitter towards me. The night John walked me to the elevator was the first time I noticed the change in you. I was going to tell you about John that night, but when I went into your room, well I just wish you'd told me everything that night." She reached out and touched Melissa's hand.

"I couldn't tell you, Jennifer. What could I say? Hey, I see you're dating my ex. The only thing I knew to do was to leave Charleston a lot sooner than I had originally planned to do so." Melissa began to cry.

"How could you just leave without talking to me about this?" Jennifer got up and grabbed a tissue from the bedroom for Melissa, handed it to her, and sat beside her on the couch.

"Listen to me, Melissa. I've got so much to tell you about John. It's nothing like what you've been thinking about him or us."

"What was I supposed to think? A man I've been with for seven years, comes home one night, tells me he's leaving me, and won't tell me why. Then while I'm in the hospital recovering from an accident, I see you hugging him at the elevator. It made me so sick I wished I had died when I fell down those stairs." Melissa's voice cracked and she began to sob uncontrollably.

"My God, Melissa. I wish you'd told me. All of this hurt was so unnecessary. John was in the hospital because he has prostate cancer. He is an old friend of mine from college. We both dated other people back then. There is absolutely nothing but friendship going on with us. I know he never meant to hurt you, Melissa. He thought he was protecting you from his inability to have children."

"What do you mean?" Melissa sat up and wiped the tears from her cheeks. "He never even gave me a reason for leaving. How could he not have intended to hurt me? You don't just walk out on someone you're married to without some explanation."

"He thought once treatment started that he wouldn't be able to have a normal sexual relationship with you. He had just started the cancer treatment when you saw us together."

"What? Why didn't he tell me? The night he left me I had just found out I was pregnant that day. I was going to surprise him at dinner. We could have shared the excitement of the baby together, and he never would have had to go through cancer treatment without me."

"I know, Melissa, but he thought he was doing what was best for you."

"I was pregnant, Jennifer. His leaving was not going to make me go have sex with someone else. Like he could just leave me and I'd go jump in bed with another man. It wouldn't have mattered about sex."

"I told him that. Even though I didn't know it was you I was referring to."

"Why didn't you ever tell me about John or tell him about me?"

"We ran into each other in the parking garage when I was going to pick you up at your doctor's appointment. I told him I was going to the doctor's office to pick up my pregnant boss. I don't guess I ever said your name and he never would have guessed my pregnant boss was you."

"So when did you learn he had cancer?"

"He called that night and we were going to meet for dinner one night on the weekend. He told me what he was doing at the medical building that day. You fell in your garage that same night John and I talked on the phone. I was going to tell you, but we just never had the chance. When you saw us in the hospital John had just found out he was well enough to go have a special treatment in Baltimore. He told me the great news and walked me to the elevator. That's when you saw me hug him."

Melissa's heart began to pound. What did this mean? Now what? Would he be coming back into her life? That thought excited her and frightened her at the same time. She was almost afraid to let John back into her life. She had built so many walls around her emotions she didn't know if she'd be able to get back into his life. What guarantee did she have that things would ever be like they used to be, and what if he didn't want her back?

"I can't believe it, Jennifer. I can't believe he left because he was sick. If he had only told me, we could have worked it out together. Now what? Where do we go from here?" Melissa asked.

"I think I need to call John. He should be home by now or you could call him if you want to."

"No, you call. What if he still doesn't want to see me? Maybe he doesn't feel the same way about me and doesn't want to get involved in my life again."

"I don't think that could possibly be true, but if you rather I called, I will."

"Yes, you call. If he sounds like he doesn't want to see me then please don't push it."

"That's ridiculous. Of course he'll want to see you." She dialed the number.

Melissa's heart was beating wildly. She wasn't sure she could handle it if he didn't want to see her. She walked out on the deck of the porch and looked out at the ocean. The sun was out again. There was no trace of the rain of the day before, but it was still very cold and windy.

The blueness of the ocean seemed to beckon her towards it. The splashing sound of the waves seemed to be in sync with her own pulse. The winter sun was a welcomed sight. It was as though even nature was smiling. She breathed in the crisp cool air of winter and received a deeper feeling of healing. Her spirit felt lighter. She was nervous about seeing John for the first time, but she felt free from the pain she'd carried all those months. She exhaled a sigh of relief. What a great feeling to know the reason he had left her was an admirable one. She wished she could have been by John's side during his sickness. She wanted to be with him, to hold him, to make love to him. Even though the latter might be an impossibility at this point in his sickness.

"I'm finally free from all of this confusion!" She yelled out at the waves and sky. A wonderful liberating laugh left her chest. The lies that filled her heart were gone. She smiled to herself and went back in the house. She prayed silently that John wanted to see her again as badly as she wanted to see him.

Chapter Twenty-Three

Jennifer decided not to tell John about Melissa. Instead she would just ask him to come to the beach house and help her with a problem she was having with her boss. She wanted him to be surprised at seeing Melissa for the first time.

"Hello, John. This is Jennifer. How are you feeling? Did everything turn out all right for you in Baltimore?"

"I'm feeling great, Jennifer. I'm so excited over this new procedure for prostate cancer. As far as Doctor Williams can tell everything was a success. I feel like I'm getting a second chance at life and it feels fantastic. Boy, am I ready for a new beginning. How about you? How is everything going for you? Are you at home? You sound kind of far away."

"Actually, I'm at the beach with my boss. It's a long story, but I was calling to see if you might want to come here for a couple of days. I've wanted you to meet my boss anyway and we've been fighting for most of the time I've been here. Maybe having a third party would calm things down a bit. You're probably the key to easing all the tension that's been going on between us." Jennifer smiled to herself and continued.

"It's a great place to get away. Maybe you could use a little vacation. Please say you'll come? Of course the offer is only good if you're well enough to drive. I wouldn't want you to push yourself. What do you think? Could you help me out here? In your old college days you'd never have turned down an opportunity to be with two beautiful women alone at the beach?"

"Are you kidding? I feel better than I've felt in such a long time. A trip to the beach sounds great. I just hope your boss isn't still having problems from the fall she had."

"She's been out of sorts lately, but nothing seeing you for the first time couldn't help alleviate, I'm sure. If you want to stay longer than a couple of days, that'll be fine, too. I just need to get back to work on Monday."

"Well, tell me how to get there and I'll leave as soon as I can throw some clothes together. I'll bring some extra clothes in case I do stay longer. Maybe I should bring a nice bottle of wine or champagne so we can celebrate my successful surgery."

"That would be perfect. We might have a lot of things to celebrate, like new beginnings, happy bosses and great friendships." Jennifer smiled at the thought that John and Melissa would be able to celebrate their reunion and be alone for a few days after she went back to Charleston.

"Great! Well, tell me how to get there and I'll be on my way."

Jennifer hung up the phone after giving explicit directions. Now, she'd have to figure out how to keep Melissa from knowing that John still didn't know who her boss was. She wasn't going to lie to her, but she wasn't going to tell her right up front that John didn't know she was there. About that time Melissa came walking through the door.

"Well, I called John and he should be here in a couple of hours. As soon as he can pack a few clothes he'll be leaving Charleston. See I told you he would want to come."

"Oh my God, Jennifer. I can't believe this is happening to me. How do I look? I must look terrible. I'll go take a shower and change clothes. What did he say when you told him?"

Jennifer cleared her throat. "He was very excited and asked me how to get here. He said as soon as he could throw some clothes together, pick up a nice bottle of wine or champagne, he'd leave Charleston."

Melissa was glowing. The transformation in her face and eyes looked like a wilted flower that had just been given water. She was more alive than Jennifer had ever seen her, so hopeful, so expectant, so full of love for this man who had caused so much grief in her life before.

"I better get ready. I'm so excited! Thank you, Jen." She gave Jennifer a big hug, kissed her on the cheek, and ran to take her shower.

Jennifer smiled to herself. This is great. She could almost say it was worth going through all the trauma if it brought those two back together. She was relieved that the truth was finally out between her and Melissa. Now she could go on with her own life and try and find her brother Jay.

She decided to get dinner ready. They would finally get to cook the steaks Melissa was marinating in the fridge. She was glad they hadn't eaten them. A steak dinner cooked on the grill would be a perfect meal for Melissa and John. She thought about how romantic that evening could be for them. She wished she could go ahead and leave, but Melissa might need help with the first moments of getting back together and with preparing dinner. She'd wait to see how things went and then ask Melissa if she could take her car back to Charleston. She and John could use his car whenever they were ready to leave.

She began to pack a few of her things. She decided not to say anything to Melissa about leaving early until after John got there. It might make her more nervous if she had to go through seeing him for the first time alone.

Jennifer was in the kitchen when Melissa came out of her room.

"You are just glowing. I don't think I've ever seen you look so happy."

Melissa blushed. "Thank you. It feels so good finally knowing the truth, Jennifer." She went over and gave her another big hug.

Jennifer smiled. "I've started getting the grill ready for the steaks. I'm sure John will be hungry when he gets here, which should be in the next 30 minutes. I'll wait and start the fire then."

"Jennifer, am I dreaming all of this? Is he really coming to see me? Am I really going to see John come through that door after all these months? It seems impossible. I don't know if I'll be able to eat a bite of food, I'm so nervous and excited."

Jennifer smiled knowingly. "I'm sure all your appetites will return after your initial reunion. Personally, I'm starving. Remember I was sick last night and I haven't really had a lot to eat, yet."

"Oh my goodness, I forgot. I'm sorry Jennifer, since you told me about John, I haven't been able to think of anything else. I made a salad and it's in the refrigerator."

"I think I might go ahead and eat something if you don't mind. The potatoes have been cooking for a little over an hour. I think I'll eat one with some salad. Besides you and John may want to have a romantic dinner alone."

"Please don't leave me alone with John. What am I going to say to him? Both of us may need help getting through the transition of seeing each other for the first time. Jen, I couldn't handle it if he rejects me."

"Don't be silly, Melissa. He's not going to reject you. Come outside with me while I put the charcoal on the grill." She opened the door for Melissa to follow her out.

They both looked at the ocean. The rain clouds had scattered although they were calling for more showers during the night. The sea was glimmering and there was a rainbow covering the sky with streaks of the evening sun reflected on the water.

"Look, Melissa, a rainbow. It couldn't be a more perfect sign for you and John to be together. Things are going to work out fine for both of you. I just know it."

Melissa's eyes followed the sky. "I hope you're right, Jennifer. I'm not sure why, but I have a very uneasy feeling."

Chapter Twenty-Four

The ache in John's heart had only partially healed and he wanted so much to tell Melissa what had been going on in his life. He had this irresistible urge to call her on the phone, but he knew she probably didn't want anything to do with him. Now that he was going to be all right, he wanted her back, especially with all the good news he had to share with her.

He picked up the receiver and dialed Melissa's number before leaving to go to the beach. He let the phone ring ten times, but she never answered. I wonder if she is still living in Charleston. The thought that she might have moved made him sick at his stomach.

Well, there wasn't anything he could do about that right then. Maybe when he got back in town, he could actively see about finding her. Right then he needed to concentrate on the fact that he was going to the beach with a good friend and her boss. At least he didn't have to be by himself for the next couple of days and for the moment that made him happy.

Taking the keys out of his pocket he unlocked the trunk and started packing the car. He would need to get some gas before leaving town. Maybe he could ride by The Cranberry Tree and just see if Melissa were working late. He stopped at a gas station not far from his apartment, filled the car up, grabbed some cokes, wine, and champagne to take with him to the beach.

Then he drove to The Cranberry Tree and parked out front. He had avoided driving anywhere near the shop for such a long time. He got out of the car and walked to the door. Peering inside he realized no one was there. He felt sad when he looked in the window remembering all the times he and Melissa had spent there. He got back in the car, relieved that he was getting out of town. Just going near the shop made him ache inside.

The scenic route to the beach had a calming effect on John. For some reason the road seemed so isolated without much traffic on it. He let his eyes scan the horizon. There were marshes and swamps that looked so tranquil from the car. He was glad he wasn't having to walk beside any of them. The thought of copperhead snakes and creeping things didn't make it look very inviting for a stroll.

John took a deep breath and began to think about what he would like to happen in his life now that he was going to recover. He wanted to recapture his soul, find a way to get Melissa back into his life, and plan their future together not apart. He wished she would feel the same way when he told her the truth about his sickness, but she might not give him the chance to talk to her at all.

He turned on the radio. It was just too quiet in the car and he was tired of the silence that had been with him for months. He rolled down the window and breathed in the fresh air. He was enjoying the breeze when all of a sudden the car started making a thumping noise and began wobbling from side to side.

"What the-Oh, no. I've got a flat tire!" He pulled over to the edge of the road about the same time the car began to grind on the rim of the tire.

"Great, that's all I need. I don't think I put that regular sized spare in the trunk. The cannister for the little spare that came with the car might be empty." John mumbled out loud. He hated those little tires that have to be driven at only 50 miles an hour.

"Those canisters never seem to work properly when you need them too." He continued to complain. He searched everywhere in the trunk and couldn't find it anyway. His frustration began to grow. Not one car passed while he searched for a way to fix his tire. He wondered which way he should go to find the nearest gas station.

John waited a few moments longer before he started walking in the direction of Edisto. He was somewhat fearful about walking so closely to swamp lands. Hesitant he leaned against the driver's side of the car and watched the road hoping desperately that a car would drive up.

He still had not regained his strength since his radiation treatments. The wind whipped against John's body with a fierceness that made him shiver. Soon it became too cold to stand outside without a sweater or a coat. He got back in the car, reached in the backseat for his suitcase, and grabbed a sweater out of it. He chose one that Melissa had given him. The wind had picked up and he slipped it on before starting his dreaded walk alongside the desolate road.

The darkness from the storm had covered the skyline hours before sunset and the night creatures were already making their presence known. He kept envisioning poisonous snakes and alligators in the shadows of those big trees with Spanish moss hanging from their limbs. He was aware these creatures existed, he just didn't know if they were out in the winter.

What luck. He's finally getting out and going to spend some time with a friend and her boss and he has to have a flat. It was getting darker so he got out of the car and started walking.

He watched both sides of the road to see if there were any houses with their lights on. He needed to find a home where they would let him use the phone. Then he could call AAA and they would come fix the flat. Too bad he left his mobile at home. If he didn't find a house soon, it would be too dark to see. He also wished he had gotten the number from Jennifer, so he could tell them he was going to be late.

He started walking even faster. The eerie sounds of the night began to bother him. He plunged his hands in his pockets and continued to walk toward the beach. Whatever was moving around out there made him want to start running. And why wasn't there any traffic on that road. Jennifer had probably started to worry about him by now. She probably thought he had changed his mind and had gone back home.

He heard it thunder in the distance and the wind blew even harder. He shivered all over. Crazy thoughts were going through his head. Jennifer would probably read about him being eaten by an alligator in The Post and Courier. He turned and sprinted to the car. He found it hard to catch his breath, but was glad to make it back.

Chapter Twenty-Five

Jennifer went back into the house to check on the time. John should have already been there. She hoped he hadn't gotten lost. She and Jennifer were waiting to put the steaks on the grill. The coals were at that perfect stage to start cooking. If John didn't get there soon, they might have to dump the old coals and put on fresh ones.

Melissa began to get that sick worried look. "You don't think he changed his mind do you? Maybe he decided he doesn't want to see me at all?"

"Of course he does, Melissa. Maybe he got a later start than he thought he would or he forgot his cell phone. He might be lost somewhere. I don't know, but I do know his not being here had nothing to do with you. He didn't change his mind about you. Trust me on that one."

"I hope you're right, Jennifer because I can't handle any more rejection right now."

"I know, Melissa. He's not going to disappoint you this time. We just need to be patient. He'll be here, okay?"

"I can't help but be worried. John's only been late one time since I've known him. That was when he walked in the door and told me he was leaving me."

"You've just got to let the past go, Melissa. He'll be here. I'm going for a short walk. You stay here in case he shows up. All right?"

"Do you have to leave? I'm not sure I can handle seeing him for the first time by myself."

"I'll be right back. If he comes just go meet him at his car. I'm sure you'll get over your nervousness when you see him."

"Okay, but hurry. I don't really want to be alone right now."

"You could go with me, but if no one's here when he knocks on the door he might leave thinking he has the wrong address."

"You're right. I'll wait. It would be terrible if he drove all the way here and then turned around and drove all the way back to Charleston."

Jennifer headed for the beach. She was trying to hide the fact that she was beginning to worry about John. She knew something must have happened. Especially since he didn't even know Melissa was there.

She started to walk faster in hopes of releasing some of the tension she was feeling. She was also trying to avoid Melissa's anxiety. She decided to give him 20 more minutes and then she was going to take Melissa's car and go look for him. She could only hope he'd be there when she got back to the beach house. Somehow deep inside she knew he wouldn't be. There was something wrong, but what could it possibly be? Where could John be? Something must have happened or he would be there.

She began to fear the worse. What if he had gotten in a wreck? With that thought her heart rate increased. Maybe they needed to go look for him as soon as she got back. She would try to call him at his house first and if he were not there she would leave with or without Melissa.

She had to keep Melissa from knowing how concerned she was. She ran half the way back, caught her breath before climbing the stairs, and hoped John somehow had gotten there while she was out walking.

Chapter Twenty-Six

Another 30 minutes passed and still no cars drove by. John turned on the radio in hopes of catching a current weather report. The news report called for more rain and some thunderstorms for the rest of the evening. The night was already blistering cold and now it would be damp cold, cold to the bone as most southerners call it. He pulled his coat from the back seat and stuck his arms through the arm holes, covering the front of him like a blanket. He was still shivering as he opened a coke in an attempt to quench his thirst.

John turned on the interior light to check the time. It was 9:30. He grabbed one of his shirts and balled it up to use as a pillow. He had a feeling it was going to be a long night. He only hoped no criminals were out and about. He'd hate to be awakened by thugs breaking into his car. He turned on the emergency flashers, closed his eyes, and listened to the clicking noise the flashers made as it came on and off. He missed Melissa so much. He longed for the beach and the warmth of being around an old friend from Atlanta.

Time continued to tick by. He wished a car would come up, help him fix his flat or call AAA for him on their cell phone. The waiting seemed unbearable. In two hours not one single car had passed by him. If an evil person did come up they would find him defenseless in these marshlands. They could rob him, leave him for dead, and no one would even know he was missing for days. He had to stop thinking this way. He had begun to warm up and he was grateful that the temperature hadn't dropped any lower.

John was about to fall asleep when he heard a car approach. He wiped the window and looked out. He watched the car brake, and then it kept going down the road. It looked like one of those old Pintos. He turned on the headlights and leaned up so he could see better. The car passed slowly through his headlights. It definitely looked like a rusted old yellow pinto. Thank goodness that car didn't stop, John thought. He watched as it went around the curve.

It was quiet for another five minutes except for the ticking of the clock and the emergency lights coming on and off. Everything around him reminded John that time was ticking by. He sighed deeply and fell asleep.

Melissa looked out the window in hopes John would pull into the driveway. He obviously had not left Charleston when he told Jennifer he would. She knew he should have been there an hour ago. Her excited mood had changed to one of despair. She felt sick at her stomach for trusting him again. It didn't matter if he were sick, there was no excuse for not showing up when he said he would, outside of a disaster. There was just no excuse.

Jennifer finally opened the door and peeped inside. "Well did he make it yet?" She asked hoping her gut feelings were wrong this time. She looked anxiously in the den.

"No, he didn't. I told you he wouldn't come if he knew I was here and I was right."

"Look, Melissa, I know he's late but that doesn't mean he isn't coming here because of you. Believe me something must have happened on his way here. It had nothing to do with you. I'll call his house and see if he got a later start than he thought he would." She dialed his number and let it ring for several minutes. No answer. She hung up the phone.

"He's not there, Melissa and to be honest with you I'm worried about him. I hope he's not lost or even worse that he didn't have a wreck somewhere on the way here."

"No, you're wrong, Jennifer. I'll tell you what happened. He got cold feet, that's all. He doesn't want to see me."

"That's not true. It has to be something else. I want to take your car and go look for him. Do you want to come with me or not?"

"Why should I? I'll just make my own supper and get some rest. We can leave tomorrow."

"Suit yourself, but I'm going. I want you to come with me, but I'm not waiting any longer. It's almost ten o'clock now." She didn't wait for an answer. She went in the bedroom, changed her shoes, grabbed a jacket then headed for the door. "Can I get the keys to your car?" She waited. "Well?"

"Yes. I'll go with you. Not because I think we'll find him, but because I'd worry about your riding around alone not knowing the area very well." Melissa picked up her coat, handed Jennifer the keys, turned out the light, and walked out the door.

As soon as they left the beach house it began raining. Neither of them said a word for miles. The roads were totally desolate except for one car. It was hard to see, but it looked like an old Pinto. Melissa knew that wasn't John's car. There was almost a spookiness about the way the Spanish moss hung down from the trees.

Melissa was the first to break the silence. "What exactly are we hoping to find?"

"We're looking for John's car on the side of the road, a wreck, John walking down the road, or John's car riding around lost."

"How far are we going before you give this up?" Melissa asked rather sarcastically.

"I don't know. I'm going to drive at least 45 miles. If we don't find him by then, I'll assume he got lost and went back to his house."

Neither of them said anything for several more miles. It started raining really hard and it was difficult to see out of the window. They were fogged up and the wipers beat in a rhythm slower than the rain. Visibility was almost impossible. Jennifer wondered if she should just turn the car around and head back to the beach house. She was contemplating telling Melissa that John didn't know she was her boss.

"Melissa?"

"What?"

Jennifer began to speak when she suddenly saw a car on the side of the road with it's emergency lights flashing

"Oh, my God. I think that's John's car!" Melissa yelled as they drove up beside it. "That's definitely his car."

"I can't see anyone in the car. I hope nothing's happened to him out here in the middle of nowhere."

Melissa couldn't speak. Her heart was beating wildly. She wasn't sure what frightened her more, that something may have happened to John, or that she was about to see him for the first time. She found it hard to breath and didn't want to get out of the car.

"Jennifer, I can't do this. I'm not getting out of the car. You go see if he's in there."

Melissa struggled to get her words out. "I'm serious, you go. I'll just sit in the car."

"Oh no, you're not. I'm not getting out of this car by myself. What if something's wrong with him? You need to go with me in case he needs some help."

"But it's raining so hard."

"Melissa, I'm not going alone. After what you've put me through these last few months, rain or no rain, you're going to see this man."

Melissa's hands were trembling as she opened the car door. She reached for one of her umbrellas and began opening it outside the car. Everything inside of her wanted to run, but she knew she couldn't. She wanted to cry, scream, and laugh all at the same time. Instead she walked silently towards John's car.

Chapter Twenty-Seven

John could hear a car approaching. He wasn't sure if he should be excited or afraid. He hoped for the best. It was raining, but he could hear two doors slam. He was lying down in the seat and no one would be able to tell he was in the car. He was about to sit up and look out the window when he heard someone call his name.

"John, it's Jennifer. John, are you in there?" The only light was the blinking of the emergency flashers. The rain and condensation clouded the view of the window. Jennifer couldn't see in the car so she tapped on the window.

John raised up to look out and there was Jennifer peering in at him.

"Thank goodness it's you." He smiled at the glass.

"I had a feeling something was wrong and decided to come look for you." Jennifer wondered when he would notice Melissa. The hood of Melissa's coat partially covered her face and she held her umbrella in such a way that it was almost impossible to see her face.

John grabbed his umbrella and got out of the car. He looked toward Melissa and said, "You must be Jennifer's boss?" He extended his one free hand to introduce himself and he looked directly into Melissa's face. He couldn't believe his eyes.

"Me-Melissa? What are you doing, here? I-I didn't know you and Jennifer knew each other." His face turned bright red with surprise.

"Hi, John." Melissa replied nervously. She resisted the urge to hug his neck.

Both their hearts were beating loudly in their ears. John couldn't believe Melissa was actually standing a couple of feet in front of him and struggled with what to say next. He had so many questions. Was this Jennifer's boss? Whose baby? Was she remarried already? He continued.

"This sure is a surprise. I didn't realize you were Jennifer's boss."

Melissa shot Jennifer an angry look for not telling John she was at the beach with her. She got her message across with just a glance.

Jennifer interjected, "John, what's wrong with your car?"

"I had a flat on the way and I don't have my spare or my cannister to temporarily inflate the tire. I walked for a long time, but didn't see a single house and only one car passed by me. I finally decided to come back and wait for someone to come and find me. Thank goodness I made it back to the car before it started raining so hard."

"Well, why don't we put your spare in Melissa's trunk and we'll get some air in it in the morning? We'll help you get your things out of the car. All of us need to get out of this monsoon before we get sick. Let's hurry. I don't know about the rest of you, but I'm starving. We can finish cooking supper as soon as we get back to the house." Jennifer added.

"That sounds great to me. I haven't eaten in hours. I've just been sipping on a coke all evening." He reached in the car, got his keys and luggage, and put the tire and everything in Melissa's trunk.

John sat in the back seat of the car while Melissa sat up front with Jennifer. For a few minutes no one said anything. Everyone was caught up in their own thoughts. Jennifer broke the silence.

"Well, this certainly has been a weekend of revelations, hasn't it? I don't guess any of us ever dreamed we were somehow a part of each others' life. I never dreamed the two of you knew each other."

Melissa was silent. There was so much she wanted to ask them both. John was the first to say anything.

"I didn't know the two of you were working together. How and when did you meet?"

"Well, I interviewed with Melissa for a managerial position at The Cranberry Tree. I had no idea that you and Melissa were ever married. I didn't find that out until last night and I have to tell you that I was totally shocked. I was on my way to the doctor's office the day I ran into you in the parking lot. I don't know why her name never came up. I wanted to introduce you to each other from the very beginning, but I never really had the opportunity. So there you have it. I'll let the two of you fill in all the other details."

Jennifer pulled into the driveway before anyone had a chance to say anything else. If John had gotten there earlier, she would have asked Melissa if she could use her car and go on back to Charleston. She felt like the two of them really needed some time alone to hash out all their feelings, but now it was so late she'd just have to wait until the morning.

After they helped John bring his suitcase and the rest of his belongings in from the car, Melissa showed him his room. They both ached at the thought of not sleeping together.

"I don't know about the two of you, but I'm just going to have a salad and potato. By the time the charcoal gets ready again it will just be too late to eat." They all agreed to wait to cook steaks sometime the next day. Jennifer put three baking potatoes in the microwave and Melissa got the salad out of the fridge.

After dinner Melissa added more wood to the fire, and they all sat around the fire warming themselves near the embers. After a couple of minutes Jennifer excused herself.

"Well, I'm sure the two of you have a lot of catching up to do so I'm going on to bed. I just want to say how happy it makes me to see the two of you together." She went over and gave Melissa a hug and then John.

"This has turned out to be the happiest night I've had at the beach." She smiled warmly at Melissa and hoped she wasn't still mad that she didn't tell John everything before he got there. Melissa did hug her back and looked as though she were really glad that she was finally getting to be with John again.

"Good night. I'll talk to you in the morning." Jennifer put her wine glass in the sink and headed for the bedroom.

"Good night." John and Melissa said in unison.

For a long time they didn't say anything. Melissa was sitting on the floor near the fire and John was sitting on the couch opposite her finishing his Shiraz. Her face seemed radiant to him. He longed to hold her and to tell her he loved her, but for the moment he refrained.

At first Melissa avoided his eyes. She was afraid he could read her desire for him. Her pulse increased slightly when he began to speak.

"Melissa, I really don't know where to begin. You may not be open to anything I have to say, but I want to explain everything to you. If you'll let me?"

"John, Jennifer told me you're sick. Why didn't you just tell me? Couldn't you trust me enough to talk to me about any problem you were having? Didn't you know I love you enough to go through anything with you? I could have handled your being sick so much easier than the rejection and abandonment I felt. Can you see that now?"

John squirmed on the couch and leaned forward. "Melissa, I just couldn't tell you. I knew you'd stay no matter what, but I wanted more for you than that. I couldn't put that burden on you. I knew you wanted children and I didn't want you to stay with me out of pity. The doctor told me the treatment would keep me from having any children and our sex life would change. I couldn't stay. Can't you see that?"

"I wouldn't have pitied you, John. Love isn't about pity. Most of what you feared had nothing to do with what I wanted or needed. I was pregnant, John. I was pregnant the night you came home and told me you were leaving. I found out that day." Melissa began to cry.

John reached down and pulled her up toward him on the couch and held her. "You mean the baby is ours?"

"Whose else could he be, John? Do you think I've been with anyone else? Did you think after you left me that the next day I found someone else who fathered my child?"

"Why didn't you tell me you were pregnant?"

"Why should I have told you? You were leaving me without a reason."

John had a sick feeling inside. He could have been with Melissa the whole time. Her accident may never have happened if he had not walked out on her. He regretted the pain he had caused them both. John squeezed her closer to himself. He wondered if she had given their child up for adoption.

"Melissa, where is our baby now? You did say he, didn't you?"

"Yes, John, you have a son named John Michael and Maddie is keeping him for me this weekend."

John had a huge grin on his face and squeezed Melissa again.

"That's fantastic, Melissa. I want to see John Michael. Maybe when we get back to Charleston I could go by your house and see him." John was just overcome with excitement.

"Yes, I'd like that." Her crystal blue eyes sparkled as she looked into John's eyes. She wanted him so badly.

John continued to smile at Melissa, reached down, touched her chin, and pulled her toward his mouth to kiss her. "May I kiss you, Melissa? I don't want to do anything you're not ready to do."

Melissa swallowed and whispered, "Yes, John, I'd like that very much."

He leaned closer and gently kissed her. She responded with a hunger that surprised him. He pulled her closer to himself on the couch. At that moment they were both overcome with emotions. They began to cry relieved to finally be back together.

"I've missed you so much, John. Please don't ever leave me again." She wrapped her arms around his neck and kissed the tears on his cheeks.

"I won't, baby. I was so wrong in not talking to you. I never should have left. Please forgive me, Melissa. I didn't mean to hurt you. I thought I wanted you to find someone else because I wanted you to have a chance at a real family."

"A real family, John? What's that supposed to be? We are a real family and of course I forgive you. We survived it and that's all that matters now. Our love survived it and destiny brought us back together." All of a sudden she noticed the tiredness in John's eyes and remembered he had just gone through intensive laser treatment. He needed to get some sleep.

"You look tired. Why don't we get ready for bed? I'll bring some more wood inside and you can stay out here with me on the couch or I'll make the bed for you in your bedroom."

"I want to sleep with you, Melissa. I want us to sleep together out here near the fire. That is if you want to be near me tonight?"

"I do want to be near you, John. I want you more than I've ever wanted you in my life." She kissed him passionately. She longed for the old days when they made love every time they were even the least bit rowdy near the roaring fire in her fireplace at home.

"Come on let's get ready for bed. Do you want to shower first or just change into pajamas?" She smiled at him knowing he wasn't real keen on wearing pajamas.

He shrugged his shoulders. "I took a shower earlier before I left Charleston, but it's been a long night. I probably need to take another one since my jog next to the swamp lands. I was kind of stressed out not knowing which way I should go for help."

John headed for the bedroom to get his robe and pajamas. He hated wearing pajamas. He had to wear them in the hospital, but he hated the thought of wearing them his first time back with Melissa.

Melissa came in his room before going outside to get the firewood. John had already taken off his shirt. She admired his physique. Although he was much thinner, he still had strong looking shoulders. All those years of exercise and a healthy diet had paid off.

She looked at the hair on his chest the way it swirled upward. That was the place she had rested her head the last time they were together. She always loved his appearance and his dark head of hair. She found him very handsome and very desirable at that moment. She blushed, afraid he might be able to read her mind.

"Do you want something hot to drink? Or some more wine?" She asked, turning her gaze from his body to his eyes.

"Yes, that would be nice. Do you have any cocoa?"

"Yeah. I'll put the water on. It should be ready by the time you get out of the shower." She went into the kitchen, put the water in the tea kettle, and then went outside on the porch to get more wood for the fire.

She stood outside and breathed in the coldness of the night. Although it was hard to see, she could hear the ocean beating against the shore. Her love of the sea, God's creation, its beauty, its savage strength, always healed her soul.

She looked up at the sky and whispered, "Thank you, God for bringing him back to me. I didn't know if I'd ever hold him again. Thank you so much."

The icy wind blew against the hotness of her cheeks. Being near John caused a warm feeling inside of Melissa and even her limbs ached for him. She had to be patient. She had to keep in mind that John was still fighting his sickness and her longings might have to be bridled or restrained until he was strong enough to be with her. Being outside in the cold helped, but she couldn't endure the wind's bitterness much longer. She looked toward the beach for a little longer. For a moment she thought she saw someone walking, but decided she was mistaken. She grabbed four more logs and headed inside.

The tea kettle would be shrilling soon. It was probably whistling even now. She went inside, made herself some hot tea and waited before pouring water for John's cocoa. The fire needed some of the fresh logs she had just brought inside. After she stoked the fire, she sat down on the couch, gazed at the embers and drank in the warmth. She cradled her cup of tea and relished the peace she felt about her relationship with John. She thought of John Michael and smiled. He and John were going to love each other so much. She just knew it.

John came out of the kitchen carrying his cup of cocoa. He had poured it himself. His hair was wet and he smelled so good and clean. She had missed his smell all of these months. She looked at his face, struggled with her desire to make love with him, and tried to make small talk. She placed covers and blankets on the couch.

John finished his cocoa and snuggled close to Melissa. She put their cups on the coasters on the coffee table. Holding John close to her, she combed his partially dried hair with her fingertips. He looked so peaceful and content. Tired but content.

"I love you, John." She gently kissed his lips.

"I love you, too, Melissa. I wish I could make love to you, but I don't think that's possible yet."

"That's okay, John. We're together and that's more than I ever could have hoped for even a week ago. Sometimes delayed gratification makes us appreciate things even more. Don't get me wrong. I do want you more than ever, but I'm just glad to have you near me again." She wrapped her arms even tighter around him. She caressed him tenderly, kissed him gently on his face. His eyes closed. The fire crackled in the background. They were both so exhausted from the stress of the day. They soon slept the night in each other's arms.

Chapter Twenty-Eight

Jennifer twisted from side to side throughout the night. So many questions were finally answered, so many problems resolved. She wondered what was ahead for everyone. It seemed as though everything had come full circle. For some reason she had a sad empty feeling inside, like something was still wrong. She turned on the light and began to write in her journal.

She wrote of everything that had happened in the past few weeks. How much better she felt after finding out the truth. She read her own words out loud to herself.

"What a move this turned out to be for me. Here I am coming to South Carolina in hopes of finding my brother and instead I find John and go to work for his estranged wife. Who would have thought I'd have any part in their reconciliation. I'd have to say all the pain and the misunderstandings were worth it just to see them back together.

Now I need to concentrate on the reason I moved here in the first place. I wonder if Jay still goes by the same name or if he goes by something different. He was adopted when he was only eight years old. His name on his birth certificate is Jay Crawson, but after he ran away and got into trouble with the law, who knows what name he's using now."

Jennifer put down the journal and turned out the light. She was planning to go for a run first thing in the morning. She missed her daily run these past couple of weeks. She loved to run. Something about running made her feel healthier, helped her clear her mind, and relieved the stress in her life. When she got back to the beach house, she'd eat some breakfast, take a shower, and ask Melissa if she could drive her car back to Charleston. She could go get John's tire fixed, and then they could drive John's car back to the beach house. She could even keep John Michael instead of Maddie if they wanted to stay at Edisto for a few days longer.

Finally, Jennifer gave up on trying to sleep. She put on her running shoes, went to the bathroom, and walked out to the den. It seemed a little chilly, so she added another log on the fire for John and Melissa. They were wrapped into one lump on the couch. She smiled and whispered, "peace at last." Their troubled hearts were finally at peace. They finally found healing by being back together.

She decided not to eat anything or make any coffee before going on her jog. She wouldn't be gone for very long. Picking up her jacket, she left for the beach. It was still dark and it would probably be another hour before the sun came up. She paced herself for a longer run than she normally ran. The air was cool but refreshing. It was low tide and Jennifer had plenty of room to run right beside the ocean.

Her thoughts began to turn inward. It seemed that with John and Melissa finally back together she would need to concentrate on her own future. Would she find Jay before she had to leave South Carolina? Where would she be sent next?

"Oh, well my mission is accomplished, now what?" Jennifer said out loud between deep breaths. The waves began to crash closer to her feet. It was time to go back. She was hungry for breakfast and hoped if John and Melissa were awake that they were prepared for her return. She certainly didn't want to interrupt anything when she walked in the door.

As she started to turn around and go back to the house, her head began to spin. She lost her footing and fell in the sand. She tried to pull herself up, but felt nauseous. Oh, no, she thought. I'm about to lose it. Surely I'm not about to go into a diabetic coma.

"I should have taken my insulin before I left." She whispered.

All of a sudden she could hear a stranger's voice piercing through her thoughts frightening her. Jennifer tried to pull herself up, so she could see the man's face, but she was so dizzy that she just dropped back down on the sand.

She wasn't aware that anyone was out walking on the beach, or that anyone could possibly be only a couple of feet away from her. It was still dark and she couldn't make out his image, but he continued to speak. She wanted to scream but couldn't. Jennifer rested her head against the ground and listened to the sound of the waves crashing. That was the last thing she remembered before she lost consciousness.

"Hey, baby. What's a pretty young thing like you doing out here all alone?" He stumbled toward her.

"A girl like you shouldn't be walking around alone in the dark." He stepped forward and reached for Jennifer's shoulder.

She didn't answer.

"Hey, lady. I'm talking to you. Answer me!"

She didn't move.

He tightened his grip on her shoulder and shook her. "You aren't fooling me, lady. I guess I'll just have to get my knife out and make you talk." He reached for the knife in his back pocket.

"Now open those eyes of yours."

Jennifer was still unconscious and did not respond to any of his tactics.

"If that's the way you want to play, okay, but I got to get me something to eat. I'm taking you up to the shack across the road. When I get back, I'm gonna have to teach you a lesson with Mr. Knife here." He swirled the knife in the air to emphasize his point.

The man grabbed Jennifer under her arms and dragged her up an embankment. Twice he dropped her in a sand dune then finally reached the abandoned shed.

Chapter Twenty-Nine

Melissa was the first to get up. It was cold in the room, so she got the last two logs she had brought inside and placed them on the fire. She made coffee and ran back to warm her feet against John's warm legs. He recoiled for the moment and then pulled her close to him.

She couldn't believe they were back together sharing the same space on the couch. "I've made coffee. Do you want a cup?" Melissa asked John.

"Sure, here I can get it. I'm getting hungry. How about you?" He followed her into the kitchen. The sun was streaking through the window.

"Yes, I'm hungry. I'm surprised Jennifer's not out and about yet. She's usually such an early riser. I hope she's not hiding in her room just to give us some privacy. If she doesn't come out soon, I'll go in and check on her. I bet she's really starving by now and missing her coffee, too. I made Almond Amaretto just for her this morning."

Melissa poured cream first and added the coffee to both their cups. John took his cup from Melissa letting his hand linger on hers for a moment. She noticed the gesture and looked directly into his eyes. He's so good looking, she thought as she continued to stare at him. He smiled as if reading her mind.

"Sometimes, Mr. Isaacson you're irresistible." She put her cup down on the counter, walked back over to him, wrapped her arms around his neck, and pulled him toward her so she could kiss him.

He responded and smiled. Letting go, Melissa turned toward the refrigerator to begin making breakfast.

"I was thinking we could call John Michael and see how he's doing." She said as she headed for the phone.

"That would be great!" John's voice sounded so excited about talking to his son for the first time.

"I was going to wait until Jennifer got up before I called, but I think I've waited long enough. Maybe I should just peep inside her door and see what's going on with her." She walked over to the door, gently tapped on it, then quietly opened it, but Jennifer was not in the bed.

"H'm, I guess she got up early and went for a jog. She's not in her room, John." She said as she closed the door.

"Jennifer sure has been gone a long time. I hope she's all right. Knowing her, she's just trying to give us plenty of time to be alone. I didn't even hear her leave, did you?"

"No, but she must have left a couple of hours ago. We've been up for over an hour. Does she always walk this long?" John asked.

"I don't think so, but if she's not back by the time we finish calling John Michael and eating breakfast, we better go look for her." Melissa started dialing the number to her house. They could hardly wait to find out how John Michael was doing. John's face was just beaming.

Melissa waited for Maddie to answer the phone.

"Hello?"

"Maddie, this is Melissa. How's John Michael doing?"

"Oh, he's doing fine, Ms. Johnson. He just misses his mother but he's fine."

"I miss him so much, too. Is he sleeping or can you bring him to the phone?"

"I just put him down for a nap, but I'm sure he's not asleep yet. Hold just a moment and I'll go get him."

Melissa waited while Maddie went to get John Michael. She turned to John and said, "Let me talk first and then I'll give the phone to you, all right?"

John nodded yes. He was so excited. The smile didn't leave his face while he stood there. He couldn't wait to get back to Charleston, so he could hold his son for the first time.

Maddie held the phone to John Michael's ear while he and his mother cooed and spoke in baby talk. After several minutes, they finally said good-bye and Melissa handed the phone to John. She went to the kitchen and started making breakfast, giving the boys some time to get acquainted and bond a little.

Melissa looked at the clock. It was already 9:30 and Jennifer still wasn't home from walking on the beach. She wished she'd hurry back. She made all Jennifer's favorite foods for breakfast as a "thank you" for bringing John and her back together. She wanted to hug Jennifer, and tell her how grateful she was to have her as a friend.

After John reluctantly hung up the phone, he poured the orange juice and walked out on the porch to see if he could see Jennifer in either direction. He couldn't. The beach appeared isolated.

"Wonder where she is?" He mumbled out loud to himself. Like Melissa, he had started to worry about Jennifer. He went back inside. The wind was biting cold and he wasn't dressed warm enough to endure the cold.

"Well, did you see her?" Melissa looked up from cooking an omelet in hopes she would see them both walking in the door.

"No, I didn't. I didn't see anyone for miles to be honest. I'm beginning to worry about her too, Melissa."

"Maybe we shouldn't be worried, but I can't help but think something must have happened to her. I know she probably wants to give us some time to be alone, but I think something else is going on here. Maybe she got a cramp in her leg, or maybe she took the car to get the flat fixed. Did you check to see if the car is gone?"

"No, but I bet you're right. She's probably riding around looking for a place that repairs tires. I'm glad you thought of that." John looked out the front window, but there was Melissa's car still parked in the driveway.

John sighed. "The car is still out there. Where could she be?"

"I don't know, but we've got to go look for her before we eat. I've got a sick feeling, John and I feel we need to get to her right now. We can all eat together once we bring her back."

"You're right. Let's grab a couple of muffins and drink this juice I poured. We may be in for a long walk."

Melissa agreed. She opted to get dressed first, and then grab something to take with her.

John drank his orange juice, grabbed a blueberry muffin, and headed for the bedroom to put on some warm clothes. They both put on sweats and warm jackets. Melissa drank some juice and got two warm muffins from the oven. She wrapped them in a napkin and stuffed them in her coat pocket. They headed out the door.

"Maybe we should split up to save time. You could walk to the right and I'll go to the left. That way we could cover more territory in half the time."

"I guess you're right. If we both head in the wrong direction, it could waste a lot of time. Let's set our watches to walk 45 minutes then we'll turn around and meet back in front of the beach house."

Melissa agreed. They kissed each other and started walking in opposite directions. It just so happened that she was heading in the same direction Jennifer had walked earlier that morning. She was unaware that she was headed straight for the stranger. She felt a sick feeling in her gut. Something was wrong, she just knew it. Jennifer always ate a big breakfast. Especially if she were going to walk or run for a long distance. Fear filled Melissa's thoughts as she began to jog down the beach. She was certain Jennifer was in trouble and needed her.

The wind was icy in her lungs. She started running. The thought of her own frailty never occurred to her. Her chest tightened. Her heart skipped a beat when she saw the stranger pacing back and forth in front of the crashing waves. He stopped as if waiting for her arrival. She slowed down to a walk hoping she could catch her breath before she reached him. The sound of her own heart was louder than the waves.

Chapter Thirty

The stranger had dragged Jennifer's body along the sand just moments before Melissa arrived. The dilapidated old house was the place he had been hiding from the police for the past couple of months. He was wanted in several states, was apprehended in Columbia, but he and another inmate had escaped two months earlier. His buddy had been gone for days breaking into beach homes in search of food.

He was notorious for cruel acts of violence against women including rape and murder. He was sentenced to 47 years for the murder of two women in North Carolina. There were suspicions that he'd killed four women in the Aiken area, but nothing had been confirmed. There was not enough evidence for an arrest or conviction in those cases.

His buddy only had a record of theft, breaking and entering, and minor violations of the law like driving without a license, no insurance, and trespassing.

Jennifer was still unconscious and could not feel the guy drag her body across the road. The gravel scraped her hands and face. His viselike grip, bruised her wrist as he pulled her along. The anger and hatred he felt toward his victims seemed to be without purpose or meaning. If someone didn't intervene soon to disrupt his plans, there would be no hope for Jennifer.

He carried her inside lifting her passed the rotting structure of the porch and let her body slam against the back of the wall and floor.

She slumped forward still not aware of what was happening to her. He left her there and went back towards the beach. He was hungry and started scanning the houses to see if he could see any sign of the one where Jennifer was staying.

The wind beat against his tattered clothing. He had stolen them weeks before from one of the campsites coming into Edisto. He walked along the edge of the shore letting his feet sink in the waves and sand unaware of how cold he was. He didn't seem to notice anything, but the hunger in his stomach. He kept envisioning the hot breakfast his victim would have been eating by now. There was sure to be someone else with her at the beach, maybe several people and he could crash the party. He would kill someone if he had too. He smiled to himself as he imagined how good it would feel to finally get his gut full.

His eyes glanced up the beach. A smirk creased his dirty cheek. A woman approached him, coming from the same direction the other girl had been jogging. She also looked out of breath. He smiled to himself as he imagined the fate of his new prey. He wanted to laugh as he thought, two in one day. He tried to conceal his joy as she approached.

Melissa suddenly saw the man walking in her direction and immediately felt uneasy. The closer she got to him the more alarmed she became. The undershirt and dull brown khakis he wore looked as though they had never been washed. His hair had that matted unwashed look as well. She braced herself as he came closer, not sure if she should turn around and run back to the beach house. Melissa decided to ignore the man and walk straight ahead with purpose. She would have followed her first instincts were it not for the hope that she would find Jennifer. She had a feeling she was somewhere near by. She was only a few feet in front of the man when she heard him speak.

"You looking for your friend?" He said as Melissa went past him.

"What?"

"I said, you looking for your friend? A lady with long dark hair, who was jogging this same way. Jogging. She was jogging earlier this morning. You looking for her?"

All Melissa's intentions of ignoring the stranger came to a halt. The sound of her heart was pounding in her ear. She couldn't ignore him if he knew where Jennifer was. She had to answer him.

"Yes. Yes, I am. Did you see where she went?"

"Well, it just so happens I did."

She waited feeling more and more nervous. The pungent odor that emanated from him made Melissa nauseous. The smell of urine and waste filled her nostrils, not to mention the stench of his body odor. She tried to appear calm, but failed. She had to find Jennifer and whatever she had to endure to do that she would. Looking at this man, knowing he had seen Jennifer, made her fear the worse. She only hoped Jennifer was still alive.

The man began to speak. "She went up there to the house. My wife and I have been living in that shack since I lost my job. We've had it mighty bad. No money. No food. You know what I mean, Ma'am?" He looked her up and down and then locked into her eyes to see if she were swallowing his story.

Melissa felt sick. He looked at her as if he were undressing her with his eyes. She tried to pretend she believed every word.

"Well, I'm sorry about your misfortune. Maybe we can get you and your wife some food and get you a job somewhere. Is your wife sick?" She tried to sound sincere.

He seemed to jump on that idea. "Yes, Ma'am and your friend went to see about her. She wanted me to come look for you and bring you back to help her."

Melissa didn't believe a word of it, but knew she would have to play along if she wanted to find Jennifer. As much as she hated to, she would have to go with him to the old shelter across the road. Reluctantly she followed him. She turned her nose toward the wind and walked a little ahead of him so she wouldn't have to smell his stench.

As they approached the rotting building, she wondered how anyone could be living in such a dilapidated old place. The rotting wood of the porch seemed too fragile to support the weight of one person much less three. No wonder his wife was sick, that is if he even had a wife. Melissa jumped on the porch or what piece of one that was left. She was thinking hurricane Hugo may have caused most of the damage to the property years ago and no one had spent the money to rebuild the structure. She walked cautiously across the crumbling planks. Fear was beating in her heart. She was afraid to look inside, afraid Jennifer might already be dead.

As she reached the door, the man pushed her hard inside the building. She lost her balance and fell headlong onto the dirt covered flooring. Portions of the wood broke into pieces under the weight of her body. She rolled in front of Jennifer and let out a loud scream.

"Oh my God. Jennifer! Jennifer!" She reached over for her friend. There was a trace of blood coming from her mouth, but thank goodness she was still breathing.

"What did you do to her?" She glared at the man and rocked Jennifer back and forth in her arms trying to awaken and comfort her friend.

"Now, now. Is that anyway for you to be talking to me? I just helped you find your friend, you ungrateful...". He didn't finish his sentence. Instead, he went over and kicked Melissa in the side.

"Ugh." She groaned and doubled over. Her mind was spinning as she tried to think of a way to get Jennifer out of there. She decided to pretend to be hurt worse than she really was.

He started to kick her harder, but decided to finish them both off later. "This is your lucky day, lady. I'm hungry and I'm going to find some food down at your place. You better still be here when I get back or I'll go ahead and finish you off. You got that? You better stay right here or I'll kill you and your friend. You got me?" When she didn't answer, he kicked her again.

"Ugh." Melissa grunted and then stayed perfectly still to give the impression she couldn't get up. She didn't want him to kick her anymore. She feigned unconsciousness until he left the shed.

When he finally went back outside, she still didn't move. She silently prayed John was heading their way looking for them. He would not be a match for this man, but maybe he could go call the police. She prayed for John that he wouldn't get killed trying to save them. Her side was bruised and she ached all over. Her heart hurt for Jennifer. She feared that none of them were going to survive the night, not even John.

150

Chapter Thirty-One

John turned around and started walking back toward Melissa again. He finished his 45 minutes without any trace of Jennifer. When he got back to the beach house and didn't see Melissa or Jennifer, he knew something was wrong. He began to walk in the direction Melissa had gone, not sure what else to do.

He wondered what could have possibly happened to them both. Maybe Jennifer had fallen and couldn't walk and Melissa was finding it hard to get her back to the house. That would explain the long delay. Then his reasoning turned to doubt and fear. What if there were a gang hanging out on the beach? Or there was someone who had ill intent toward the girls out there? He might need to go back to the beach house to get some kind of protection. He jogged back to the house.

John sprinted the last hundred yards, ran up the steps, and flung the door open. He looked in Melissa's bedroom for a gun, searched her dresser drawers, and under the mattress, but found nothing. He looked in the den, but didn't see any guns anywhere. Time was going by so fast, he had to find something to protect himself and the girls. Maybe he was jumping to conclusions, but he didn't want to take any chances. Maybe he should just go ahead and call the police. Jennifer might need medical attention. God only knows what's happened to them out there.

All John knew was neither Melissa nor Jennifer was back after several hours on the beach. He at least needed to report that much information to 911. Even if there was no danger at all, he wanted something on record.

He dialed 911 and an operator answered immediately.

"Yes, I'd like to report two missing persons. One has been gone since 5:00 this morning and the other has been gone for a couple of hours. We're at the beach at Edisto and I have reason to believe that something bad has happened to them."

"Sir, I'm sorry, but a person has to be missing for over 24 hours before we can declare them truly missing. You'll just have to call us back then if they still haven't shown up."

"Listen, we're at the beach. My wife was worried about our friend who had been gone for hours. She was supposed to be back in 45 minutes and she never came back. I'm telling you something is terribly wrong. Whether it's an accidental drowning or whatever, I need the police to check this out. How do I go about reporting that?"

"Well, I can put a call through, but I'm not sure they'll respond until they get something more concrete."

"You mean I have to wait until someone is hurt or dead before you'll send a policeman out here?"

"I know that sounds cruel to you right now, but if we send a car out for every call we get we wouldn't have one available when a real emergency happens."

"That's ridiculous. This is a real emergency. You need to send a car out right now." He gave her the address and hung up the phone not knowing if she would call in the request or not.

He was so disgusted with the system. Looking around the room, the only thing he saw that he could use for protection was a fire poker. He picked it up, looked at it, and decided it would have to do. Anything was better than going empty handed. Melissa and Jennifer might laugh at him when they saw him with a fire poker, but he didn't care. He may look stupid, but he needed something to fight with. Somehow he knew that he was going to have to use it and it might be the only thing around to save his life.

Chapter Thirty-Two

As soon as Melissa knew the man was gone she immediately began trying to get Jennifer up from the floor. She knew she'd probably only have one chance to escape and there was very little time to get them both out of there. She tugged on Jennifer from the front and tried lifting her, but was unable to maintain her balance. Jennifer was not a heavy person, but because she was unconscious, she was nothing but dead weight. Melissa tried again, but could barely budge her.

She ran to the door and looked out to make sure the stranger was not outside the door. She checked out their surroundings to figure out the best way to escape. She would have to find a good place for them to hide. The sand would be hard for them to walk in especially trying to carry someone else. She decided to hide back in the woods behind the shack rather than risk running into their assailant somewhere on the beach trying to make it to the beach house. She knew he would kill them. There was no doubt in her mind, they had to get out of there right then.

Going back to Jennifer she wrapped her arms around her from behind, right at the base of her rib cage and preceded to drag her across the floor towards the door. Jennifer was still breathing, but still had not regained consciousness. The heels of her shoes made a trail in the dirt.

Getting her down from the porch would be the tricky part. Melissa thought as she sat Jennifer in front of what was left of the front steps. She jumped down and reached up for Jennifer. When she looked at her friends face, she suddenly began crying.

"What in the world are we doing in this mess?" She sobbed out loud as she tried to get Jennifer down from the porch. Losing her balance, they both fell to the ground with a thud.

"Oh!" She cried out. Her body shielded Jennifer from directly hitting the ground. She needed to get control of her emotions or she wouldn't have the strength to get them both out of there. In the back of her mind she kept worrying about the man coming back and catching her trying to escape. She'd have to hurry or they'd both end up dead.

The area around the dilapidated house was grown over with tall grass, weeds, and debris. Some of the surrounding area was made up of marshes and swamp land. Just the thought of what might be out there in the swamps was enough to frighten anyone. The brush became so thick Melissa could barely drag Jennifer away from the shed. Melissa's back ached and her side throbbed where the stranger had kicked her. She didn't know what he had done to Jennifer before she had a chance to get to her, but the blood coming from her mouth and nose definitely meant something terrible had happened.

Instead of taking Jennifer in the direction of the beach house, she went in the opposite direction to mislead their assailant, sliding her first to the right a few yards and then away from the shed a few yards. Finally, they were engulfed in the woods. She counted twelve steps in one direction and then twelve steps in the other direction until she was deep in the woods. By the time it got dark it would be very easy to get lost if she didn't keep up with her steps. The ground made a sucking sound as her feet began to sink deeper in the mire. She cringed over what she might be touching in the mud.

Soon she didn't have the strength to go any further. The ground was two inches deep in water. There was no place for them to sit down without getting wet. She wondered what was happening with John. She prayed that the attacker hadn't hurt him in any way. She squatted in the mud, pulled Jennifer up against her, so that only her feet were touching the water. Melissa shivered. It seemed to be getting colder as the wind picked up and it was almost impossible for her to keep crouching in the same position. She sobbed under the guilt of seeing Jennifer in such bad shape.

"This never would have happened if I hadn't been so stubborn. I'm responsible for your being here in the first place. I wish I had told you everything in the beginning. None of us would be here." She whispered and continued talking to her friend as if she could hear every word.

"Please forgive me, Jennifer. I'm so sorry for getting you involved with my life." She sobbed even harder. Her words and tears went unheard by her friend. Only the cold wind resounded with a whipping, haunting sound.

Chapter Thirty-Three

John walked down the beach searching earnestly along the shore for any sign of Melissa or Jennifer. It was several minutes before he noticed the man walking toward him. He felt his heart begin to beat rapidly, and tried to hide the fire poker, hanging it on the back pocket of his jeans in case the guy was watching him. Somehow he knew this man was responsible for the girls not making it back to the house. When John reached him he was startled to hear him speak so abruptly.

"Hey mister, you got a cigarette?" He asked watching John's every movement and trying to read his face.

"No, no I don't. I don't smoke." John replied rather coldly. He tried not to appear anxious or upset. He tried to keep his tone low and unemotional.

"Well, that's too bad. Cause I really need a smoke. You know what I mean?"

"Not really. I don't like the smell of smoke."

"That's too bad. You don't know what you're missing." He reached in his pocket for his knife and continued.

"That's too bad you don't have a cigarette. I'm just gonna have to take your money and go get me some!" He pulled out the knife and lunged toward John.

John slung the poker around with all his strength. The force gashed the man's arm and caused the knife to go flying. He had obviously caught the man off guard. John knew for the moment he had the advantage, but he also knew he had only stunned the man. He drew back, hit him again with all the force he could muster.

The convict having lost his balance, struggled to pick himself up from the sand. "Why you little."

The man tried to get up, but John hit him again before he had a chance to and jumped on top of him. He pressed the poker against the man's throat.

"Now where are they you slime-bag?" John's adrenalin was flowing and he was surprised by his own strength.

The stranger struggled to get free but could not. John used all of his body weight to press against the man's throat.

"I said where are they? What did you do with them?"

The man gasped for air. "They're in the old shed back there across the road." He croaked. His eyes darted in the direction of the shed.

John got up, started to run toward that direction when the man grabbed him by the foot. John swirled around and knocked the man in the side of the head with the poker. Blood began to gush out and the stranger slumped to the ground. John closed his eyes and tried to block out what had just happened. He had never hurt anyone in his life and now he thought he may have killed someone. He groaned, grabbed his stomach, and continued to run toward the shed.

If only the police had come as soon as he had called them. It was getting late and it would be getting dark soon. Finally, he saw the old shelter and wondered what he would find there. The girls might not even be alive or they might not be there at all.

He reached the shelter and tried climbing up on the porch. The rotting wood made it difficult to secure his footing. He wished he had brought the fire poker with him in case there were other men with the guy. He had dropped it in the sand somewhere while he was running. He peered in the doorway and felt disappointed. There was no one inside. His heart sank and his mind raced. Where were the girls? He had to find them.

He began yelling out their names, but the wind and waves seemed to drown out his cries. He went back inside to see if there was any sign that they'd ever been there in the first place. He carefully walked across the porch, stepped over the broken boards again, and went inside. Most of the flooring was covered with sand. It was possible someone had been there, but he couldn't be sure the girls had ever been there. He went back outside and circled the house, calling Melissa and Jennifer's names as he walked.

It was time to call the police again before it got too dark to see anything without a flashlight. The hours had just flown by and the sun would be setting by 5:00. He'd have to hurry.

It would be very hard to see his footing in the taller grass that surrounded the area and he might find it difficult to find the house since there wouldn't be any lights on. He ran most of the way and prayed he'd be able to distinguish Melissa's beach house from all of the rest.

When he finally spotted the stairs leading to the house, he cleared two steps at a time until he reached the porch. Once inside he called 911 and reminded the operator that he had called earlier and left the address at Edisto. He quickly told her about the episode on the beach.

"The other man is either dead or badly wounded. My wife and friend are still missing and that guy was the last to see them. Please send the police out here now!"

She said she'd send a trooper, asked him to repeat the address, and asked his full name. John hung up the phone disgusted with the system. They should have already sent someone out the first time he called.

Finding a flashlight in the kitchen drawer he checked to see if it worked. It did. He grabbed some matches and ran out the door in the direction of the shed. God, he hoped the girls were still alive. Maybe they were hiding some place nearby.

The dispatcher radioed a state trooper and reported the incident. There happened to be a car in the vicinity of the beach, so they would be able to get to the residence within five minutes. She also contacted the hospital emergency center so they could send an ambulance to the area. The ambulance would take longer. They would have to send it from East Cooper Community Hospital in Mt. Pleasant.

John followed the shore line until his flashlight picked up on the stranger's body still crumpled in the sand. He went over to him, shined the light in his face, trying not to look at the gash and blood on the side of his head. He wasn't sure if he were dead or alive. He hoped he hadn't killed anyone and he hoped even more that the girls were still alive. The thought that he may have killed someone made him feel kind of numb inside.

He continued to walk in the same direction. Finally the light shone on a window. John walked toward it until he reached the steps. He looked inside again to make sure no one was inside, took some of the dry brush that the wind had blown up on the porch, added some dry rot from the old structure and started a small fire in the right corner of the shed. He hoped the girls would see it and maybe if they were hiding somewhere, they would come closer to the house and respond to his cries for them.

After the fire was started, John went back outside with the flashlight and began to search the thick brush behind the shed. He called for Melissa and then Jennifer, but there was no response only the waves crashing in the background. He was determined not to stop looking until he found them.

In the meantime, the troopers pulled into the driveway of Melissa's beach house. They rang the doorbell, but didn't get an answer. One of the officer's walked around to the back and found the door opened. He cautiously entered the house not knowing who would be inside or what he might find there. The other officer joined him around back and checked out the carport. After they both made sure the house was empty, that no one was hiding outside on the property, they headed for the beach calling John's name. There was no answer.

The dispatcher had told them there was an accident on the beach, knowing only that there was a victim and an attacker, yet not knowing who was hurt. They traced the sand with their flashlights in a mechanical thorough way, so as not to overlook any bodies on the ground. They were about to turn around and walk in the opposite direction when they saw a fire burning in the distance.

"Maybe we better check that out before we head back. We might need to contact the dispatcher and let them know about the fire."

His partner agreed. They were walking toward the fire when they saw the convict in a heap in the sand. They knelt down to check his breathing. He was not dead, but he might not make it much longer.

They radioed for back up and to let the EMS guys know where they could find the body. They continued toward the fire. Flames were consuming the whole structure.

John didn't expect the building to burn so quickly. The rain earlier in the weekend didn't seem to affect the flames at all. The structure went up like a huge bonfire. He could only pray the wind would not carry the flames to the surrounding area, catching the woods on fire. At least he could see easier. Light was spread out for several yards in all directions around the shed making it easier for him to search for Melissa and Jennifer. He hoped they would see the flames and be able to escape from where the stranger had taken them.

The fire climbed higher and higher towards the heavens. Small fragments of burning embers were tossed around by the wind. He watched the flames tilt toward the ocean. The wind was obviously in his favor. As long as it continued to blow east there was no danger of the woods catching on fire. John's voice was hoarse from yelling for the girls, but there was still no sign of either of them.

Chapter Thirty-Four

Melissa was shivering as she tried to maintain her stance in the murk that surrounded her. She knew she couldn't stay there any longer. She could not endure the dampness or the cold. The joints in her fingers and knees began to throb with pain. The sound of the night creatures was out in full force. Images of snakes, spiders and alligators filled her thoughts. Although it was supposedly too cold for copperheads, she still hoped her feet had not found their way into the places they had bedded down for the winter. Every time something brushed against her leg she had to suppress a scream.

Her first efforts to stand were unsuccessful. She tried again this time rolling her weight forward as she pulled up on Jennifer. She retracted until they were finally out of the marsh.

"Now what?" She thought out loud. She turned around to look in the direction of the shed. To her surprise it was engulfed in flames.

"My God." She whispered. "Has he caught the place on fire thinking we're still inside?" She shook inside and continued to head back toward the beach house. She stopped every few steps to rest and to set Jennifer's body down for a few moments. She felt Jennifer's pulse. It felt weak, but at least she still had one. Melissa had to get her to a doctor as soon as she could.

Her plans were to get to the house, call the police, and find John. She knew, neither she nor Jennifer could make it much longer in the cold. She was thirsty. A dryness from the wind and her own fear parched her throat. Jennifer was probably dehydrated as well. She wondered if John were alive. Had he run into the stranger? She tried not to think about it, but was afraid he might be caught in the shed that was burning up. She shuddered. Just the thought that he might be dead made her start crying.

She tried to get control of herself. "You've got to get control of your emotions or you won't have the strength to save Jennifer or yourself." She spoke softly through the tears.

"Be strong, Melissa." She fussed at herself as she tried picking up Jennifer again. She grabbed her under her arms below the rib cage and continued to try to drag her backwards through the debris on the side of the road. She could see the shed burning out of the corner of her eye. Her heart hurt just thinking John might be there. She prayed for John and Jennifer.

For a brief moment she thought of John Michael. Thank goodness she hadn't brought him with her. At least he was safe and warm. The tears rolled down her cheeks. She considered hiding Jennifer somewhere and running to the beach house, but was afraid the stranger might find her. Their best chance of survival was to stay together. Even if it took longer, she would not leave her behind. Melissa kept moving determined not to give up. She had run several marathons, but nothing compared to the fatigue she was feeling at that moment.

The tears continued to fall down her cheeks. Memories filled her mind. Melissa thought of her mother and wondered what her life would be like if her own mother had lived. Right then she wanted her mother. Melissa wished her mom was there to hold her, make the fear go away, and tell her everything was going to be all right. In reality she didn't believe they would be okay.

The wind rustled a bush near her left arm startling her. She watched the leaves shake and tremble in the wind. Her own mind and body imitated the tremor and she felt just as fragile. A limb snapped to the right of her. She suppressed her scream, but could not stop her body from shaking. Like dead leaves where no breeze blew, she froze in her steps unable to move her feet.

Chapter Thirty-Five

John was backing away from the flying embers that were swirling in the wind when he heard a voice yell out behind him. He jumped and slowly turned around.

"Hold it right there, buddy. You're under arrest." One of the troopers pulled his gun from its holster and got his cuffs out.

"Wait a minute, officer. I'm so glad to see you. I'm the one that called to report my wife and friend are missing. You're trying to arrest the wrong person."

"Looks to me like you just started a fire. There's a man back there who could be dead by now. You can talk all you want back at the dispatch unit when we take you in for questioning." He clamped the cuffs around John's wrists and told him to keep walking toward the beach house.

"But officer, I'm John Isaacson. I'm the one who called to report the incident. Don't you think you should be looking for my wife and Jennifer? They're out here somewhere. Time is running out and they may be hurt and need medical attention." John's voice was filled with anger and despair as he continued.

"We don't have a moment to spare!" John was covered with soot from the fire and didn't realize he looked as rugged as the guy on the beach minus the stench.

"Look buddy, you can tell us all the details later. Until we can run a check on you and get some identification, we don't want to hear your stories. You might as well keep your trap closed and keep walking."

John continued to walk in silence. He was tired and his legs ached from fatigue. His throat was parched and sore, and he had very little strength to put one foot in front of the other.

They reached the man John had hit with the fire poker. Just the sight of him made John's stomach ache.

The officer reached down to check the man's pulse. When he did, the stranger pulled his knife on him and stabbed his arm.

"What the...he's not dead and he's armed!"

The man slit the officer's arm with another jab.

"Help me out here, Bob. Shoot him!"

Robert pulled his gun and shot three times. The stranger slumped over without a sound.

"I killed him, Sam."

"There was no way to help it. He probably would have killed me with that knife if you hadn't stopped him."

Robert got his handkerchief out of his pocket and wrapped it around Sam's arm.

John was relieved that he wasn't the one to kill the guy. "See sir, I told you I was the good guy here."

"Not so fast. How do I know you two weren't working together? Just keep walking."

The three of them kept walking down the shore toward the beach house. The officers studied the wooded area of the beach as they walked. They didn't want any surprise visits from any of the stranger's friends. In the distance they thought they saw a dark figure moving very slowly, but it was too dark and too far away to tell. They both unlatched their guns as they got closer. Waves were pounding to their left, so it was impossible to hear anything. The dark form became clearer as they approached, but they were too far away to determine who or what it was.

John didn't notice the shadowy image at first, but as they walked closer toward the Palmetto trees, he could see what appeared to be someone dragging a body. His heart began to race. Could this be an accomplice of the man or was that Melissa and Jennifer?

The officer closest to John motioned for his buddy to head toward the thicket. He signaled for John to keep quiet. They turned off their flashlights and continued to walk toward the frame.

The fire from the burning shed illuminated the sky more than normal, allowing them to see better than usual, especially without a moon glowing in the sky. They reached the thicket and began to walk cautiously toward the figure silhouetted against the night. The officer who was in front stepped on a dry limb as they entered the thickest part of the woods.

The limb snapped and all of them stopped dead in their tracks. That much of a warning was enough to get them all shot. Everyone froze, suddenly aware that the dark form they had seen earlier suddenly vanished. That one sound scared someone off. Who was that person and what connection did they have with the stranger?

Chapter Thirty-Six

Melissa was close enough to the path leading to the house to rest Jennifer against a tree and run for the phone. She knew someone was nearby, she had heard three shots sound in the darkness. Not even the waves could drown out that sound. This was one time the darkness would be an advantage to her. No one knew the area better than she did. As a child she had played hide and seek in these trees.

She placed Jennifer between two trees that were knotted together. This had been a perfect hiding place for her when she was a little girl and it would be a perfect chair for Jennifer. Her mother could never find her when she had hidden in those branches. She lay Jennifer in the crook of the trunk, pushed her jacket under Jennifer's head, and started running up the path that led to the beach house. Finding the back door open, she tiptoed inside, checked to make sure no one was hiding there, and ran and locked the door. She then ran to the phone and dialed 911.

Out of breath, she could barely get the words out. "Hello, operator? I need an ambulance. My friend has been assaulted and she barely has a pulse. Also, the police need to get here as soon as possible. The person who did this is still out there somewhere." She gave the lady the address.

"Ma'am, according to my records someone has already made that call. The troopers should already be there and an ambulance is already on the way."

"Thank, God! Thank you operator. I'll just wait for them to get here."

"I suggest you keep the door locked. The police are already on the beach and they radioed in that they had located a male body in critical condition. You and your friend may be in danger."

Melissa began to cry out. "Oh, my God, Jennifer is still out there. Let me get her and try to bring her inside."

"Maybe you should just wait on the paramedics!"

"I can't, she might not make it until they get here."

"You might not make it if you go back out there. They should be there in less than 10 minutes. Just wait until you see them."

"Thank you for your help." She put the phone down still in a daze. She was not going to wait. She grabbed a glass of water, wet a bath cloth, and carried the first aid kit under her arm. She wasn't sure she'd be able to carry Jennifer up the stairs, so she decided to carry a blanket with her to wrap around Jennifer, and they could both just wait outside the beach house until the ambulance got there. The reality that John might be almost dead on the beach made her sob as she walked down the stairs. She only hoped this night had not taken away everyone she loved.

As she turned the corner, she saw the ambulance pull into the drive. The lights were flashing, but they did not have the siren on.

The paramedics jumped out and asked where the person who was in critical condition was located.

"You'll have to follow me. There may actually be two people in critical condition. I left my friend hidden in the woods until I could run and call for help. She's this way." Melissa pointed toward the trees and walked hurriedly down the path. The blanket was dragging in the sand and the water kept splashing over the sides of the glass she was carrying.

"Here, let me help you with that," one of the paramedics offered. He took the water and first aid kit. "I don't think you're going to need the kit. We have our own supplies with us." He smiled warmly at Melissa trying to ease the tension.

She was still reeling from the thought that a man was dead on the beach. Jennifer was barely breathing and she had no idea where the killer was. The tears began to streak down her cheeks again as she realized her world was caving in around her.

Finally, they reached Jennifer. Immediately the paramedics checked her vital signs, wrapped a sheet around her, and placed her on a stretcher. Melissa could see the alarm in their faces.

"We're gonna need to get her to the hospital as soon as we can. Do you want to ride with us?"

Melissa dropped the glass on the ground and tried to wrap the blanket around Jennifer.

"I want to go with you, but my husband is out there somewhere and I need to find out what's happened to him. As soon as I can, I'll come to the hospital." She squeezed Jennifer's hand promising her she'd get there as soon as she could.

She followed the men as they carried Jennifer back to the beach house to put her in the ambulance. They immediately began to radio the dispatcher to let them know they were taking one of the victims to the hospital. The dispatcher had already scheduled another ambulance for the other victim when they heard from the trooper that the guy was dead.

Melissa grabbed another pair of running shoes, put on a heavy sweater and a jacket, and headed out the door. The next steps she took were some of the hardest she'd ever made. Not knowing where the killer was, or if John were alive, made her sad and anxious. Her head was pounding.

The walk back to the beach was a lonely journey of fear and emptiness: the waves crashing, the wind icy cold against her cheeks, her legs heavy with dread. She felt her stomach churn. She stopped and gagged. She wanted to throw up, but only had dry heaves like a drunk with nothing left inside to vomit. She felt in her left pocket for a tissue and there was the cold blueberry muffin she had brought with her earlier that morning. For a brief moment she remembered being so peaceful with John the night before. About that time she saw a crumpled body in the sand. She was not close enough to see and it was too dark to determine who it was. She gagged, so afraid she was about to see the face of her husband. She wanted to run, but something kept drawing her closer.

The police and John were walking towards Melissa. Before she had a chance to determine the identity of the man, an officer yelled out to her.

"Hold it right there. Don't move."

She saw what appeared to be three men walking toward her. Two were carrying flashlights and the other appeared to be in hand cuffs. She assumed it was the stranger on the beach in hand cuffs. John must be the figure of the man that was in front of her. Her greatest fears were realized. John must be dead. She became dizzy and disoriented and collapsed on the sand.

Robert ran to her to see if she were wounded or carrying a weapon. He swung the light up and down her body, but didn't see any wounds or blood stains, nor did she have a weapon in her hand. He leaned down, picked her up, and carried her back to where John and the other officer were waiting.

When John saw that it was Melissa, he cried out. "That's my wife Melissa. Is she all right?"

"Just keep it down, buddy. Until we get some identification on you and this one too, you're still a suspect."

"We have another friend with us. She may be hurt as well. Please don't take us until you find her."

"What did I tell you? Keep it quiet until we can check you out." He radioed the dispatcher and reported the woman and their present situation. "There may be another young woman out here somewhere. We may need some back up. Also, the woman needs medical attention." He reported.

"That's a copy. We'll send another unit out there."

They finally reached the beach house and one of the officers went in first to make sure no one was inside. When he had searched the house, he notified the other officer, everything was clear for him to come upstairs. They put Melissa on the couch and wrapped her in a blanket.

John asked them if he could get his wallet to show them his drivers license.

"You just show me where it is and I'll get it for you."

John walked toward the bedroom and pointed toward the chest of drawers. "It's up there with my extra change." He pointed toward the chest.

The officer had him repeat his address and date of birth. John looked thinner than the picture on the license, also he hadn't shaved and he looked as bad as the guy on the beach, but he did give his address correctly and his date of birth.

"Okay, you want to tell me what happened to that guy out there?"

John felt relief. He began to tell the officer everything that happened to them since Jennifer had left the cottage that morning.

Both men listened. Neither commented until John had finished his side of the story. They were concerned for the missing female.

"We need to find Jennifer. Is that what her name is?"

"Yes, Jennifer Crawson. She works at my wife's gift shop in Charleston."

"We'll call the dispatcher to give her the status on our findings." The officer uncuffed John's wrists and apologized if they had hurt him in any way. John rubbed his wrists where the cuffs had pinched his skin.

Robert walked out on the porch to radio the dispatcher. He listened as she explained.

"The other female, identity unknown, was picked up by the paramedics. Her condition is critical. She might not make it. The next two hours are critical, Officer Simpson. You may need to prepare her friends for the worst."

"All right. We still need to pick up the body on the beach, identity unknown. The Isaacson guy says the female at the hospital is named Jennifer Crawson. She works and lives in Charleston. I'll have a full report when Officer Pelham and I return to the station."

John knelt down and looked at Melissa's face and worried that the stranger had abused her in some way. Her face was dirty yet pale underneath the smudges. He wondered where Jennifer could be.

In a few moments, the officer came back into the room and began to tell them what the dispatcher told him.

"The ambulance picked up your friend over an hour ago. She's in critical condition. They've taken her to East Cooper Community

Hospital and to be honest she may not make it. They didn't have any identification on her when she was admitted, so you'll need to contact them with her insurance company, next of kin, drivers' license number, any health problems or allergic reactions to any medications that you may know about her."

John cleared his throat and tried to suppress his emotions. "How about Melissa, can you get her to the hospital? I don't know how badly she may be hurt."

"They're sending another ambulance out and a car to pick up the body on the beach. Do you know anything about that guy?"

"No. Before this morning, I didn't know anyone was on the beach, but us." He went to the phone book and got the number to the hospital in Mt. Pleasant.

John continued to explain what he was doing. "I'm going to call the hospital and get that info to them on Jennifer." He searched Jennifer's purse to get her drivers' license and her address book. He remembered her mother's name and got her phone number to give to the hospital front desk clerk. When he finished, he hung up the phone, and waited for the ambulance with the others.

"One more thing, Mr. Isaacson, we'll need you to come by the station as soon as possible to sign a sworn affidavit that your involvement with the man on the beach was purely in self-defense. They will also be doing a DNA and finger print investigation on the man to try and determine his identification. He may have some prior convictions. We'll let you know anything we can and we might be calling to ask more questions."

They checked Melissa's vital signs again. She had a strong heartbeat and appeared to be suffering from exhaustion and dehydration. However, it would take a total examination to determine what else may have been done to her by the stranger.

The officers told John the ambulance should probably be there in the next fifteen minutes and they headed back to the beach to pick up the man's body. John closed the door behind them and waited for the ambulance. He added some wood to the fire and went back over to be with Melissa. He sat on the floor in front of her and held her hand. He decided to get her some juice to see if he could get her to drink a little.

Groggily she responded to his urges. She whispered his name and reached out for him.

He finally got her to drink a little fluid when the phone rang.

"Hello? Yes it is. What? When? Oh my God. Are you sure? I, I... as soon as I can. I'll take care of everything." John let the phone slip through his fingers and drop to the floor. Tears trickled down his cheeks. The sound of the recording on the phone interrupted the silence in the room.

"A phone is off the hook on your line." The message kept repeating itself as he walked over to Melissa. He dreaded having to tell her the bad news.

Chapter Thirty-Seven

John struggled with the next words he had to tell Melissa. He stretched out on the couch beside her and waited for her to awaken. He wiped the tears from his eyes. Jennifer was one of his best friends in college. He had grown to rely heavily on her kindness and friendship during the last few weeks. The knowledge that she had just died made John burst into tears. The shaking of his body as he cried woke Melissa up.

"John, it's all right. I'm okay. Don't cry. I'm the one that should be crying. I thought that man killed you." She kissed him repeatedly on the face and continued. "I was so afraid I lost you again."

He returned her kiss with warmth and compassion. "I love you, Melissa. Did he hurt you in anyway? What did he do to you?" He braced himself for her answer.

"He didn't hurt me very badly. My ribs are sore where he kicked me around, but he didn't rape me or anything. I don't know what he did to Jennifer. I think he almost killed her. Blood was coming from her mouth, but I don't know if he violated her in any way. She was unconscious when I found her, so I couldn't ask her any questions. Thank goodness I got to her when I did and the ambulance came as quickly as they did." Before she got the last word out, there was a knock at the door.

"That must be the emergency medical team coming to see about you. I didn't know if you'd need to go to the hospital. A doctor may need to see you to make sure there are no broken bones or anything else wrong."

"I'm fine, John, really. Tell them I don't need to go to the hospital."

John opened the door. "Come on in."

"Mr. Isaacson, how's your wife doing?"

Melissa answered for John. "I'm fine, really. I don't need to go to the hospital with you guys. I'm a little sore, but that's all." They were the same men who had taken Jennifer to the hospital.

"Okay if you're sure we don't need to take you in to get x-rays."

"I'm sure. I'm just glad you got Jennifer to the hospital in time."

The men looked at each other somewhat confused. They wondered if the dispatcher had gotten the message to the Isaacsons before they got there. "We were real sorry about your friend."

"What do you mean? Jennifer's all right, isn't she?" Melissa asked, looking to John for some reassurance.

"I just got the call right before you regained consciousness. I was just getting ready to tell you."

"No, John. No. Don't say it." She started to cry.

"Mr. Isaacson, if you're sure you don't need us we'll head back to the hospital. We're so sorry for your loss." They closed the door behind them and continued down the stairs.

John felt the knot tighten in his stomach. "Come hear, baby." He pulled her close.

John could feel her heart pounding as he attempted to talk and comfort her at the same time.

"Melissa."

"No, John. Please don't say it. I don't want to hear it."

"Melissa, the paramedics did everything they could, but Jennifer died." His voice cracked.

"No, No, No. Why John? How could she die? What did that man do to her?" Her body shook as she sobbed into John's neck. He cried silently as he held his wife.

Finally, when he was able to talk he continued. "She didn't die of what you think she did. It wasn't dehydration or being out in the cold."

"What do you mean? How did she die?"

"She died from kidney failure. She was diabetic. She went into a diabetic coma. They called her doctor and he was treating her for diabetes. She's been diabetic since she was an infant. They never expected her to live as long as she did. Maybe that's one reason she never got married."

Melissa just stared at John in disbelief. "My God, why didn't she tell us? I had no idea. Jennifer alluded to her blood sugar level at times. I knew she went to the doctor on a regular basis, but I never suspected she was seriously sick."

"In school she had a hard time doing anything that required commitment for the future. She didn't pursue medical school, although that was a big dream of hers. She dropped out of school twice and went home to her mother's. I just thought her mother must have needed her."

Melissa sobbed into John's shirt. "I feel so guilty, John. She'd probably still be alive if it weren't for me. Jennifer was so worried about me that she insisted on coming to the beach. Everything that happened to Jennifer was all my fault." Melissa continued to cry.

"That's not true. You don't know that. She might have died this weekend at home. Her kidneys could have failed anywhere at any time. We just need to be grateful we had her in our lives as long as we did. She's really responsible for our getting back together and for saving your life."

Nothing John said made Melissa feel any better. She continued to cry as she remembered how mean she had been to Jennifer the past few weeks.

John held her and just let her cry, rubbing her shoulders and back. The embers in the fireplace began to go out one by one. A cold feeling filled the room. Without Jennifer being there, knowing she would never be back, a void settled over them both. John noticed that Melissa began to shiver.

"We're freezing. Let me get some more wood for the fire." John whispered.

Melissa clung to John not wanting him to leave her yet. She reluctantly let go of the grip she had on him. He pulled away to get more logs.

They were still awake when the morning came. It was cold and gray with no sign of the sun coming out. The emptiness continued to stay with them as they realized they had lost a very good friend. It just did not seem real. They would never hear her laughter again.

A wintery rain began to beat against the windows, winter seemed to come in its fullness during the night, and winter described the sadness that had settled over Melissa as well.

John was still awake when Melissa began to move around. He was thinking about the details for Jennifer's funeral. They would need to call her mother right away.

Melissa didn't say anything when she got up. She grabbed her robe and headed for the shower. John put more wood on the fire and started some coffee. He was tired and weak and would need extra caffeine to make it through the day. He went back and got under the covers and waited for the coffee to brew. The floor was icy cold as he walked barefoot down the hall.

Although the shower was hot, it didn't take away the coldness Melissa felt. She felt like a stranger in her own house and numbness permeated her every move. Nothing seemed right. She began to sob into the spray of the shower.

"Please forgive me, Jennifer. I'm so sorry for the way I treated you these past months. Please forgive me." She turned off the faucets, but could not turn off the pain that lodged inside of her. She wanted to leave the beach and never come back. She wanted John Michael. She wanted to hold her little baby, wrap her arms around him, and never let him go.

The next hour seemed like a blur. John packed most of Jennifer's things. Melissa could not bring herself to go in Jennifer's room. He was trying to make it as easy on Melissa as he could. He put everything in the trunk of the car, threw out most of the food that was left in the refrigerator, and scrubbed the counter tops. He got out fresh clothes to put on before he put his suitcase in the car and headed for the shower.

While John was in the shower, Melissa kept walking out on the porch, and staring out at the waves. Maybe she was hoping to get a glimpse of Jennifer somewhere out at sea. Maybe she wished she could leave all the sadness out there.

Going back inside, she grabbed a cup of coffee and sat in the chair closest to the fire. She was staring at the flames when John came back into the room.

"Melissa, I know you're probably not hungry, but we both need to eat something."

She did not move, only stared more intently at the fire. He walked over to her and looked at her swollen eyes and face.

"Come here baby, you look so tired and fragile." He pulled her over to him and held her in his arms. She didn't respond, just continued to have a blank look on her face.

"I know it will be hard, Melissa, but we have to try and get things back to normal as soon as possible."

"Back to normal? Do you really think anything will be normal again? Will we ever forget this horrible weekend?" She pulled away and glared at him.

"No, Melissa, but we have to get back into some sort of routine. We have to make some steps toward normalcy." He reached over and pulled her closer to him.

At first Melissa clung to John, releasing all her pain, frustration, and angry tears onto his shoulder. Later she began to withdraw, to pull away from him emotionally and physically. She knew he sensed it as soon as she began to withdraw. She didn't want to hurt him. In a way she wanted to hurt herself to get rid of the guilt she was feeling. She felt so responsible for Jennifer's death. Why didn't Jennifer tell her she was dying? She could have tried to help her. They could have talked about kidney transplants.

Melissa felt like she needed to be punished for what happened to Jennifer, that somehow she had to feel pain. When John reached out to her, she recoiled. Why should he comfort her, she didn't deserve to be comforted?

John interrupted her thoughts. "Melissa, don't let all these negative thoughts fill your mind. Whatever you're thinking right now isn't true." He reached out for her, but she pulled away.

"Maybe we should finish getting ready so we can leave." She said, avoiding his eyes.

"Okay, whatever. You didn't hear a word I said, did you? I just wish you'd fight this guilt thing. If you don't stay with the truth, you'll end up depressed. That's how it was for me when I tried to live my life without you. I didn't even know you were pregnant. Just remember how useless all that pain was for us."

Melissa pulled away and walked outside on the porch. The wind whipped against her body. She didn't have on her coat and her hair was still damp. Her thoughts were even harsher than the weather and the wind.

Meanwhile John felt helpless in getting through to Melissa. He took his shower. The hot water pounded against his face and chest. He wanted to cry, but couldn't. He tried to organize his thoughts around everything they needed to do. He'd have to get the tire fixed first, which meant they'd end up driving separately back to Charleston. He hated that. The more they weren't together the farther away Melissa might withdraw from him. He wanted them to start their life and marriage over with John Michael in the center of it. He believed this would be what Jennifer would want.

They said very little while cleaning up the beach house. John turned off the hot water heater, locked all the windows and doors, and cleaned out the fireplace. He watched Melissa stand at the window and stare out at the ocean. He felt like he was losing her all over again. When they were finally ready to leave, Melissa walked to the car totally unemotional like a prisoner getting into a police car. She didn't even look at John. He got in the driver's seat, buckled his seatbelt, turned toward her and began to speak.

"Melissa, I want you to listen to me. You're not responsible for Jennifer's death. It made her very happy to be a part of our being together again and I'll forever be grateful to her for that. She was very sick, but for some reason she chose not to tell either one of us how sick she was. She wouldn't want you to feel guilty about her death, and she wouldn't want to see you this depressed."

Melissa shrugged her shoulders and looked out the window, tears were streaking down her cheeks. She put on her sunglasses even though the sky was gray and cloudy.

Reluctantly, John started the car. Once again there was a cold silence between them. He sighed, put the car in reverse, and pulled out of the driveway.

As they drove away, Melissa did not look at him or the beach house. Instead she closed her eyes not to sleep, but to keep from weeping. The drive to John's car seemed to take forever. They took his tire to the nearest gas station. Melissa dropped John off at his car and waited until he changed the flat.

He walked over to her window and motioned for her to roll it down.

"Are you sure you're going to be all right driving back by yourself? I could take my car back to the beach house or leave yours there."

"I'll be fine, John."

"Melissa, you look so sad. Are you sure you need to be alone right now?"

Her bottom lip began to tremble. She shook her head yes, started the motor, and began to drive away. John stepped back just in time to keep her from running over his foot.

Chapter Thirty-Eight

The next few days were spent taking care of Jennifer's affairs. John agreed to make all of the phone calls. He even contemplated giving Andy a call to see if he wanted to come to the funeral.

Melissa still wasn't able to get beyond her grief or her guilt. She passed the time by putting her mind and her affections on John Michael. No matter what she did, there was always something to remind her of what a good friend Jennifer had been to her. She regretted the two of them never spent a lot of time talking about Jennifer's health or her life dreams.

Melissa felt so selfish and self-centered now. If only she could go back and start over. Now that she knew the truth, Melissa would have been a much kinder friend to Jennifer and she regretted that the most.

The phone rang interrupting her thoughts. It was Jennifer's mother. She wanted Melissa to help her go through Jennifer's belongings. She would need Melissa's advice on what to do with everything and she hoped they would be able to find Jennifer's will somewhere in her apartment.

"I'll be glad to help in anyway you need me to, Mrs. Crawson, and I'm so sorry about Jennifer's death. It must be so hard on you as well, since she was so young."

"Well, I know you might not understand what I'm about to say, but Jennifer has been sick all her life. In some ways I'm almost relieved that it's over. We never expected to have her with us as long as we did. It was probably sheer determination on her part that she endured her illness. I think she's been on this mission to find her brother, to help him, and somehow that kept her living as well. Maybe she was afraid he suffered from the same illness. All I know was she was consumed with the desire to help him in some way."

"She did tell me about him. I'm just so sorry she never got to achieve her goal. Maybe I can do some research and locate him. She believed he was living somewhere in South Carolina. Maybe there is some website that could lead me to where he is. As soon as things settle down around here, I'll make that a priority."

"That's very kind of you, Melissa. He's had such a rough life compared to Jennifer's. I wish we had adopted both of them at the same time. It would have made such a difference in the way he turned out."

"Mrs. Crawson, it's been so good talking with you. I've got a little one in the other room who is crying for his mommy. I'll start on Jennifer's apartment right away, and I'll call you if I find her will anywhere."

"Thank you, Melissa. I'll be waiting for your call. Also, I'm not sure if she wanted to be buried in Atlanta or Charleston. Maybe you can check and see if she made any arrangements about that as well?"

"Sure. Good-bye, Mrs. Crawson." She hung up the phone and ran and got John Michael out of his crib.

The next day Melissa headed over to Jennifer's to start cleaning her apartment. She pulled into her driveway. She let the car run for a while before she could get the courage to go inside.

This was her first attempt to go near her friend's home. She almost put the car in reverse and headed back to the office. Instead she took a deep breath, switched off the ignition, and just sat in the car for what seemed like hours. She heard the clock tick, the keys clink against the steering post, and listened to her own breathing. She wiped the tears that fell down her cheeks.

Finally, she took another deep breath, gathered all the strength she had to go inside, grabbed her purse, and closed the car door behind her. It didn't close all the way, but she didn't stop to close it.

She was afraid any delay would cause her to change her mind and keep her from facing her fears. Jennifer's apartment needed to be cleaned out, and it had to be done today, or she might not ever be able to come back.

Walking toward the door, she stopped to check the mail in the mailbox, then pressed the key into the door that Jennifer gave her when she first came to work at The Cranberry Tree. It opened easily. Melissa closed it behind her, rested against it for a few moments, and continued toward the kitchen to put the mail on the counter. Her heart pounded loudly in her ears. She breathed deeply before taking another step toward the hallway. She passed the couch and could almost see Jennifer sitting there, laughing as she often did.

Along the walls were several pictures of friends and family members. There were pictures of happy times with college friends, weddings, her mom and dad, and childhood memories. She even saw a picture of herself (very much pregnant) with the staff. She looked at Jennifer's face and then her own. Jennifer looked so happy and vibrant, with no sign that she was sick. While her own eyes looked so sad. She fought back the tears as she placed the frame back on the mantle.

The house smelled like Jennifer. Melissa continued to walk toward the bedroom thinking that might be the logical place to begin. The closets would have to be emptied and all Jennifer's clothes packed. She would wait and see what Mrs. Crawson wanted to do with the clothes. Jennifer's mother might be the same size as Jennifer and might want some of them for herself.

Jennifer's suitcase was still packed and sitting on the bed where John must have left it. She would need to wash all the dirty clothes that were in there, including everything in the bag on the floor that contained the clothes Jennifer was wearing on the day of the tragedy. It was so hard to bring herself to take them out and put them in the washing machine. Melissa remembered how dirty they got being in that shed along the swamp lands.

She unpacked the suitcase first, folded everything that didn't need washing, and put them in neat piles on the bed. As she got closer to the bottom of the luggage, she found a journal Jennifer had been writing in. She flipped through a few pages and realized Jennifer was keeping a daily account of everything that she was going through before she died. Melissa's spirit rejoiced. She held it close to her chest as if it were a priceless jewel. Here was the unadulterated truth in Jennifer's own writing. Now she'd know if Jennifer truly forgave her for everything. She flipped to the last page of the journal to the last words Jennifer had entered. They appeared to be Jennifer's thoughts just minutes before her tragic walk on the beach. It was the night she and John had reconciled. She closed the journal and decided to wait until she got home and was snuggled in her bed to begin reading it.

Melissa would contact Mrs. Crawson to see if she would let her keep the journal for a few days. For the first time since Jennifer's death she felt excited and encouraged. She started cleaning out Jennifer's closet and her drawers as fast as she could, so she could hurry home and begin reading the journal. She also started cleaning the kitchen and packed all of the utensils. She cleaned both the bathrooms and boxed all the linens.

Finally, she stopped when she had no energy left. She decided to leave the rest for Jennifer's mother, but at least this would be a start. She'd try and return on Saturday when Mrs. Crawson arrived. Then she could decide what to do with everything. They had two weeks to vacate the premises and what she accomplished in the last three hours would help somewhat.

Now it was time to find Jennifer's important papers and a Will if she had one. She searched the desk in her office. This was the one place she had not tried to clean. There was a large drawer on the right side of the desk with a metal box in it. It wasn't locked. Thank goodness, she thought.

She was glad Jennifer was such an organized person. She had a big paper clip holding a group of papers which turned out to be everything Jennifer's mother could possibly need to plan her funeral. There was a Will, all her insurance papers including life insurance, her desire for what to do with all her personal effects, and a complete set of all her medical records.

Jennifer wanted to be buried in Atlanta where her father was already buried and in the plot next to where her mother would be. She would like to have a Memorial Service in Charleston at the Presbyterian Church on Meeting Street.

Melissa would call Mrs. Crawson as soon as she got home and let her know everything she found. She'd also ask her if she could read Jennifer's journal. It was getting late, so she turned on a couple of lights. She tucked the journal under her arm, locked all the doors, and headed back to the house. After she put John Michael to bed, she took a shower, and made some green tea. She finally called Mrs. Crawson to let her know what all she had gotten done at the apartment and to ask her about keeping the journal for a few days until she could read it.

Mrs. Crawson thanked her for all that she had done and told her of course she could keep the journal. They planned on meeting that next weekend. Melissa was so excited about reading her friend's words. It somehow made her feel close to Jennifer having her last thoughts before she died. She snuggled between the fresh sheets she had just put on the bed, took a swallow of green tea, and felt comforted by the fact that she had a part of Jennifer still with her.

Now she would have so many questions answered. In some way the journal seemed to preserve Jennifer's memory. When Melissa opened to the first page, the phone rang. She sighed, wishing she had the whole weekend to herself so she could read without any interruptions.

"Hello?"

Chapter Thirty-Nine

John was still finding it hard to communicate with Melissa. He had called her several times, but she didn't have much to say. She was polite, but reserved and this irritated him. He wasn't sure if she even thought of him anymore. The only real joy he had was the time he spent with John Michael. He beamed with pride and joy when he saw his son for the first time. He loved showing him off to others.

He was thinking about asking Melissa if he could move back in with her. They could get remarried first if she wanted to, but he was tired of having to go home to his apartment every night alone. He picked up the phone, dialed her number, and waited for her to answer.

"Melissa? It's John. I thought I'd come by and see you. Are you up for a visit? I need to talk to you about something."

"Hi, John. I've already put John Michael to bed and I'm in bed, too." Melissa put the journal down beside her and took a swallow of tea.

"H'm, sounds like a perfect time to come over." He smiled to himself.

Melissa waited a moment, ignoring John's last statement, then she asked him if they could just talk on the phone instead of his coming over.

"Melissa, I don't want to talk on the phone. I want to see you in person."

"Let me ask you something first, then if you want to come over you can." She continued talking without waiting for a response from John.

"I found Jennifer's journal today. It seems she wrote something down every day. I want to go back to the beach house alone and read it. Maybe she wrote something that will help me feel better about my relationship with her before she died. At least I can know the truth whether good or bad. What do you think? If I were to go, I'd need you to stay here with John Michael for the weekend."

"I'd love to stay with John Michael, but Melissa, are you sure you should go back to the beach house alone so soon? Are you really ready for that? Couldn't you just lock yourself up in one of the bedrooms here or get a motel in Charleston?"

"John, I need to do this. If I don't go back now, I don't know if I'll ever be able to go back. If I stayed here to read it, I'd be tempted to spend time with you and John Michael. Besides I'll only be gone Friday and Saturday and I'm planning on driving back on Sunday. You might not understand this, but I need to go back to the beach. It's important for me to do that and I don't really know why. Jennifer's mom will be here next weekend and she might want to take the journal with her. I want to read the whole thing before she gets here. Will you do this for me?"

"Baby, if its going to make things better for you and for us, that's all that matters. I want to see that smile back on your face. What time did you plan on leaving?"

"What about tomorrow evening when you get off work? I'll have my things packed and ready to go. I'll make supper for you, and have John Michael's bottles and food prepared for you for this weekend. Maddie would probably come by and help you if you need her, too. She told me she'd come anytime, just let her know."

"All right. That'll work."

"John, when I get back, we can have a long talk about us. Maybe it's time to plan our lives together with John Michael."

John smiled. "That's what I want more than anything. I want us to be a family again, Melissa. I want the three of us to be a real family."

"Just give me this little bit of time, be patient with me a little longer, and I'll do every thing I can to make that happen." Melissa continued, "So, I'll see you tomorrow night and John, I do love you."

"I love you too, baby. Goodnight." He still wanted to go over and spend the night with her, but decided not to push it since he might be moving back in with her after the weekend. He'd just have to wait a little longer."

"Night, night." Melissa hung up the phone and went and checked on John Michael. She couldn't resist the urge to pick him up. She grabbed his blanket, wrapped him in it, and carried him to her bed without his even waking up. Once they were in her bed, he nuzzled close to her.

She decided not to read the journal until she got to the beach. She would wait and call a cab first thing in the morning to pick her up at around 6:00 that evening. The decision not to drive had a lot to do with John. He might insist on driving her if she tried to go alone. In reality she was a little afraid of going back there for the first time, but she was determined to face her fears.

In the morning she would pack her things. She'd pack lighter than she had before, taking only jeans, a sweater, a jacket and running shoes to wear during the day, sweats and a robe for the nighttime. She had not decided yet if she would run on the beach. Probably not, she wasn't that courageous. Basically, she planned on lying near the fire, reading the journal, and then coming back to Charleston.

She hated to leave John Michael again, but she promised herself she'd take him with her one day when all of this craziness was over. John Michael stirred a little and nestled closer to Melissa. She held him close, played with his curly dark hair, and admired his contented angelic face. Finally, she turned out the light. She wished she could take John Michael with her for his first beach trip. Melissa knew this wasn't the right time for him to be with her. He would need her undivided attention and she knew it would be hard to give him that. For some reason she just knew she needed to go alone.

Chapter Forty

The cab driver turned down the last paved road toward the beach house. Melissa knew it would take at least thirty minutes to get there from that point. Her eyes trailed the marshlands on both sides of the country road they traveled. The sun had melted into the western sky. There had been many such skies on her trips to Edisto. Those memories were chiseled in her mind the same way the sea had carved its mark on the shore. Etched there in her thoughts were the peach and orange shadows of the sky at sunset: Reflecting, glistening on the sea in the evening.

She watched the sky where the trees were not blocking the view. She was waiting for that moment when the sun is no longer visible, when a residue of hue masks the sky, leaving only streaks in the darkening horizon. Sometimes they were purple and red, sometimes orange and yellow. This evening they would be more purple and red because it was winter. She longed for that sight. She continued to watch the sky, hoping to catch a glimpse before the colors evaporated into the night.

Melissa was grateful to have the quiet and solitude on the ride down. Joe turned the music down when she got into the cab. He had driven her before and taken her to the airport on several occasions. He seemed friendly enough. She was glad to have a familiar face to drive her there, someone who wouldn't talk much. She wasn't in the mood to talk.

Melissa took the journal from her purse. She held it close to her chest, believing she held onto the truth about what had been going on with her friend all of these months. Tears filled her eyes. She was finally going to know the truth.

Joe pulled into the driveway and removed her one suitcase from the trunk. She tipped him generously and informed him she would call a day early to have him pick her up. He nodded, got in the cab, and drove in the opposite direction from the way he had just driven.

Melissa picked up her suitcase, climbed the steep steps on the ocean side of the cottage, unlocked the door, and went inside. She retrieved some logs from the porch for the fire to remove the chill that always accompanied the winter months. She unpacked her suitcase and put away the few groceries she brought with her. Then she placed the journal on the table beside the couch and decided to wait until morning to begin reading it.

She made hot chocolate, grabbed the phone, and called John to check on John Michael and to let him know she made it to the beach all right. He was waiting anxiously for her call. She assured him she was fine and she would not be venturing out on any walks in the dark. Then she asked him to put John Michael on the phone, so he could hear her voice. No one wanted to hang up, but John knew Melissa was probably very tired. Finally, he and John Michael reluctantly hung up the phone.

The full moon shone through the kitchen window beckoning Melissa to come out on the porch to face the ocean for the first time since her last visit. She held the cup in her hand while waiting for the water to boil, took a deep breath, and walked outside to look at the beauty of the night. The view of the ocean was intoxicating, as it reflected the moon's light. The waves exhibited their own massive beauty, spraying white against the shore. She breathed deeply again. This night reminded her of the hundreds of times she had walked the beach at night when the moon was full.

As she looked toward the left, those pleasant thoughts were suddenly tainted by the memory of the stranger who abducted Jennifer. Every event of that evening resurfaced in her mind. Melissa shuddered and resisted the urge to run back inside. The magic of the night lost its beauty as the sadness of Jennifer's death overpowered Melissa's emotions. Fear soon replaced the peace she had felt earlier, and an eerie feeling came over her as she sensed that someone was watching her every move.

Suddenly standing outside alone seemed like a dangerous thing to do. She ran back inside, locked the door behind her, and heard the kettle whistling in the background. She poured the hot water over the cocoa in her mug, grabbed a blanket from the hall closet, and stretched out on the couch. Jennifer's journal caught her eye. Picking it up, she put her mug down, and turned to the month when Jennifer first came to work for her.

Melissa excitedly read each word, skimming the pages until she got to the part where Jennifer came to the shop for an interview. She smiled as Jennifer wrote of her first opinion of Melissa, those first couple of times they were together. Melissa never knew how Jennifer perceived her. Jennifer described her as both attractive and unbelievably sad. She wrote of her frustration of not being able to help Melissa get over her pain or at least to talk about it some.

Jennifer also wrote about the night Melissa fell down the stairs in the garage. It was refreshing to hear Jennifer's take on what had happened. She hung on every word, as Jennifer described Melissa's near bout with death. She was afraid that Melissa might die before John Michael was born. What comforted her the most was the way Jennifer compared their relationship to being as close as sisters. Jennifer described her love for Melissa as deep as any family member's would be. Melissa found great encouragement over those words.

The hours passed and finally Melissa put down the journal, wiped the tears from her cheeks, and threw three more logs on the fire. She looked one last time out the window. The moon was shining directly across from where she peered outside. She pulled the blinds, dressed for bed, poured some more hot water for cocoa and returned to the journal. She spent the next hour reading, crying, and laughing until she couldn't keep her eyes open any longer. Finally, she put the journal on the coffee table. Curled up in front of the fire, wrapped in several blankets, she felt at peace. She breathed a sigh of relief. She was finally home and was finally going to know the truth.

Her eyes closed. Her spirit rested. At that moment she had no fear or concern. She had no idea that someone walked those beaches waiting for her return. Someone was standing there, taking a drag off of his cigarette, looking up at her window, watching the smoke from the fireplace, smiling to himself as he watched the light go out. She had no idea of the danger that awaited her there.

Chapter Forty-One

Melissa was still sleeping when the sun came up. She would have slept all day had it not been for the phone. At first she thought she was dreaming then she realized she was still at the beach house and there was no answer machine to catch the call.

She reached over and grabbed the receiver. "Hello?" She said rather groggily.

"Melissa, this is John. Are you all right? I thought I'd hear from you by now."

Melissa could hear the concern in his voice. "John, I'm sorry. I was still asleep. I stayed up most of the night, reading Jennifer's journal. Is everything all right with you and John Michael?"

"We're fine other than worried about you. I was afraid something had happened. When will you be coming home?"

"I thought I'd have the driver come and get me late Sunday afternoon. I should get back to Charleston no later than eight." She turned toward the kitchen and glanced at the clock. It was 2:30 in the afternoon.

"I was hoping you could come home sooner. I'm still nervous about your being there alone. Are you sure you don't want me to come and pick you up?"

"I'm positive. There's something I have to do here and when it's over, I'll be back home for good. I'll come back to you and John Michael and love both of you the way you deserve to be loved."

John felt a rush of passion. He wanted to make love to her. He sighed. "Well, since you put it that way, I guess we'll just have to wait until Sunday night. John Michael and I will be anxiously waiting for your return. Would you rather I didn't call to check on you?"

"I love you, John. Sunday will be here before you know it. Let's just wait and talk then. All I'm doing is reading and I'm sure I'll be just fine. All right? If anything happens here, I'll call you. Is that a deal?"

"Okay that's a deal. I won't even call to hear your voice. I'll see you Sunday night. I love you, Melissa. Good night." He reluctantly hung up the phone.

Melissa headed for the kitchen and began making Almond Amaretto coffee. Now every time she drank that flavor she thought of Jennifer. She remembered the day Jennifer came in for her interview before everything went bad. That was the first time they drank coffee together and they had many good times before she thought Jennifer was dating John.

After grabbing an apple from the bowl on the counter she stepped out on the porch. There was not a cloud in the sky. She decided to grab her coat and go for a short walk. When she got back to the beach house, she'd drink a cup of coffee and finish reading the journal.

Melissa felt so much better already. She walked briskly, headed toward the right this time, no where near where that episode had taken place with Jennifer. She was looking at the different houses she passed by when she saw a cab ride by.

"That's weird. Wonder if that's Joe coming back early to pick me up? I hope not, but I've never seen very many cabs at the beach before." She said out loud to herself.

The cab stopped and pulled in one of the driveways. The driver did not get out or blow the horn. He appeared to be sitting there with the motor running looking at her. There was a glare on the windshield so she wasn't sure if he were actually watching her or if it were Joe, but she began to get an uneasy feeling. Maybe she was just becoming too paranoid about seeing anyone at the beach. Regardless of whether she had reason to be fearful, she turned around and headed back to the beach house.

The coffee would be ready and she needed to finish the journal. Still feeling uneasy she broke out into a full run. In only a moment she was locking the door behind her, grabbing a mug from the cabinet, and sitting in front of the fire with Jennifer's journal. She started reading the part where Jennifer wondered why she was being so cold and indifferent. Melissa read page after page of the emotional strain her actions had put Jennifer through. She cried as she realized her silent warfare with John, and her jealousy of seeing the two of them together had affected Jennifer in such a hurtful way. In reality everyone's pain had been so unnecessary.

From the journal entries, Melissa could tell Jennifer questioned the motive behind her coldness. Jennifer had wanted to walk away from her job at The Cranberry Tree, but made herself stay out of fear that Melissa might be sick and unable to help herself. Even her decision to come to the beach, as painful as the ride down had been, was unselfish.

Melissa marked her place in the journal, and decided to shower and change clothes, before reading any further. Afterwards, she made a salad, drank some cranberry juice, and added more wood to the fire. It was almost sunset, and she suddenly got the urge to go outside. It was a part of her heritage that any time you visited the beach you had to take a swim in the ocean no matter how cold it was and you could never miss a sunset. It would be like missing the unveiling of a famous painting or the curtain closing at the end of brilliant performance. A sunset at the beach was like the sun taking a bow at the end of his performance. Sunsets, what a perfect ending to each day.

Dark clouds dominated the sky for most of the day and there were showers all along the coast, but in the late afternoon the sun broke through. This evening a mauve and purple hue spread across the darkening sky. Melissa could not resist going outside. She took a deep breath as she beheld one of the most glorious sunsets she had ever seen. She continued to watch until it slid into the nighttime sky. All at once it felt colder outside, she crossed her arms to protect herself from the wind that was blowing straight off of the ocean. When the sun was completely buried in the shadows of the night, she reluctantly went back inside.

The fire produced warmth that brought comfort and peace. Melissa opened a bottle of Chianti, got the smoked cheddar cheese from the refrigerator, sliced part of the sunflower seed bread she bought at the Fresh Market, and carried them all back to the coffee table in front of the fire. She placed two large pillows on the floor in front of the fire, watched the embers, and sipped on her glass of wine. She was thinking about time and how precious it had become to her since Jennifer's death.

She watched the flames sizzle and pop as they chiseled away at the logs. Somehow the sunset, the ocean, the fire and the wine released her emotions to a place of total abandonment. All her suppressed feelings of grief came to the surface. She wept over the death of her friend and wished for the hundredth time that all the things not said would have been.

What would it have hurt to have talked about everything, to have spoken the truth no matter how hard it was to hear it out loud, to give voice to the most vulnerable parts of their lives, to bring all their insecurities into the light regardless of the rejection? If John could have shared his deepest fears, if Jennifer could have talked about her sickness, if she had only talked to John about her pregnancy and shared her own feelings of rejection with Jennifer. Would they have come to the beach at all that weekend? Was life intended to be this way? Had destiny played any part in the way things had turned out? It was hard to say.

Melissa wiped the tears from her cheeks. She felt better just allowing herself to think through all the difficult questions. She sighed deeply, took another swallow of wine, threw the pillows back on the couch, and snuggled back under the blankets to read the end of the journal. Finally she reached the part where she told Jennifer the truth about John.

According to Jennifer's words everything finally made sense. "How refreshing to finally know the reason for Melissa's pain and attitude toward me, and to know that John and Melissa were married. Wow what a revelation. Seeing my two closest friends come back together, watching them talk in front of a fire after so many months of being separated, makes it all worthwhile."

Melissa read the final night that Jennifer wrote in her journal. Her last words were so very comforting to Melissa. Reading those words brought a healing to her soul.

Jennifer wrote, "I can finally have peace after all these months of worry. Watching Melissa and John go through so much pain, both of them sick and close to death and so very sad. If I had only known the truth sooner. Now they can finally enjoy John Michael and be the family they were meant to be.

"To see love conquer all their fear and despair, makes me feel so good inside. I can almost believe for my own healing. I know my time is limited. If I make it one more month, one more week, or just one more day it would be longer than I could ever have hoped for. Now my life seems to have had some meaning or purpose these last few months. Maybe when they have a baby girl they'll name her after me, that way I can continue to live in their memory.

"The medicine doesn't seem to be working anymore. They say my kidneys are failing to respond without my getting outside support. I refuse to take that path. When my body shuts down that's it for me. I've lived a full life and I've spent most of my adult life knowing I was on borrowed time. So, whatever happens at this point I'm ready for it. I don't have children to worry about or a husband. My mom has worried about me for years. In some ways the end of life for me will mean less worry for her."

Melissa sobbed as she read the last words of Jennifer's journal. She marveled at the courage and unselfishness of her friend. She wished Jennifer would come walking through the door so she could tell her goodbye and have one more time to apologize. She promised to grant Jennifer's last request. If she and John had any more children and they had a girl, they would certainly name her after Jennifer.

Finally, Melissa wiped the tears from her cheeks and wrapped herself tightly in the blanket on the couch. For the first time in weeks she felt peace. She also made a promise to herself to never let anything keep her from being a good wife to John and a good mother to John Michael. Life was too short for them not to be together.

Melissa breathed a deep sigh of relief. She was so glad she found Jennifer's journal. Thank goodness Jennifer thought it was important to keep one. It was one of those Oprah, 'Thankful or Grateful' journals, and it was filled with so many things Jennifer was grateful for; like her job at The Cranberry Tree and the friends she had met through that connection. She also wrote over and over that she was grateful for her friendship with Melissa and the strength she received from that relationship.

Melissa flipped through a few pages in the front of the book and couldn't believe what Jennifer had written. Jennifer was grateful that Andy was no longer in her life and that he had not been able to find out where she lived now. She wrote. "Although he was so unfaithful to me for all those years, he still didn't want me to have a life of my own. His compulsive behaviors frightened me most of the time. Thank goodness I am free at last and that he has no idea that I moved to Charleston. At least I don't think he knows where I am."

"My God!" Melissa spoke out loud. "Jennifer never said one word to me about Andy stalking her, or that she hoped he wouldn't be able to find her in South Carolina. Wonder what else she didn't tell me. There's no telling what's written between these pages. I'll have to finish the whole journal in the morning. I'm just too tired to read anymore, tonight." Melissa closed the book and looked intently at the orange blaze of the fire. She wished John were there so she could just hold him and make love to him. She felt so lucky to have him back in her life. Poor Jennifer never really had a decent guy, at least she never talked about one. Melissa couldn't wait to see John. She wanted to call him right that minute, but decided to just wait until Sunday like they had agreed.

Instead she closed her eyes and tried to sleep but couldn't. She wrestled with her desire to be with John and to see John Michael. Turning her back to the fire, closing her eyelids even tighter together, she tried to turn her mind off. Frustrated she sat up, turned on the light, and started to dial the phone.

"No, I told John we weren't going to talk until Sunday so I'm just going to wait. It's too late to call anyway." Melissa continued talking out loud.

The wind blew hard against the windows. She looked at the wood stack and decided she had enough wood to last all night and the early morning. She tried to ignore the clock and concentrated instead on the popping sound of the fire. The wind and the ocean concealed the creaking sound of the bottom step leading up to the porch. A dark figure crept up the other four without making a sound.

Chapter Forty-Two

The old rusted mustard yellow pinto pulled into the driveway of the beach cottage exactly four houses down from Melissa's house. The cottage was vacant during the winter and was used primarily as a rental during the peak season. The man sat in his car and finished smoking his cigarette. He was waiting to see if there was any activity along the shore before breaking into the house.

The beach appeared to be isolated with no winter visitors. His routine barely deviated from this ritual. He picked a house, broke into it, stayed for a week, and moved onto the next cottage. Since his prison buddy had been killed, he had determined to vindicate his death by finding someone at the beach to kill. It didn't matter if he found the people involved in his friend's death, he only wanted one of these rich people to pay for it. He had been planning the way they should suffer for over three weeks.

Like a caged bird, he'd trap someone and he'd make them pay. He knew some of the beach people come back to check on their property in the winter. He might have to be patient, but he was going to torture the first one that crossed his path. His obscure religious background mixed with a hellish past of abuse made his philosophy of "an eye for an eye" take on a distorted version. He didn't care whose eye, he just intended to perform his own style of vengeance on them. He might need more than one person to completely pay the debt.

He opened the door on the passenger's side of the car and crawled out. The driver's door was still jammed from an old accident. His jeans were torn right above the right knee and were a bit ragged at the ankles, but his hands were meticulously clean. The rest of his attire looked like he had been wading in a swamp. Ironically he spent hours washing his hands and cleaning his nails. This was a compulsion he had developed from childhood after his stepmother kept making him wash his hands, screaming at him, "You have filthy hands. You'll never amount to anything!"

In his mind he was never able to get his hands clean. Even as an adult he always thought they looked dirty, oily and grimy. In reality they weren't dirty, but he thought they were. Sometimes he had his nails manicured, polished and filed, but no matter what he did they reminded him of a mechanic's hands. He constantly kept them hidden in his pockets, ever mindful not to run his fingers through his greasy hair or to touch anything that might get his hands dirty, sticky, or change their soft appearance.

After closing the car door, he took out a handkerchief and wiped his hands off to remove any germs that may have been on the door handle. He walked around to the trunk and got out two towels. He swiped a push cart full of towels from the Holiday Inn down the beach and hid them in his trunk. Even when he murdered his first victim he would have to be careful not to mess up his hands.

He walked toward the back of the beach house, wrapped a towel around his right hand, broke the glass near the door knob, and let himself in. He left the towel that was full of glass from the window outside, and used the other one to clean his hands.

The house had white rattan furniture with cushions covered in a blue sailboat print. The cottage had all the conveniences of home; a television, VCR, cable, stove and refrigerator. There was some food in the cabinets and refrigerator, but very little.

He guzzled down a can of coke and wiped his mouth with the other side of the towel. He found a can of chili and some crackers, and began eating right out of the can. They had a plastic hand soap dispenser beside the sink. He pumped it three times and filled his hands with antibacterial Dial Soap. He washed them four times before feeling halfway satisfied. He used their bathroom, washed his hands a few more times, and decided to walk up and down the beach a couple of times.

It was nearing sunset when he noticed the light on in the beach house right down from where he was planning on spending the night. He watched intently, his heart racing, lit another cigarette, and watched the upstairs window.

The wind was blowing so coldly, he stuck his hands in his arm pits to keep them from getting chapped, and headed for the back stairs to see if he could get a better view inside the house. A woman came to the window and looked out. He waited until she moved away before he started climbing the stairs.

The bottom step creaked as he crouched stealthily in the shadows. He waited a moment and continued the climb. His heart raced with excitement and anticipation. The wind began to blow even harder against him and the house. He began to tremble from the cold and the anticipation of killing his victim. It would be his first time to ever kill anyone, but he felt he had to if he was going to settle the score for his buddy. He smiled and wiped his hands on the towel he held in his left hand. He waited quietly not wanting to warn his prey that someone was waiting outside.

He smiled again as he saw the woman's shadow move toward another room. This was going to be easier than he thought. He could actually wait until daylight, just knock on the door, and she would politely let him inside.

Chapter Forty-Three

Melissa slept late the next morning. When she finally woke up she decided to take her time getting dressed. She was dozing, reading, resting, and refeeding the fire when she heard a car pull into the driveway. Her heart leapt inside. John must have decided to come to the beach and surprise her. He said he wouldn't call, but he didn't say anything about driving down to the beach. "Oh my goodness. Why didn't I get up earlier, take my shower and already have on my makeup?" She mumbled to herself.

She glanced out the window before making a dash to the bathroom to brush her teeth. Pulling the curtain back, she peered out the window. Her heart stopped beating. It wasn't John. It was a man she had never seen before, driving a rusty old Pinto. She cringed. The man was heading to the back of the beach house with two towels in his hands. His clothes looked worn and dirty. She felt pure fear as she watched him walk out of her sight passed the window.

Melissa ran to her suitcase and pulled out the gun she had brought with her from Charleston. After the incident on the beach, she was afraid to travel anywhere without it. Her hands were shaking so badly she wasn't sure if she'd be able to hold the pistol straight, if she needed to use it. Melissa's eyes darted around the room. Her mind was racing. Should she hide, sit in the chair near the fireplace with a pillow on top of the gun, or just go to the door and point the gun in the man's face and tell him to get off of her property?

She heard the stranger climb the stairs. Her heart was beating louder than the steps he was taking. She heard him knock on the door. He began to bang on it when he didn't get a response.

"Open the door! I know someone's in there." His voice was harsh.

Suddenly Melissa heard the window in the door shatter. Glass splintered on the floor.

"Seems kind of odd that a house with smoke coming out of the chimney, would be empty. Don't make me have to come in there and find you. You're being rude to your company. Didn't your mama teach you what happens to people who are rude?"

Melissa suppressed a scream when she heard the glass break. She positioned herself in the rocking chair and faced the door. She rested the gun between her knees, aimed it toward the direction of the intruder, and hid it underneath a pillow from the couch. She waited and did not utter a sound. She started shaking on the inside when she heard the man enter the house. She heard his feet crunch against the broken glass on the floor.

Melissa kept remembering Jennifer, imagining what she might have gone through before she found her, and this gave her the courage to defend herself against this intruder. Melissa was determined this creep was not going to kill, rape, or rob her without a fight. She waited.

The man continued to talk as he unlatched the door from the outside. "If you don't answer me soon, I'll come in there and make you talk." He opened the door and came inside.

Just the thought that someone had broken into the house so easily made Melissa nauseous. She was poised and ready until she heard the screen door slam. Then she jumped and her hands started shaking uncontrollably.

He walked slowly into the entrance of the house and looked around. He lifted his nose and took a deep breath to see if he could smell any breakfast cooking, but he couldn't even smell any coffee. He looked around the kitchen. It was clean except for a bowl of fresh fruit. He stopped to wash his hands and let the water run until it was hot. He scrubbed and scrubbed until the skin was red. He dried them with one of the towels he had brought with him, picked up an apple, and turned toward the direction of the den. He felt the warmth of the fire burning and could hear it crackle and pop.

Melissa watched him from her chair as he came down the hallway. She heard the water running and thought it odd that someone would take the time to wash their hands right after breaking into a home. She wondered if he cut himself on the glass. She continued to wait for him to appear in the doorway. She could hear him getting closer as his steps echoed against the hardwood floor. She watched him dry his hands on a towel as he turned the corner. She swallowed hard still trembling inside. He took three more steps, stopped, and stared at her.

She looked quite calm, unusually calm, and stared straight at him without any apparent fear. For some reason her hands were covered. This sight reminded him of his stepmother. A flashback of her cruel words started ringing in his mind. He suspected this woman had dirty hands, filthy hands like his. Why else would she be trying to hide them?

Melissa was still shaking inside, but her outward appearance was cold and elusive. Memories of how Jennifer looked when she found her in that shed kept coming into her mind. She knew this man, just like Jennifer's assailant, was capable of anything.

Melissa set her eyes on the towel in the man's hands still wondering why he spent so much time cleaning them. He noticed her looking at his hands. He became self-conscious, afraid his stepmother's words would begin to come out of this lady's mouth. He threw down the towel and stuffed his hands in his pockets.

"You messed up, lady. You never should have come here. I've been waiting for weeks for you. My partner is dead and you're my choice for repaying the debt." He used his right hand and pulled a knife out of his back pocket.

"What's wrong with your hands, lady? Your hands dirty, lady? Maybe I need to cut off your hands with this knife."

Melissa tightened her grip on the gun handle. She was prepared to shoot him if he came any closer. Finally, she spoke.

"I don't believe you're going to do anything." She pushed the pillow on the floor to reveal the gun. She held the handle with both hands.

The stranger seemed surprised to hear her speak. His eyes spied the gun for the first time. "Well, now aren't we full of surprises. The silent one finally speaks and I can see your hands are very dirty."

Melissa wondered why he kept alluding to her hands in that way. She kept her eyes directly on his. He seemed to be inching his way toward her, ever so slowly.

"Don't come any closer or I'll shoot." She pointed the gun up toward his face.

He attempted to distract her by talking incessantly. "Well I'm just not sure you have the guts to pull that trigger. Looks to me like you're not sure either."

"I wouldn't bet on that if I were you. I'm the one with the score to settle. Your friend was responsible for the death of my friend. You might say I have more of a reason to want to kill you than you have to kill me. For the record, I never killed your friend, but I'm very capable of defending myself against you. You might say I feel I owe it to my friend." Melissa didn't seem to notice the more she talked the closer he was getting to her. She was somehow overcome with thoughts of Jennifer.

"I guess I don't have a chance in hell of getting out of this one. Looks like you've got me. So now what? What do you want me to do?" He looked at her in feigned surrender. In reality his concern was to get that gun out of Melissa's hand.

"I haven't decided yet." She thought of going to the phone and calling the police, but was afraid her hands would shake. If this man thought there was any chance she was afraid of him, he would probably jump her. As a matter of fact she suddenly realized he was close enough right then to do that.

"Hey mister, back up and sit down on the couch. I don't want you to get any ideas." She shook the gun back and forth and motioned toward the couch to let him know she was serious.

His face turned red. She infuriated him, he was just seconds away from grabbing the gun out of her hand. Melissa was trying to figure out what to do next when the phone rang. It startled both of them. When she got up from the chair, her right foot was asleep from sitting in the same position for so long. She hesitated for a moment to give her foot some time for the circulation to return to normal. The phone continued to ring.

"What's wrong? You crippled or something? If you don't hurry, the person on the phone is going to hang up."

"Just be quiet and wait there on the couch!" She walked over to the phone, but watched the man carefully with every step she took.

"Hello?"

"Melissa, it's John. I called Maddie and asked her if she would be able to keep John Michael for tonight and tomorrow and she said she would be glad to. I thought I would-"

"John, listen to me very carefully. Someone broke into the house and he's here right now. I'm holding him at gun point right this minute. I need you to call the police and get someone over here as soon as possible. Hang the phone up right now and call. He's a friend of that guy that died on the beach. Hang up John and call."

"My God, Melissa did he hurt you? How long has he been there?"

"John, listen to me! Hang up the phone and call the police. I need to go. I love you, John." She hung up the phone.

John slung the phone down and picked it back up to dial 911. He then called Maddie to see if he could just drop John Michael by her house. He told her there was an emergency at the beach house and he needed to leave right that minute.

"Sure, Mr. Isaacson. Bring him and we'll go back to the house after I pack a few of my things. That way, you won't have to wait on me to get there."

"That'll be great. I'm on the way." John grabbed John Michael, buckled him in the car seat and screeched out of the driveway. He began to panic inside. What if he didn't make it in time and this guy killed Melissa?

John pulled into Maddie's driveway. She was waiting outside for him. She took John Michael out of his arms.

"Is everything all right with Mrs. Isaacson? Is she okay?"

"There's another intruder in the house. She has a gun. I hope and I pray to God she's all right."

John jumped in the car and headed for the beach. He was running red lights when he decided he'd better pay attention. It wouldn't help

Melissa if he got in a wreck and got killed on the way to the beach. He prayed every minute she was smart enough not to let that man get the gun away from her. It would kill him if something happened to Melissa. John would kill the guy himself if he laid one hand on her.

Chapter Forty-Four

Melissa walked back to the chair constantly keeping her eyes on the man as she walked. She wasn't about to let him get away or attack her by surprise. Thank God, John called when he did.

"So, ma'am, do you think I could go to the bathroom? My stomach sure is torn up and I'd hate to mess up this pretty white couch of yours."

"Yeah, I bet you could care less about my couch. What a perfect opportunity for you to try something. I guess I'll just have to follow you down the hall, and I want that door left opened while you're in there. Got it?" She stood up and walked over to the couch where the man was sitting.

"Whatever turns you on, but I'm warning you it won't be a pretty sight." He roared with laughter and continued. "My stomach's been torn up since I ate that chili from the house down the beach." He laughed out loud again, got up, and walked toward the bathroom.

Melissa didn't trust him. She knew his only chance to escape was to do something before the police got there. She certainly didn't want to be anywhere near him with an upset stomach, but she couldn't allow him the freedom to escape. He laughed the whole time while he held her captive outside the bathroom door. She was beginning to get nauseous just listening to him.

The intruder spent about five minutes washing his hands. She thought to herself, what a neat freak he is. Finally, he finished and

215

she walked him back to the couch. She was surprised he didn't try to grab the gun, lock himself in the bathroom, or crawl out the window. Melissa went back and sat in the rocking chair and waited anxiously for the police to get there. Every minute she spent with him, the more nervous she became. She wished they would hurry.

"Aren't you hungry? I'm starving and I left my apple in the bathroom."

She normally would have been very hungry by this time of the morning, but his bathroom trip made her sick at her stomach, and she was just too nervous to eat anything.

"No, I'm not hungry and I'm not taking any chances with you. So you might as well sit there and be quiet."

"Yeah, right. I'm hungry and I'm not gonna shut up until you get me something to eat. You'll just have to shoot me and I don't think you have it in you to shoot anybody."

"I don't really care what you think. You come near me and I'll pull the trigger faster than you can change your mind. I don't particularly want my tax dollars going toward keeping scum like you in prison, and stop rubbing your dirty hands all over my couch. I should have made you sit on the floor." For some reason the man kept rubbing his hands back and forth across the couch.

His face turned red. "What did you say?"

"You heard me."

"My hands aren't dirty!"

"What?"

"I said my hands aren't dirty! I'm gonna be sick again, so you better let me go back to the bathroom. Your couch is going to be real ugly in just a few minutes."

"You wouldn't dare."

"I'm starting to mess in my pants. If you don't want your precious white couch to change colors you better..." He couldn't finish his sentence.

Melissa began to smell a terrible odor. "Get up! Get up! Get off my couch, right now!"

"I hope your hands don't get dirty cleaning all this mess off of your sofa."

"You filthy creep! Go back in the bathroom and stay there."

He began to scream like a child and seemed terrified by her words.

"I'm not filthy. I'm not filthy. Don't lock me in the bathroom. I'm not a bad boy!" For a brief moment Melissa felt sorry for the guy. His pants were soiled and he left a dark stain on the couch. He started freaking out and screaming uncontrollably.

"Dear God, what's wrong with you?" Melissa yelled out loud.

He stumbled toward her crying with a glazed look in his eyes.

"If you don't get in the bathroom, I'm going to shoot." She pulled the hammer back on the gun and pointed it toward the man.

"No, don't shoot me, lady! Don't shoot!" He was running down the hall when the back door opened. It was two state troopers."

"Hold it right there. Get your hands up. You're not going anywhere." The officers restrained the man before he could get any farther down the hall. They took him outside and handcuffed him. They put a plastic sheet on the seat to keep him from staining the car seat.

Then they went back inside to ask Melissa some questions.

Once the officers arrived, Melissa no longer had the strength to hold it all together. Pretending not to be afraid and suppressing her emotions had been so hard. Suddenly, she began to shake inside, especially when she realized how close to being killed she truly had been. Thank goodness the police got there as quickly as they did.

"Did he hurt you in any way?"

"No. Other than breaking into my house and ruining my couch, he never laid a hand on me."

"Have you ever seen him before?"

"There was a man who was killed by some officers out here last month. This guy had escaped from prison with him. He kept telling me he was at the beach to avenge his friend's death."

One officer made notes on everything Melissa said while the other one asked her more questions. "Is that your old car out in the driveway?"

"No, it belongs to the intruder."

They radioed into dispatch everything that had happened, and gave the dispatcher the license plate number of the pinto to find out if it were stolen. Then they finished writing up their report.

"Do you want us to take you anywhere? We didn't see any other cars out there."

"No, my husband John should be here any minute. He can take me back home." Those words sounded so good to her ears. She breathed a sigh of relief.

"Do you want us to stay with you until your husband gets here? We don't mind. Besides neither of us are looking forward to riding back to headquarters in that smelly car."

She smiled knowingly and replied. "No, I'll be fine. Just so he can't get out of the car and come back here before you lock him up in jail, I'll be fine."

"We've got that taken care of. He's handcuffed and locked in the patrol car. Just call us if you need anything. We might need your testimony in court before we can convict him of any new charges, so we'll be notifying you in a few days."

"Okay."

"That should do it. We'll be heading back to the station."

"Officers, thank you for getting here so soon. I wasn't sure what was about to happen. I appreciate everything."

She closed the door behind them and went back to the fire to put more wood on it. She wished she could stand to stay near it, but couldn't even stand to look at the couch where the stranger had been sitting. Just the thought made her nauseous. She decided to take a shower. She felt violated by having an intruder get into the house. She wished she could wash the memories away as well.

The water felt good as it beat against her face. She couldn't move. The tension in her shoulders and neck seemed to ease the longer she stood there. So many thoughts were running through her mind. It was time to go home. It was time to be with her family and to love them with all the desire and passion she had inside. She sighed deeply in the comfort that thought brought. Finally, she turned off the water after bathing and washing her hair, toweled dry, and slipped on some jeans and a sweater.

She flipped her head down and blew dry her hair. The heat blowing on her neck continued to relieve the tightness in her shoulders. She was numb inside and couldn't even cry. Thank goodness all of this was finally over. They could finally go on with their lives.

Melissa put on her Keds without socks, packed her things, and began sweeping up all the glass from the door before John got there. She sprayed an air freshener in each room. The couch made her sick. She'd have to get it replaced as soon as possible. There was no way she was going to attempt to clean it. Everything was ready before John got there. She had just put the bag of garbage next to the door when she heard John's car pull into the driveway. She immediately started to cry and ran outside to meet him. These were tears of relief. He opened the car door and ran toward her. She threw her arms around his neck and cried in his arms.

"Baby, are you all right?"

Melissa couldn't talk, she just nodded her head yes.

"Did he hurt you? Did the police make it in time?"

"He didn't hurt me and they've already taken him to jail. He messed up the house though. He broke the glass in the door when he broke in and he soiled my couch and ruined it. I just want it thrown out. I'm so glad I brought a gun or he would have killed me. There's no doubt about that. Thanks so much for calling when you did, and not listening to me when I told you not to call. One of us would have been killed because I was determined this guy was not going to touch me without a fight." She kissed John pressing against him with her need to be comforted.

John hugged her even closer. "Thank God he didn't touch you. If anything had happened to you, I don't know what I would do. Come on let's get your things and get out of here."

"I've already packed my things and cleaned everything. My suitcase and some groceries are on the porch. All that's left is to clean any hot coals out of the fireplace, turn off the hot water heater, and lock up."

Melissa walked over to John and looked at him in the eyes. "I just want to go home. I want to be with my husband and my baby. I don't want to leave either one of you ever again. I love you, John. I've missed you so much."

"I've missed you too, Melissa." He took her hand and led her into the bedroom. He pulled her beside him on the bed.

"I've waited so long to hear you say those words. I wasn't sure you'd ever be able to trust me again." He kissed her gently on the forehead, then her cheek, and then her neck.

Melissa closed her eyes, cherishing the moment.

John lifted her chin, kissed her softly on the lips, opened her mouth with his tongue, and felt the passion run through her body. She moaned in surrender to his gentleness. Trembling as he held her close to him.

"I want you, John more than ever. I want to make love with you, but I want to wait until we're back at home. Somehow the whole scene here is still lingering in my mind. Right now I don't care if I ever come back to this place. I'm not sure I have the strength to stop what we're doing, but I want the memory of our being together to be perfect."

John smiled, took her hand and lifted it to his lips, and kissed her fingers. "Let's go home." He helped Melissa up from the bed and walked her out to the car. He opened the car door for Melissa and ran inside to finish cleaning everything.

He looked around the den and saw the stain on the couch. His stomach churned. The Lysol spray didn't totally disguise the odor. He got a piece of cardboard and placed it over the opening where the glass was broken in the door.

While Melissa waited on John, she looked up and saw a cab drive by. It headed down the road passed their beach house.

"That's odd why do I keep seeing that cab out here?" Melissa said out loud to herself. She squinted in the direction that he had gone. He seemed to stop at the same house he parked at the last time she saw him.

John was gone for at least 30 minutes and the cab never picked anyone up or drove off. She never saw the driver get out. That is so weird. I know the couple that owns that house and it's only used for summer rental. It had been several years since she talked with them last, but still, what's he doing over there?

John returned to the car and told Melissa about the makeshift repair he made on the window.

"I need to call about that window first thing in the morning. Anyone could get inside. A strong wind might blow out the card board. I'll call Smith's Window Repair on Monday."

Right then Melissa didn't care what happened to the beach house. She didn't care if she ever saw it again.

"John, listen. Do you see that cab a couple of houses down right behind me?"

John glanced out the window. "Yeah, why?"

"Nothing, really. I just keep seeing it out here, it never seems to pick anyone up, and I've never seen the driver."

"Yeah?"

"Well, what's going on? I think it's odd. Let's drive by there and see if we see anything suspicious."

"Melissa, please. Let's just get out of here. Who cares what he's doing out here?"

"I'm curious that's all. Humor me and drive that way past the cab."

John started the car, but when he cranked up so did the cab. The driver pulled out of the driveway and headed in the opposite direction.

"Well, looks like it's too late to check him out. There goes your cabby."

"What?" Melissa turned around in time to see the brake lights on the cab. "Oh, forget it. Let's just get out of here."

For most of the ride back they were silent. Melissa rested her head on John's shoulder and slept. John was thinking that he wanted to remarry Melissa. He was tired of living separately and knew it was time for a new beginning. He had decided to purchase a new emerald ring with diamonds for Melissa this week and planned to propose to her the next weekend. He would not stay with her tonight. She needed rest. He would wait until after he proposed to her to spend the night for the first time.

When they pulled into the driveway, John brought all of Melissa's things into the house while she ran in and scooped John Michael into her arms and kissed him all over his face. He giggled with excitement. She had missed him and his innocent, angelic face smiling up into hers.

"Mommy missed her angel so much." He giggled again as she squeezed his chubby little cheeks.

John hated to interrupt such a joyful moment, but interjected. "Melissa, I'm going to leave and head back to my apartment. I'll call you as soon as I get there, okay?"

Melissa looked so disappointed. "Do you have to leave? I mean you just got here. You can stay over if you want to, John."

"I better go. I know you need to get rest and you need to spend time with John Michael before you put him down to sleep."

"I really wish you wouldn't go." She held onto John Michael with one arm and reached for John with her free hand. It saddened her that he wanted to leave so soon. She wanted them to spend time alone after John Michael went to bed. Maddie had already left and they'd have the house to themselves. She wanted to make love to him and share the healing she had received from reading Jennifer's journal.

John started to give in, but remained committed to his original plan.

"No, I better get on home. You need rest and I'd probably interfere with that. I'll call as soon as I get home." He kissed her forehead.

"No, John. I don't need rest. I, I..." She didn't finish her sentence. "I guess I'll just have to wait until tomorrow night to spend some quality time with you, but I'm disappointed that you don't want to stay. I've got so much to tell you. Will you be able to come over tomorrow?" She looked longingly into John's eyes and put John Michael down in his play pen.

"Sure, I'll check my schedule at work and maybe we can meet for lunch. I'm so far behind right now because of the time I missed during my surgery."

"John, I'm not talking about meeting you for lunch. I want to be with you. You know, be with you intimately. I want to be close to you. I want us to make up for lost time." She put her arms around his neck and pulled him close to her.

"I want that too, Melissa, but this whole week we're working on the budget at the office. I'll have to work late every night. How about Saturday night? We could go out to dinner and then come back here and talk, or we could get Maddie to keep John Michael and we could go to my apartment for the night. How about that?" He smiled into her face as he envisioned the look on her face when he gave her the ring.

She still wanted him to stay the night and didn't understand his big hurry to leave. Why couldn't he at least stay for another hour? She tried to hide her disappointment and answered his question. "All right. I'll just have to wait until Saturday night." She poked her bottom lip out to express her sadness over having to wait.

"Good. I'll see you then. As soon as I get to the apartment, I'll call and check on you and John Michael." He touched her bottom lip and continued. "Hey, don't look so sad. Saturday will be here before you know it." He hugged her gently one last time before heading out the door.

Melissa released her hold on him, letting her arms hang by her side. Her smile was gone, but she courteously walked him to the door, and reluctantly said good night.

Chapter Forty-Five

Melissa was missing John more each day. He was so busy working at the office, he barely had time to call. Now she wished she had accepted his invitation to go to lunch. The only upside to his being busy was that she had time to work with Jennifer's mother on taking care of Jennifer's arrangements. The funeral would be the next Saturday in Atlanta. Jennifer had dedicated her body to medical science for research on diabetes and liver disease. So the funeral had been postponed for another week.

Also, she had spent days on line trying to locate Jennifer's brother Jay. The only Jay Crawson she had been able to find was living in Atlanta. Wouldn't that be the greatest irony of all? Jennifer moves to Charleston to find her brother and he is living in Atlanta the whole time. He might be in prison, but that was his last known location.

She was committed to finding him at any cost. Maybe she and John could stay in Atlanta a couple of days after the funeral and try and locate him. It was possible that Jay would need some kind of rehabilitation and Melissa would pay for it if that were the case. As much as it was possible, she was going to help Jennifer's brother in some way. That was a promise she made in her heart to Jennifer.

It was Saturday morning and Melissa was so excited about seeing John that night. She went shopping for a new dress to wear for dinner. This was the first time she'd been shopping since Jennifer had died. She felt like she was getting ready for the prom. She hoped John wouldn't call to cancel because he was just too tired to go.

Shopping was fun. She picked a turquoise green dress that made her skin glow against the contrasting shade. She felt like she was falling in love with John all over again and there was a definite glow on her face. All the sales clerks said she looked delicious in that color. She graciously accepted their compliments and headed for the shoe department to pick out new shoes. The thrill of trying to look good for John felt wonderful. After shopping for herself, she would go to the little boy's section and buy John Michael several outfits to wear on the playground.

Finally, it was time to go home and get ready for her date. The answer machine was blinking and she had three messages. Her heart sank as she pressed the button to play the first message. Surely John had not changed his mind about going to dinner. One was from The Cranberry Tree, one was a solicitor, and the last one was from John. She was thrilled when he left the message about what time he would be picking her up for their date. Thank goodness he wasn't calling to cancel their plans.

Melissa soaked in the tub for about half an hour. She lit candles, put on some Luther Vandross music, and soaked in oil beads. Afterwards, she put on her favorite after-bath splash from Body Works and sprayed on a small amount of Contradiction, one of John's favorite colognes.

She wore her hair down, long dark curls falling below her shoulders. By the time the doorbell rang, she was completely ready for John's arrival. She was a little nervous, but too excited to be fearful. She felt feminine, almost sexy as she opened the door.

"Wow, you look great!" He complimented her as soon as he came in the door and gave her a kiss.

"Thank you." She blushed as she closed the door behind him.

"I mean it. You look especially beautiful tonight. I don't know what's different about you, but you are radiant." He found it hard to keep his distance.

"Well, our reservation is for seven o'clock, so I guess we better get going. Let me go hug John Michael goodnight and then we can be on our way." Melissa looked at John and asked him if he wanted to go with her. He of course jumped at the chance. Maddie was in the bedroom reading John Michael a bedtime story.

He giggled when he saw his mama and reached out for her. She took him in her arms. He was so cute with his curly dark hair and the big dimple in his right cheek.

She blew bubbles on his cheek and kissed him repeatedly. He giggled even more.

"Um, sometimes little man, I could just eat you with a spoon!" Melissa smiled adoringly at her little miracle baby.

"Here's your daddy. Say Da-Da." She handed him to John.

"Hey there, buddy. It's time to go night, night. Daddy loves you." John's eyes moistened. He never thought he'd ever be able to say those words. What a miracle that he could hug his very own son.

"Got to go, but we'll see you in the morning." John reached out, tussled his son's hair, and handed him back to Maddie. She smiled at John's last statement.

"You both look very nice this evening. I have to say it is so good to see you together again."

They smiled and told her they would try not to be too late.

Dinner was wonderful. The rack of lamb, chicken Marsala and Riesling white wine were superb. John decided to give Melissa her ring and to ask her to marry him before dessert was served.

"Melissa, I need to ask you something and I don't think it can wait."

Melissa reached over and touched John's hand. "What is it? You seem so serious. Is everything all right? Did you go back to the doctor for a follow-up exam?"

"I'm fine. I just want to ask you something. I want to ask you to marry me again." He pulled the ring box out of his pocket and handed it to Melissa.

"What? You're kidding me, right?" Melissa's cheeks were flushed as she reached out for the ring box. She gasped when she saw the 3 carrot emerald with diamond baguettes. It was perfectly cut. Her mouth hung open in disbelief.

"Oh, John, it's absolutely beautiful. I had no idea you were planning all of this."

John put the ring on her finger and repeated. "Well, what do you say? Melissa will you marry me?" He admired the ring as he reached for her left hand and waited for her to answer.

"John Isaacson, nothing in this world could make me any happier. Yes, I'll marry you." She was more excited than the first time John had proposed to her.

"I love you, Melissa. Now we can start over as a family and as husband and wife. We can have a brand new beginning and leave the past behind us." He leaned over and kissed Melissa.

Their waiter came over before Melissa had time to respond. He was instantly aware that he was interrupting a very special moment. "Please excuse me, but do you want coffee or would you like to see the dessert tray?" He smiled warmly at both of them and waited.

John looked at Melissa to see if she wanted anything. She shook her head no and he declined as well.

"No, we'll skip the dessert tray. Just bring us the check please."

They were both anxious to be alone. They left the restaurant and headed to Melissa's house. Maddie couldn't stay late so they needed to go straight home as soon as they finished eating.

Melissa showed Maddie her new engagement ring as soon as they walked in the door.

"Oh, Mrs. Isaacson, it is absolutely beautiful." She had never used Melissa's maiden name even after the divorce. She never thought they should get a divorce in the first place.

John Michael had already gone to sleep. Melissa brought out a bottle of Chablis and handed it to John to open. She excused herself for a moment and ran to the bathroom to check her makeup and then joined John on the couch.

His dark eyes seemed aglow with pride as he admired the ring on Melissa's hand.

"Let's make a toast, Melissa. I want this to be a wonderful new beginning for us."

"All right. You first."

"Here's to a wonderful life together. One filled with lots of great memories, a house full of kids, and love beyond our own hopes and dreams." He waited and looked at Melissa's happy face.

"Let's see. May we leave all pain and sorrow behind, and find new joy and love in our union. May our love overshadow every hurt of the past. May our traumas finally be behind us for good with no more unfortunate surprises. May God keep all our loved ones, our friends, and ourselves safe from any harm, and may this marriage be better than it was before. Oh yeah one more thing, here's to our beautiful friend Jennifer who will forever be in our memory. We are forever grateful to you for the part you played in bringing us back together. We love you Jennifer." They clinked their glasses, emptied the contents, and placed them back on the coffee table.

John pulled Melissa close and kissed her gently on the lips. He wrapped his arm around her and she could hear the steady beating of his heart. He squeezed her even closer against himself and smelled her hair. He kissed her gently again until he could feel her respond and melt under his embrace. He could have made love to her right then, and it was very hard not yielding to his passion.

He cleared his throat and asked her what she wanted to do. "Should we wait? Do you want to wait until we get married?"

She was flustered and took a moment to catch her breath. "You're asking me that now? It would have been easier to answer that question 10 minutes ago. I don't know if I can even say those words. You need to help me out here. I know there's something really good about delayed gratification, but for the life of me I can't remember what it is right now."

John laughed out loud. "We can do it. Let's wait until our wedding night just like we're making love for the first time."

"It's been so long I might as well be a virgin. I'm not sure I remember how to make love any more."

John smiled. "Trust me, it'll come back to you."

Melissa began to wonder if this had anything to do with John's surgery. Was he not sure of himself? Did he need more time? She continued. "Well, now what, John? If we wait, what are we going to do tonight? Do you want to spend the night, but sleep separately? I want to sleep with you, John. I want to be near you even if we don't do anything."

"Melissa, I don't think I can get in the same bed with you and not touch you. I don't trust myself or you at this stage of our relationship."

Melissa smiled at John. "Are you afraid that I might attack you in the middle of the night?"

"You might. I can be pretty irresistible in my shorts." He winked at her, leaned down, kissed her on the cheek, and continued.

"I guess I really better get going before neither one of us can control ourselves."

Melissa felt so strongly that part of John's desire to wait had to do with his health. In her mind they were married, but whatever John wanted to do she would go along with it. If he needed to wait then she was willing to do so until he was ready for intimacy. It took her a few moments to regain her composure before telling him though.

"John, I wish you could stay. We could just cuddle on the couch. You could leave after I fall asleep. What do you say?"

"Melissa, it would be too hard. Surely you know that."

She decided not to push the issue. "Okay, we'll totally wait until our wedding day." She stood up and walked him to the door. Before she said goodnight, she wrapped her arms around John and hugged him tightly. "I love you so much, John and I love my ring. I can't wait to give myself completely to you again.

He kissed her feeling the heat and passion of her mouth. He almost told her he wanted to stay the night, but resisted the urge.

"I love you too, Melissa and I want you more than you'll ever know." He hugged her again, said goodnight and went home frustrated, but happy.

That night Melissa looked at her ring over and over again. Even after she turned off the light on the night stand, she would sit straight up in bed and turn the light on again. Her ring sparkled in the light when she moved her hand. She squealed out loud. "I must be dreaming!" She just couldn't believe everything had changed so much in her life.

She finally turned off the light and pulled the covers over her head. Even under the covers she couldn't stop grinning. It seemed impossible that she and John were going to be married again. Sleep did not come easily. Thoughts of John swirled in her mind for most of the night.

John also had a sleepless night. He worked on his plans to remodel the beach house. He wanted to surprise Melissa with the changes he was making to the house as a wedding gift to her. Their world was finally coming together. There had been so many storms, but somehow they had endured them all. The worst was finally behind them.

John emptied the pencil sharpener on his desk, turned out the lamp, and attempted to go to sleep. All of his dreams were finally coming to pass.

Chapter Forty-Six

Melissa and John were planning on going to Jennifer's funeral the weekend before their wedding. Melissa had spent hours on the internet and phone trying to locate Jennifer's brother. The last report of Jay's whereabouts was in Atlanta. He was incarcerated there and moved to the State Mental Hospital. Because of the lack of funds and space he was released into the streets of Atlanta. No one was certain where he might actually be at this time.

There was no record that he owned a car. His driver's license had expired and there was no activity on record anywhere that could totally pinpoint his whereabouts. In all probability he was homeless, and other than walking the streets of Atlanta there was not much chance of finding him.

John had agreed to help Melissa look for Jay. They would spend Saturday afternoon walking in downtown Atlanta to see if they could locate him. The funeral was so sad, but inspiring. So many individuals would be helped by the dedication of Jennifer's body and organs to medical research. She would have wanted it that way. Jennifer's mother was such a nice lady. They all went out to eat after the grave side service. Mrs. Crawson was so impressed with Melissa's commitment to Jennifer to find Jay.

It seemed by the time they came to the funeral Melissa had searched every possible avenue to find Jay. He had to be somewhere in Atlanta.

John was more familiar with Atlanta than Melissa. He knew the whole downtown area because of the length of time he had lived there. He also knew where most of the homeless people hung out. The only problem they both had was not knowing what Jay looked like. Their walk was unsuccessful as they inquired amongst the homeless community. Almost all of them had a nickname and did not ever identify each other by their real name. Although their search was unsuccessful, Melissa still did not give up on her plans to find Jay. She was more determined than ever. After their honeymoon she would continue her search, even if she had to come back to Atlanta alone.

The next week went by so quickly as Melissa finished all the last minute details for the wedding. It would be small, but elegant with only the closest of friends and family to attend. She and John had decided to spend the first two days of their honeymoon at the beach house and then they would fly to Switzerland for a five day tour of the area. They'd begin in Zurich and end in Geneva. John Michael would stay with Maddie until they returned to Charleston. Then they would take him and Maddie to the beach house for the next couple of weeks after they returned.

John had planned to surprise Melissa by having the beach house totally remodeled. He had all new furniture and new hardwood floors put in. He had included a front door to the structure that included a spiral inlay for the front of the house. No longer would there only be a back entrance. He extended the porch area to surround the entire house. The squeaky steps had all been replaced as well. He didn't want there to be anything that reminded Melissa of the tragedies that had taken place there.

He had someone design two new doors for the front and back entrance to the house.

They were sculptured in solid oak two inches thick, one to replace the door in the back that had the glass windows, and one created especially for a new entrance. This time there would be no glass inlays, so as to discourage any thieves from breaking inside. He couldn't wait to see Melissa's face as he carried her up the front steps.

The closer it got to the wedding, the more beautiful Melissa seemed to become. She seemed so peaceful and full of joy. At least she wasn't still feeling guilty about what had happened to Jennifer.

They hadn't talked about the journal much. There just hadn't been time and John had been so preoccupied with things at the office and the remodeling project. All he knew was Melissa seemed to have peace with herself after having read it.

He wished Jennifer could be there to share in their wedding and reunion. She was totally responsible for their getting back together and would be so excited about the wedding. He smiled to himself as he imagined Jennifer looking down from heaven at all the festivities taking place.

The wedding went as planned. After the reception, he and Melissa hugged their guests and waved good-bye. Melissa held John Michael close to her up to the very moment they left. She really didn't want to leave him again.

She and John rode back to the house in a limo, packed their suitcases, grabbed some groceries, and left for the beach. It was such a different ride than the last time they traveled to Edisto. Melissa had a picture made of herself and John Michael to give to John as a wedding gift. One of her vendors at The Cranberry Tree designed a frame for her. She had it engraved with the words, "All Our Love, Always". While John was driving, she pulled the picture from her bag and handed it to him.

"Here's a little something from John Michael and me for your wedding gift."

"Oh, no Melissa. I've been so busy with work, I didn't get you anything. I guess I was so excited about getting married that I didn't think about doing something special for you. Do you forgive me?" He looked innocently into her eyes.

"Of course I forgive you and besides you gave me this beautiful ring. I didn't expect you to give me anything else. I had planned to give you my gift whether we ever got remarried are not."

John pulled over and stopped the car before they came into view of the beach house. He pretended to stop just to open her gift. He opened the neatly wrapped package and admired the picture of his wife and son.

"Thank you, Melissa. I love it. I never dreamed all of this would have been happening to us a year ago. I thought my life was over and now look at my family." His voice cracked as he said the word family. He fought the urge to get emotional. He leaned over, kissed Melissa, and took both her hands into his.

"I'll cherish this gift forever. The best gift you could ever give me was our son. He is truly our miracle baby." He admired the image of his wife and son, then looked lovingly into Melissa's eyes and continued.

"Melissa, are you sure you want to go back to the beach house? We don't have to go back there if you don't want to. We could go somewhere else for our first night together. There are some motels we could stay at further down the coast. I don't want anything about this night to be painful for you."

"John, this is exactly where I want us to be for our first time after getting remarried. I'm sure everything will be fine. As long as you got rid of that couch and replaced the window in the door like you said you would then everything will be fine." She squeezed his hand to reassure him and continued.

"The beach is always where I've come for healing. When my parents died I came here. This is where I came when you left me. We were reconciled here and this is where I read Jennifer's journal. I have some wonderful childhood memories here and as long as we concentrate on the good things, I believe everything will be all right." She kissed him.

"Now I want it to be the place I make love with you for the first time after so many months of separation. I love you and we've waited a long time to be together again, maybe we've waited too long. I'm just ready to be near you and I don't really care where that is, but at least our beach house will be a special place for me."

"That's all I needed to hear!" John started the car and headed toward the house. He smiled as he thought about how surprised Melissa would be to see all the changes that had been made to the house. It didn't even look like the same place. He selected new furniture that Melissa had admired when they were out shopping together. There were several things she was going to purchase sometime in the future. He had bought everything she would have wanted.

John turned on the last road toward the driveway, he watched Melissa's face as she realized there was something different about the front of the house. Also, there was a big banner across the door that said, "Happy Wedding Day" with lots of ribbons and balloons draped around it, thanks to Maddie.

Melissa screamed with excitement. "John, the house is beautiful. I absolutely love it! When did all this happen?"

John smiled with pride as he admired the work he did on the entrance of the house. The hand carved stairwell was perfect for carrying his bride up the stairs and across the threshold.

"What? I thought you did all of this." He said teasingly.

"Hurry, John. I can't wait to see everything up close."

"Just wait, there are more surprises to come." He swerved into the driveway, helped her out of the car, and lifted her into his arms to carry her across the threshold.

"Stop John, before you carry me inside. Let me look at the intricate hand carving of the bannister. Oh my goodness, it's beautiful and the door, I can't believe it. When did you have time to do all of this?"

John was still smiling. "You know all those late nights at work."

"Wow, this is so nice, John. I can't believe this door. It doesn't even have any glass. Looks like no one could break through this one." She had John put her down for a moment and she reached out and touched the carvings.

John picked Melissa back up, grabbed the key with his one free hand, unlocked the door, and continued to carry her in the house. He turned her all around so she could get a good view of all the new furnishings and wallpaper.

"Oh my gosh, look at this place! John, I absolutely love it. I just don't know how you had the time to do all of this."

"Oh, I don't know. I just worked it into my budget schedule." He finally put her down so she could walk around and look at everything on her own.

There was a new fireplace inlaid with brass and precious stone. There was a new back door that was also without windows. All the furniture she had admired in Charleston and planned to buy sometime in the future, furnished the den and bedrooms. There was an elegant new white couch, love seat and chair in the den. John had purchased an antique rocker as well, that had been newly caned just so she could rock John Michael in it.

Melissa walked out on the porch which was entirely new and wrapped around the whole house. The back stairs seemed to be hand crafted as well. No more squeaks on the steps climbing up or down from the ocean. John even had a new shower installed near the base of the stairs and a foot faucet to wash the sand off after leaving the beach.

Melissa shook her head. "I can't believe this is the same place."

When she went back inside, she noticed John used her favorite color schemes for the wallpaper. The hardwood floors were the lighter color she loved so much, and even the bathroom had been redecorated in her favorite dark hunter green color.

Finally, she turned to face John with tears streaming down her cheeks. He was of course grinning from ear to ear.

"Oh, John, I love it. This is better than anything I could have imagined or attempted to do myself. What makes it even more special is the time and thought you must have put into it. You furnished it just the way I wanted it." She wrapped her arms around his neck still aware that he might still be too sick to become very intimate.

She continued. "Why don't you get our belongings out of the car and I'll pour some Champagne? I think we left a bottle the last time we were here and John, I don't think there is anything else you could have done to make this moment more perfect."

John kissed her on the forehead. He didn't want to let her go. "That was the plan, Melissa to make this night as perfect as I could." He smiled as he went out the front door to grab their things. He turned on the hot water heater, and when he returned he turned on the gas logs. He had replaced all the fireplaces in the den and bedrooms to propane gas logs.

When Melissa opened the refrigerator, it was already stocked with food, wine, juice, champagne, and gourmet goodies including strawberries and chocolate for dipping.

She poured the champagne and handed John his glass. They walked out on the back porch to watch the waves. A bright full moon reflected romantically on the water. John wrapped his arm around Melissa's waist as they both faced the shore. He was the first to break the silence.

"Can you believe we made it to this night? It seems like a dream, doesn't it? We're finally together and a year ago I thought I had lost you forever." He spoke softly in her ear.

"Hush, John. Don't even think about anything negative from the past. Let's just remember the good things. I do miss Jennifer and I want to honor her memory in some way for getting us back together, but I don't want to relive the sadness we had back then. I just want us to live the rest of our lives making up for lost time." She turned to face him, wrapped both her arms around his neck, and kissed him passionately on the lips.

Then she took him by the hand and led him back inside. They ate some of the goodies from the refrigerator, poured another glass of champagne, and headed back to the couch in front of the fireplace. It was nice not having to worry about adding logs to the fire or cleaning up the ashes. Melissa found it hard to even remember her last time there, since it seemed like they were at a totally different place.

The fire was sizzling in the background. John tossed a new afghan on the floor with a couple of pillows, and pulled Melissa on the floor toward him. This would be their first time to make love since their reunion and for some reason they were both very nervous. Melissa was trembling inside. She was the first to speak.

"John, let's get ready for bed first, since it's so late."

He agreed. They both got up and went to the bedroom to get their suitcases and unpack their clothes. Melissa had taken a shower at her house before they left Charleston, but John had not. He decided to jump in the shower before coming to bed.

Melissa put on one of her gowns she had received as a wedding gift. She ran to one of the other bathrooms and brushed her teeth. John had turned on the gas logs in the bedroom. She looked at the new Hemingway bed with the new bedding. Everything looked so inviting and cozy. She normally always slept in front of the fireplace in the den because the flue didn't work properly in the bedroom. What a difference these new gas logs made. She couldn't help but think what a good man she was married to, so sensitive to all her needs.

When John was finished with his shower, he brought the ice bucket with the remainder of the champagne to the night stand in the bedroom. He handed Melissa her glass. He had nuked the chocolate and brought it with the strawberries to Melissa. He lit three, vanilla scented candles before getting into the bed with her.

Melissa was overwhelmed with John's sensitivity to what she might enjoy on their first night together.

"Champagne, strawberries, chocolate and vanilla candles wow, all of my favorites. John, you really know how to appeal to my romantic side."

John reached over, dipped a strawberry in chocolate, and pressed it against Melissa's lips.

Watching her enjoy the fruit and chocolate impassioned him. That's it, he couldn't wait any longer to be with his bride. He put the remainder of the strawberry on the plate and moved over to the other side of the bed to get closer to Melissa.

She snuggled up close to him and let him wrap himself around her slender body. She seemed to melt right into him. Melissa felt free, freer than she had felt in such a long time. She whispered in his ear.

"You are so good to me, so gentle. I love you, baby more than I ever dreamed I could love anyone. You heal me, John emotionally and physically. You even heal my spirit." She moved even closer to his warm body.

John was as gentle as he could be towards her, wanting to please her with his touch. He caressed her and kissed her, letting himself explore the channels of her desire. He waited with each new move until he knew he had satisfied his wife's needs. Her voice confirmed her pleasure and she responded in ways that spoke of her fulfillment.

He caressed her face, kissed her repeatedly, wishing he could stop time, wanting to keep this moment in his heart forever. He made love to his wife and experienced the most pleasure he had ever known. He thanked God for giving him back his beautiful wife, for giving him a second chance at life. He began to weep for no apparent reason.

"What's wrong, John? Are you all right? You're not in pain, are you?" Melissa kissed the tears on his face.

"I'm just so happy, Melissa. Being with you makes me so happy. We're finally where we've needed to be all along."

She responded to his words, kissing him passionately, letting him make love to her again.

He seemed more gentle than she ever remembered his being. The tears came from her own eyes as she experienced fulfillment again.

He continued to hold her, still trying to put her needs before his own. She relaxed, sighed deeply, and melted under his embrace. They both were at peace in each other's arms. All the wedding stress behind them, everything had gone as planned without any problems. Now they could sleep totally at peace, totally comforted in each other's love.

The sound of the waves lulled them to sleep. The fire in the fireplaces warmed the whole house. The bubbles in the champagne rose to the top of the glass. The vanilla candles continued to burn throughout the night giving the room a warm cozy feeling.

Sleep did come, but they would awaken to find their bodies intertwined in a warm bundle. This only helped to impassion their desire again and again. Time and truth had healed their pain. Now there was nothing to make them afraid. Switzerland would be a fun and exciting trip for both of them. The torment of the past was finally behind them.

It was after 11:00 in the morning, when they finally got out of bed. Their flight for Switzerland was not until 3:00 so they had a little time. They ate breakfast and then John decided to take another shower while Melissa went on a short walk down the beach. She would take a bath when she got back and there was more hot water.

The ocean was a brilliant blue and the sun was out as much as could be expected in the winter. Melissa just could not resist the urge to go for a run on the beach. She felt great after such an exhilarating evening. She jogged in the opposite direction of the way she and Jennifer had gone on that eventful morning. She had just started out along the shore when she saw that cab again at her neighbor's house.

"Okay that's it. I'm gonna find out what that guy is up to." Melissa ran past the house, circled back up behind another house, and snuck up beside the cab. She went over to the driver's side and knocked on the glass.

"What are you doing in there?" She obviously startled the man.

He let out a scream as Melissa's face suddenly appeared at the window. He turned the key in the ignition, so he could roll down the window.

He yelled out, "What is it? You scared me."

"I said, what are you doing parked here at the Smith's house?"

The man started to stutter a little. "I come here, eat lunch, and read my Bible after bringing people to the hotel from the airport. Then I pick them up when they leave. Check out isn't until 1:00 p.m. and it's just too far to go all the way back to Charleston, so I just wait here for my cab company to call."

Melissa was a little bit embarrassed that she interrupted his Bible reading. "You're reading your Bible?"

"Yes, ma'am. It helps me calm down to sit here in full view of the ocean. I bring a sandwich, a snack, and a coke."

Melissa felt terrible. "The Smiths might have you arrested if they find out you park here without permission. I'll call the hotel and the cab company printed on your cab to confirm your story. If everything checks out, you can park in front of my beach house." She pointed to her home.

"What is your name and your cab number?"

"They call me J. C. and my cab number is 674589."

"Have you got something I can right that number on?" Melissa asked.

He got a piece of paper out of his Bible and jotted down the info. "Here, and ma'am, please don't call the police. I promise I'm telling the truth."

"All right, but it will be another week before I can check on this. Wait until you hear from your boss before you start parking in front of my house, okay?"

"Yes, ma'am. I will."

Melissa stuffed the paper in her pocket and headed back to the beach house in case John was looking for her.

Chapter Forty-Seven

Melissa and John checked into their Zurich Hotel, Swissotel International/Nova Park, and had the rest of the day free to do whatever sightseeing they wanted. Melissa loved going into all the little shops and storefronts along the Bahnofstrasse. It was hard to believe that beneath those streets were the vaults that held the majority of the world's gold. Although they enjoyed the exclusive shopping district, it was the River Limmat and Lake Zurich with all the natural surroundings that helped to stimulate the continual romance of John and Melissa's honeymoon.

They shared bread and cheese while relaxing on the shore of Lake Zurich. John admired his bride as she sat silhouetted against the sloping hillside of the horizon. She responded to his desire to be with her and went back to the hotel to be alone with him. It was their honeymoon and they couldn't seem to get enough of each other. They toured a little and returned to their room.

Later that evening they walked down the Perterskirche and enjoyed the medieval part of the city. They admired the 13th Century tower with one of the largest clock faces in Europe. After walking through Old Town along the narrow alleys between the old Swiss homes and churches, they once again went back to their room.

John pulled Melissa onto the bed with him. He was addicted to her love and for the first time in her life she was able to give herself so completely to him without fearing she might not ever be able to give him a baby. They began not only to know Switzerland as the city of peace, but also as the city of love.

The next day they took a train to Lucerne and walked along the famous Chapel Bridge that tells the story of Lucerne in the paintings on the ceiling. This was Melissa's favorite attraction in Switzerland. Perhaps she could relate to the Lion Monument. Somehow she related to the dying lion. They had both gone through a kind of death themselves over the past year.

Their favorite cities were Lugano, St. Moritz and Zermatt. There was something unique about each place that appealed to each of them. The blue waters of Lake Lugano and the lush surroundings around the Lake took Melissa's breath away.

John enjoyed some of the world's finest private art collections in the Villa Favorite at Castagnola. They both dipped in the St. Moritz Springs, allowing the mineral waters to bring health and healing to their bodies or so the legend claims. Hitting all the high spots of Switzerland was exhausting. Melissa could not wait to get back to the motel to call John Michael.

They had one more event to go to before she could do that. They enjoyed a ski trip in Zermatt and mountain climbing. It was absolutely breath taking to ride the cable cars and to view all the peaks and glaciers that surround the area.

"Melissa, you look so beautiful. I think you look better than I've ever seen you look before. You seem so at peace with yourself. It makes me happy to see you so content." He pulled her closer to himself.

"I am at peace. The only thing missing is my baby boy. I miss him so much right now. I wish we had him and Maddie with us. Let's go shopping later to find them a gift to take back with us before we leave? You'll have to help me find them something, okay? Why don't we go ahead and give them a call? I'd like to see how they're doing."

"Sure that sounds great." He picked up the phone and struggled with the language barrier of the front desk attendant, but finally got the call to the States to go through. There was no answer.

"Wonder where they are? It's 8:30 in the morning in Charleston. That's weird, John. Did the answer machine come on?"

"No, it didn't."

"Where could they possibly be at this hour? Are you sure you dialed the right number? Try again just to make sure."

He tried again. Still, no answer. "Why don't we go buy their gifts to take back with us, and when we get back we'll call again?"

"All right, but I've got a sick gut feeling, John. I think something's wrong."

"Melissa, don't be silly, there's nothing wrong. Maybe Maddie's bathing him or she decided to take him outside to swing. Did you give her a time to expect us to call?"

"No, but I know their schedule and it's weird for Maddie not to answer the phone."

"Did you set the answer machine to come on by five rings?"

"No, the message should come on after three rings."

"Well, just in case there's a practical explanation, let's go shop for an hour, then try and call again. If there's still no answer, we'll call a neighbor and ask them to check on them, or get someone at the shop to go by there. If we still can't get them, we'll call the police, okay?"

"All right, maybe you're right. Maybe I'm just being paranoid. Let's get the gifts and call as soon as we get back." She couldn't wait to talk to her little angel. They put on their evening clothes and headed out the door. It would be time for dinner in Switzerland soon.

They had just left the hotel when the phone began to ring in their room. The attendant at the desk took a message and left it in their box. He did the best he could, trying to write in English. He struggled with the interpretation. He could speak English a little better than he could write it. So in fragmented sentences he wrote what he had been told.

"Not to worry, I'm teaching Jr. He washes his dirty hands like the book said, like the Good Book."

Melissa and John bought a beautiful hand carved Coo-Coo Clock for Maddie and arranged shipping to have it sent to her home. They found some wood carvings to take to John Michael and some handmade stuffed animals. They ate an early dinner with two glasses of red wine and walked along the wood bridge in Lucerne. They stopped by the Lion Monument again and looked at the dying lion.

"He looks so beautiful, yet he will always be dying. That's sad, but so true of life don't you think?" Melissa squeezed John's hand even tighter.

"I suppose it represents all of us. We're all dying a little every day. I'm just so glad we've survived all of our hardships, and we've been given this chance to start our lives over. Now we have only good things ahead for all of us." He wrapped his arm around Melissa and kissed her lovingly on the cheek.

"Well, I'm anxious to get back and call Maddie. I can't wait to tell her we found a surprise for her and John Michael. Maybe I'm crazy, but I still have this very uneasy feeling inside."

"Melissa, don't worry. I'm sure everything is all right. What could possibly be wrong now?"

"I don't know, but something doesn't feel right."

They turned and walked along the cobble streets and headed back to the motel. Before they went inside John took his bride in his arms and kissed her passionately.

"You've made me the happiest man in the world. Nothing will ever separate us again." He wrapped his arm around her and walked her inside.

Chapter Forty-Eight

Melissa and John bypassed the front lobby and came in the back entrance of the motel with their packages. They took the elevator up and waited for the antiquated piece of machinery to make it to the seventh floor. They missed the sound of the phone ringing by only minutes. Lieutenant Smith decided not to leave a message. He would just try again later.

They put the packages down on the table, took their shoes off, picked up the phone and rang the front desk to place a call to the United States. The new attendant placed the call without realizing they had messages waiting for them in their box. Melissa held the phone and waited anxiously for someone to pick up. The answer machine did not come on and after fifteen rings she placed the receiver down.

"There's no answer. Something's wrong, John. I just know it."

"Do you want to call Mrs. Beasley your next door neighbor? She's liable to get disoriented and we might frighten her without a reason, but we could ask her anyway."

"Yes, call her. I don't care if she gets upset. She's right next door. She could walk over there and see if Maddie and John Michael are all right."

"Okay. Let me check with the front desk to see if we have any messages first. Seems like he would have already told me if we had any though." John picked up the phone and waited on the desk clerk to pick up.

"Yes, this is Mr. Isaacson in room 703, do we have any messages?"

"One moment, please."

It seemed to take him forever to come back to the phone. "Yes, Mr. Isaacson. You have two messages. Do you want to come to the desk and get them or should I just read them to you?"

"Go ahead and read them." John held Melissa's hand and waited.

"Please excuse me, Sir. The clerk who was on before I was, does not have good English and does not write so good."

"That's all right. Do the best you can."

"The first one says, not to worry. I'm teaching, Junior. He washes his dirty hands now, like the book said, like the Good Book."

"What is that supposed to mean? Who sent that message?"

"I don't know, Sir. There is no signing at the end."

Melissa interrupted. "What John? What does it say?"

"Just a minute. There is another one."

"The second one says, I'm still waiting. We are all still waiting. I believe you recognize the number." The desk clerk read John's number.

"That's my phone number. What does it mean, we are all waiting?"

"I don't know. That is the message. There is no more. No name."

"Okay. Okay. Thank you." John hung up the phone.

"What is it? What did he say? Who's waiting?" Melissa was becoming even more worried.

"It was just some crazy message. Maybe the clerk was confused with his English. The only part I understood was my phone number."

"What? What did it say?"

"Something about not worrying about Junior. He's learned how to wash his hands, like the book, like the Good Book."

"Oh, my God! He's talking about John Michael! It's that man that broke into the beach house!" Melissa began to scream.

"It can't be, Melissa. He's in jail."

"No, he's not. He's got my baby!" She began to cry and scream uncontrollably.

"Melissa, you've got to get control of yourself. We've got to call my apartment. He's waiting on our call and he can't hear you this upset and frightened."

Melissa continued to sob into one of the pillows on the bed. "I want to go home right now. Get me out of here, John. Get on the phone and get us a flight out of here. I'm leaving right now and I don't care that he's waiting on a call."

All of a sudden the phone rang. Melissa let out another scream and John answered the phone.

"Hello."

"Mr. Isaacson?"

"Yes, this is he."

"This is Lieutenant Smith with the Charleston Police Department. I'm calling to let you know that we have a problem with an escapee from the prison in Columbia. The man who broke into your beach house has escaped and we have reason to believe he is headed this way or is already in the Charleston area. You may need to warn your sitter and we may need to keep your home under surveillance. We tried to call your wife's house and there was no answer. We called The Cranberry Tree and they gave us the number where we could reach you in Switzerland."

"We've already heard from him and I think he's hidden out in my apartment. We got a strange message and he wants us to call him. He gave us my phone number." John told the officer about the crazy messages they had gotten, and that he and Melissa were planning on returning home as soon as they could get a flight out.

"Let me know what your arrival time will be and we'll have someone pick you up at the airport. Have you called the man back yet to see what his demands are?"

"No, we just got in and got the messages. Melissa wants to leave right now to check on our son. What should I do? Call him back or just go straight to the airport? We feel so helpless to be so far away from our son."

"I know, John. I still think you need to call him back and make sure everyone is still alive. Give me the address and I'll begin to send officers out to surround the place. And John, here is my mobile phone number. Call me back as soon as you make contact with him. Also, we may be able to help you get a flight out sooner than you can get one on your own. So, let me know if you have any problems at the airport."

"Yes, Sir." John hung up the phone.

Melissa was wiping tears from her eyes as she threw their clothes in a suitcase. "What did he say?"

"He wants me to call that guy. He's sending several cars over there to surround the place. Then I'm supposed to call Lieutenant Smith back as soon as I make contact with that man. He also said he'd help us get a flight out if we have a problem getting one ourselves."

John walked back over to the phone and picked it up. He motioned for Melissa to come sit beside him so they could both listen to the conversation. He then dialed the number and it rang three times before he heard someone answer. His heart was pounding in his chest.

"Yes, you rang?" The stranger laughed into the receiver.

"Who is this and what do you want?"

"I'm an old friend of the family and you might say I've made myself at home. Nice place you've got here, but you know what the Good Book says, 'What does it profit a man if he gains the whole world and loses his soul?'"

"What's that supposed to mean?"

"Well, it all boils down to you have to pay for your sins. That's all and I'm going to help you pay for yours. You've got a nice little family here. There you are in Switzerland and here I am babysitting the kid. Don't worry I've been teaching him the importance of washing his hands."

Melissa jerked the phone out of John's hand. "You listen to me you jerk. If you lay one hand on my son, I'll personally kill you. Do you understand me? He's innocent. The Good Book as you would say, speaks strongly against hurting the innocent, especially little children. If you want to hurt someone, just wait until we get there."

"Well, if it isn't the lady at the beach house. I told you, you hadn't seen the last of me. I'm glad to hear you're planning on coming to see me. You better get here in a hurry. Junior might have to be the sacrificial lamb."

"That shows how little you know about the Good Book. It says you can't take my child for payment for my sins. To be exact it says, 'the sins of the fathers shall not be visited on the children.' Every man stands on his own. John and I stand on our own for our sins, so it would be wrong if you hurt our child. You hurt him and you'll be washing your hands, day and night for the rest of your life to get those filthy hands clean."

"It surprises me that someone like you knows anything about the Good Book. Okay, I won't hurt the child, but you need to get here as soon as you can. We're all waiting, but not for long." He hung up the phone.

Melissa turned toward John. "He hung up. He said he wouldn't hurt John Michael, but we'd better get there soon that he'd be waiting for us. We need to get home right now. You need to warn the Lieutenant not to do anything until we get there. John Michael's life may depend on it."

John called the Lieutenant. They were on a flight out of Switzerland in less than an hour. John struggled with his own guilt, fear, and pain as he tried to comfort Melissa.

She was fighting a headache and trying to decide what they should do first when they got back to Charleston. She prayed silently and rubbed her right temple. John reached for her hand. She could feel a slight tremor in his touch. He looked frightened and sad at the same time. She squeezed his fingers in the palm of her hand trying to communicate her own strength to him. Melissa kept saying to herself, that somehow they were going to make it back in time to save their son and Maddie.

Melissa was determined to stay close to John this time. She believed they would have to fight this guy together, not separately.

"I love you, John. We're going to make it through this. We're going to get our son and Maddie back safely."

This time John began to weep. "I don't think I could bare it if anything happened to that boy."

"If we can get back in time, I'm not going to allow anything to happen to John Michael or let that man hurt Maddie. We've got to get back there as soon as we can before he changes his mind and takes John Michael and Maddie somewhere else."

"Melissa, we need to be very careful. We'll have to figure out a way to get them out of the apartment and escape his craziness ourselves. I'm not sure why he is so fixated on us and our sins or why he associates some of this evil with washing his hands."

"I don't care why he believes what he does or what brought him to this place in his life. I don't care who he is, he better not hurt my baby. That's all I've got to say." She put her head on John's shoulder and tried to rest her eyes for a moment.

John gripped her arm and hand even tighter and tilted his head next to hers. Although they were exhausted, they were too restless to sleep. They arrived in Atlanta, changed planes, and headed for Charleston. They were silent for the remainder of the trip, trying to prepare themselves mentally and emotionally for what was ahead.

Chapter Forty-Nine

Lieutenant Smith was waiting at the airport for John and Melissa when they arrived. Some of his men took their luggage and then they escorted them to his car.

"Has anything happened at the apartment, yet?" Melissa asked anxiously.

"We have the whole place surrounded in case he tries to leave and take someone hostage. We thought you should drive your own car over there so he doesn't suspect anything."

"We left our cars at Melissa's and took a cab to the airport." John informed him.

"We'll take you to your home and follow behind you to the apartment." The officer instructed them.

"What should we do about entering the apartment? Do we just ring the door bell or go around to the back and try and sneak in?"

"I think you should ring the door bell and we'll try to sneak in the back while you keep him distracted. Both of you need to act as normal as possible."

"If we can get to the bathroom window that faces out the same side as the back door, we could signal to you when it's a good time to come in and get him." John suggested.

"That'll be good." The officer agreed.

Melissa and John got out of the cop car and headed inside Melissa's to go to the bathroom. Melissa grabbed the gun from under the mattress and stuffed it in the waistband of her pants. She changed her blouse to one which was longer than most and did not tuck it into her pants.

She went to the kitchen and poured two large glasses of water. She gulped one down and gave the other one to John. She remembered being so thirsty the night Jennifer died. She also stuffed a breakfast bar in her jacket pocket, gave one to John in case they were separated, or this went on for days. She was so nervous she couldn't eat a bite, but she knew they would probably both need something before the night was over.

"Melissa, we better get over there." John looked at her and pulled her close to him. "No matter what happens, remember I love you."

She kissed him gently on the lips. "I love you, too. We're gonna make it through this, John. All of us are going to make it."

"I hope so." He grabbed the keys and headed toward the front door. Melissa prayed silently as they walked toward the car. Neither of them said a word on the ride over. They were too scared. Finally, they pulled into John's parking lot.

"Let's just go to the front door, ring the door bell, and pretend we are just there for a visit. If either of us can get John Michael, we need to hold him close until we are all safely out the door."

"Okay, and John, if it's ever a matter of saving me or John Michael, you save John Michael. Understand?"

"Don't talk like that. We're all getting out of there." John pressed the door bell, held his breath, and waited. He and Melissa were both thinking they were probably being watched through the peep hole.

In a moment Maddie answered the door. She looked nervous and pale, but was grateful to see the couple. Melissa and John looked around as they walked in the door.

"Where are they?" John asked in a whisper.

"He's gone to wash his hands and to give John Michael another lesson in washing." Her lower lip began to quiver.

"He didn't hurt you, did he?"

She shook her head no and wiped a tear off her cheek.

Melissa went over and hugged Maddie. "I'm so glad you're okay. I've been so worried about you and John Michael."

"He didn't hurt either of us. He's so obsessed over washing his hands and John Michael's hands that he hasn't really had time to think about doing anything else." Maddie told them.

They all went and sat on the couch. Melissa felt the revolver rub against her side when she sat down. Finally she couldn't stand it anymore.

"This is crazy. I'm going to get my baby!"

"Don't Melissa, just sit here and pretend not to be upset. There's no telling what will put that man over the edge."

"Well, I'm the one over the edge. He better watch out for me, because there's no telling what I might do to him. I'm going to make sure my baby's okay and I really don't care about upsetting him." She jumped up and headed for the bathroom.

"What's going on in here?" Melissa tapped on the bathroom door and opened it slowly.

John Michael was sitting on the counter beside the sink with both hands lathered up waiting to have them rinsed off.

That sight made Melissa's heart ache. Seeing John Michael for the first time with this man made her lip tremble. She bit it to keep from crying and tried to sound cheerful. "Well, here you both are. I wondered where you had gotten off too."

John Michael began to cry as soon as he saw his mother. He lifted both his soapy hands and reached out his arms for her. It took all the strength Melissa had not to grab her son and run out the door with him.

"Wait! No, you don't. Not before you wash your dirty hands."

"Of course not, I was going to wash my hands." She scooped John Michael in her arms and put both their hands under the faucet to rinse them. She immediately soaped her's and reapplied soap to his so the man didn't think she had contaminated John Michael in some way.

The stranger looked shocked. "I didn't think people like you ever washed your hands."

"Oh, yes, some of us do." She continued to scrub her hands.

Finally, the convict grabbed a clean towel and began to dry his own hands. She followed suit and got a fresh towel out of the bathroom closet. She debated taking the gun out of her pants, confronting him right then, but was afraid if something were to happen to John Michael she would never forgive herself. She held her son in her arms, so grateful he was still alive.

She watched the stranger's twitching face. He was obviously troubled about what to do next. She followed him into the den. He seemed so preoccupied with his thoughts that he didn't even seem to notice everyone sitting there.

John and Maddie were relieved when they saw Melissa come out of the bathroom with John Michael in her arms. They were squirming in their seats waiting for the man's next move.

Melissa was the first to speak. "John, didn't you say you needed to go wash your hands as soon as you got to the apartment?"

"Uh, yeah. Melissa. If our friend doesn't mind, I need to go wash my hands. Didn't you want to go with me, Maddie and wash your hands?"

Maddie looked sort of confused, but went along with it.

"Yes, Sir. I've wanted to wash my hands since I got here, but I was afraid this man wouldn't want me to. If it's all right with you, I'd like to go to the bathroom also."

His face contorted on the left side as he started screaming out. "No, this isn't right. You're not supposed to clean your hands." He was tormented by indecision.

They ignored him and headed for the bathroom. Maddie turned on the water while John opened the bathroom window to motion to the police to come in the back door. He closed it back and began to wash his hands.

Melissa tried to carry on a conversation while holding tightly to John Michael.

"You know I don't even know your name. You've never told any of us your name."

"Jay Crawson." He said without any emotion. Not even aware he had told her something about himself.

Melissa felt the blood leave her cheeks. Her heart began to beat wildly in her chest. My God, it can't be, she thought to herself. She tried to act, nonchalant.

"Crawson? You must be kidding." She immediately thought of Jennifer. Here was Jennifer's brother standing a few feet in front of her. It seemed impossible.

She continued. "My best friend was named Crawson, Jennifer Crawson. Your friend from prison was partially responsible for her death. I believe you know her name. I believe you know Jennifer."

He started screaming out, "No, you're lying. You're bad. You're all bad people."

John and Maddie ran out of the bathroom. John ran over to John Michael and reached out to take him in his arms. Jay took a knife out of his pocket, grabbed Melissa, and held the blade to her throat.

"I've had it with you people. I'm not listening to any more of your lies. It's time for me to vindicate the murder of my buddy." He pushed the knife even harder against Melissa's neck.

The police slammed through the back door. Jay turned around to see five policeman push through to the den. They stood poised to shoot, but did not want to jeopardize the life of Melissa, or anyone else in the room.

"Hold it right there, Mister. Put the knife down or we'll be forced to shoot."

Melissa could see beads of sweat form on Jay's face. He was obviously nervous. She could feel the tremor in his hand and the knife began to shake against her neck. She wasn't sure what he might do next. She reached with her left hand in the side of her waistband and slowly pulled the gun from her pants. She decided to try talking to Jay first before letting him see the gun.

"Before you kill me, I want to wash my hands. You have to give me a chance to wash my dirty hands." He became even more nervous over that thought.

She pushed the gun up to his side and continued, "Jay, I'm going to wash my hands. If you don't let me, I'll shoot you and we'll both die in our sins with dirty hands." She decided to play that up as much as she could since that was the only thing that seemed to motivate him.

"Is that what you really want, Jay?"

He was sweating profusely. He shook like a leaf and began to cry uncontrollably.

"Throw the knife down and we'll both go wash our hands before they take you in." Melissa tried to reason with him and continued. "There's no need for anyone to get hurt here. You need help and there are plenty of doctors who can help you, Jay. They'll help you so you'll never have to wash your hands again to purify yourself."

He sobbed and let the knife slip from his hand. One of the cops yelled out. "We got him. Let's move in." He pulled back the hammer to his revolver.

"No, don't shoot him. He's giving himself up." Melissa heard the bang of the gun and heard the bullet whiz by her head. She shielded Jay with her body and they both hit the floor. Her gun slid under the couch. She held her breath and waited, hoping the shot missed both of them.

"Don't shoot, don't shoot, he's giving himself up!" She repeated.

John yelled from across the room, "Melissa, are you hurt?"

"No, but he may be. Please don't shoot anymore, he's turning himself in." Melissa shouted again. She examined him thoroughly and didn't see any blood anywhere. Jay was crying with his face against the floor.

Melissa couldn't get Jennifer off of her mind. She breathed a deep sigh of relief when she heard the Lieutenant yell out.

"Everyone, hold your fire!"

Chapter Fifty

By the next month John moved all of his belongings into Melissa's house. Maddie moved into the guest house. It wasn't long before John and John Michael were sleeping soundly in Melissa's arms. The past few weeks had been so hectic it was a sleep of total exhaustion.

The sheriff's department took Jay to Columbia to undergo psychological testing. John and Melissa did not press any charges. Melissa was willing to pay for any treatment to help Jennifer's brother get the help he needed.

It was Monday. Melissa would be going to The Cranberry Tree to put everything on sale for the summer. This would make room for all the new fall and Christmas merchandise. She planned on going to market in Atlanta the second week in July to restock everything in the store. They were going to have a great Christmas this year. That thought made her smile to herself.

Melissa went over to the coffee maker and began brewing some Almond Amaretto coffee in memory of Jennifer's favorite flavor. She had begun interviewing applicants for the position of assistant manager and was scheduled to meet with someone around noon. She sat down to go through last week's mail and to pay some of the bills.

Later that afternoon she would go by the farmer's market and get some vegetables to make John's favorite dinner. She could hardly wait to tell him she was pregnant. She poured his coffee, when she heard him come out of the bathroom.

"That coffee smells great. What are you doing today? Anything special?"

"I have an interview at noon. I'm going to the shop and put everything on sale. After that, I'm going for a walk down to the Battery, to the farmer's market, and who knows I might go buy some baby clothes.

"That's nice." John had already started reading the newspaper and missed that last sentence.

"Um, that sounds like a busy day to me. Well, I guess I better get to the office."

"John, did you hear the last thing I said?"

"You're going to the farmer's market."

"I said I might go buy some baby clothes."

"Who for?"

"For our new baby!"

"What did you say?"

"I said I'm pregnant, John. I did the test this morning and I'm pregnant."

John jumped up and grabbed Melissa. "That's fantastic! I can't believe it. I wasn't sure we'd be able to have any more children after all the prostate problems I had." He kissed her passionately and continued.

"You make me so happy, Melissa. We'll celebrate in some way tonight. I don't know if you can have any wine, but I'll buy a nice bottle and we can go out and eat. How's that sound?"

"Well, I wanted to cook one of your favorite meals and I just tested today, so I'm sure we can have some nice wine to celebrate the occasion. Let's just stay home tonight, okay?"

"Sounds great to me. Anything you want sounds great." He kissed her again. "Nothing you could have told me could have made me any happier and as much as I hate to, I guess I better get to the office. I'll see you tonight then." He kissed her tenderly on the forehead and walked out the door.

The time at the shop went by so quickly. Before Melissa knew it, the new applicant was walking through the door. She seemed nice. She wasn't Jennifer, but she seemed nice enough.

"Hi, I'm Melissa Isaacson. You must be, Emily?" Melissa extended her hand.

"Oh, do you mind. My hands are dirty and I really need to wash them. Your restroom?"

Melissa eyes went wide with surprise. She couldn't believe her ears. She stared at her for a moment and finally replied, "By all means. The bathroom is that way." She pointed toward the rear of the shop. She watched her walk down the hall.

Melissa continued to mumble to herself. "This is just too weird. I have a feeling she's not the one." She decided to make a fresh pot of coffee. She made Toasted Praline. Somehow this did not seem like an Almond Amaretto moment. The coffee finally stopped dripping. Melissa poured herself a cup and finished half of it before Emily came back.

When Emily finally returned to the front of the store, she extended her extremely red washed hand and said, "Now that's better. My name is Emily and I'm here to apply for the job of assistant manager."

Melissa politely shook her hand. "Would you like some coffee?"

"Uh, no thanks. I don't like coffee. Just the smell tends to make me nauseous."

"Really? Well, you might find it difficult working here. We provide coffee for our customers while they shop. We normally have coffee brewing here all the time."

Emily started making a face like the coffee was making her sick to her stomach.

Melissa felt sorry for her. "I tell you what. Why don't we go down to Poogan's Porch and have lunch? It's a wonderful restaurant only a couple of blocks away on Queen Street. We can talk there a little more and go over your resume."

"Well, if you don't mind I'd rather not. I don't really like to go out and eat. Besides, I brought an egg salad sandwich for lunch. That's what I eat every day."

"Egg salad sandwich," Melissa repeated. "Well, I can certainly see why you'd rather eat that than go to Poogan's. Oh, come on live a little. It's my treat and you'll love it. You can eat egg salad anytime."

"No, I better not." Emily looked so uncomfortable with the way things were going and the coffee continued to make her sick.

Melissa looked at Emily for a moment and decided this interview wasn't going anywhere. "Listen, you know what? I found out this week that I'm pregnant. I've just decided that I need to hire someone who is already familiar with the business here and who knows my family. The person I have in mind already has a relationship with my son and husband and probably knows me better than I know myself.

"I appreciate your coming by and I'm sorry that I wasn't able to let you know this sooner. It seems everything just hit me all at once. Besides, I don't think you'd like working here very much. The smell of coffee everyday, would probably make your working here very hard. We all go out and eat together all the time. Sorry it didn't work out, Emily." Melissa extended her hand which was not accepted by Emily, and repeated. "Thanks again for coming by."

Emily nodded as she hurried out the door. She seemed anxious to get away from the aroma that filled the shop.

"Let me get my purse and head down to Poogan's." Melissa said out loud to herself. She locked the door behind her and left the closed sign showing on the door.

She smiled to herself as she thought about how perfect Maddie would be to take over the manager's position at The Cranberry Tree. She was the one person who knew everything about the family, loved coffee, and knew what Melissa was thinking even when nothing was said.

Chapter Fifty-One

Melissa walked in Poogan's Porch and was greeted warmly by the staff. There was already a line formed down the hall to be seated. Her eyes scanned the area where people were being seated outside to see if there were any available tables. There were a couple of tables still left.

There was a young woman sitting at one of the tables near the fireplace who looked just like Jennifer from the back. Melissa felt a tug on her heart as she realized just how much she missed her friend.

About that time a waiter came to seat Melissa. She requested a table outside and he smiled and responded. "Right this way, Mrs. Isaacson."

When she reached the table where the lady was sitting. She was no longer there.

"Son, the lady that was sitting right there. Do you know where she went?"

"No, Ma'am. I don't remember anyone sitting there. It was probably just Zoe. The rumor has it that she's a ghost from the past who appears here every once in a while. Of course I don't believe any of that stuff, but some people say she hangs out at Poogan's Porch."

Melissa smiled as she thought, it's probably just Jennifer coming by to eat at one of her favorite places.

Melissa ordered her usual fish and chips, drank the delicious sweet tea, and decided to take a walk down to the Battery. She walked the several blocks toward that direction, looking at the different doors on each house. Each door had a different design that depicted an architectural masterpiece, something unique, something that reminded her of a thumb print of each home.

Finally, she reached Rainbow Row and walked toward the trees that were planted right before the sea. There weren't many leaves yet, but each branch looked as though they could embrace her and keep her in a place of total peace. She looked up through the blackened shadows of the limbs and peered at the sky beyond the branches.

Leaving Charleston would never be an option. This was her home. This was Poogan's home and Charleston seemed to be where Jennifer's spirit had decided to rest all though her body had gone to Atlanta. Melissa breathed deeply. Edisto would soothe her soul, but Charleston would be her life.

The water at the Battery was choppy and kind of grey looking. Melissa imagined the ships that used to sail there, the magnificent history of such a city: The architecture, Poogan's Porch, the horse and buggies, the basket makers, the tourists. Charleston wasn't just like every town. It had a life that had been there forever and remained much the same year after year.

The souls and spirits don't ever die and the history of the place continues to live. On any given day, like at Poogan's Porch, you might just see an old friend again, just for a moment, just a glance. Someone will pass by, maybe in the middle of a crowd, and you could swear that you saw someone you used to know years ago. Of course that would probably be one of those things not said, but was felt and believed by the people who live there.

Printed in the United States
128814LV00004B/1-105/P